KATIE ROSE

RUNAWAY HEARTS

BANTAM BOOKS

New York   Toronto   London   Sydney   Auckland

RUNAWAY HEARTS

A Bantam Fanfare Book / April 2001

FANFARE and the portrayal of a boxed "ff" are trademarks
of Bantam Books, a division of Random House, Inc.

ISBN 0-553-58142-2
Published simultaneously in the United States and Canada

Bantam Books are published by Bantam Books, a division of
Random House, Inc. Its trademark, consisting of the words
"Bantam Books" and the portrayal of a rooster, is Registered in
U.S. Patent and Trademark Office and in other countries.
Marca Registrada. Bantam Books, 1540 Broadway,
New York, New York 10036.

PRINTED IN THE UNITED STATES OF AMERICA
10 9 8 7 6 5 4 3 2 1
OPM

For Nina Benninghoff, the real horse whisperer.
You opened up a wonderful world for me.

Special thanks to: Abby Zidle,
for her inspiration and help,
Stephanie Kip, Karen Solem, Judy Spagnola
and Darryl Dupont from KYW,
Marlene Murdock, and Linda Cajio.

1

Graystone Lodge
Milltown, NY 1895

Mary Lou Finch peeked out of her hiding place in the stall, hushing every sound she might possibly make. The front gate creaked open and she froze in horror, trying not to even breathe. A stray tuft of her blonde hair caught on a protruding nail, but she didn't dare raise her hand and yank it free for fear of being caught.

The *clip-clop* of a horse's hooves broke the silence, and a groom entered the barn, leading a blood bay inside. Max, her terrier, bared his teeth and started to growl. Terrified, Mary Lou silenced him quickly, pulling him into her skirts to muffle his canine protest. Her heart pounded as the groom passed within inches of her, and she silently prayed he wouldn't see her. How on earth would she ever explain her presence if he did? She had come to Graystone Lodge to apply for a position as a governess, and getting caught snooping around the stables could definitely injure her chances.

The groom began talking softly to one of the horses in his stall, apparently in no rush to go anywhere. A tingle began in Mary Lou's nose and she realized she had to sneeze. Desperately, she struggled to quell the itch, holding a finger beneath her nostrils and swallowing hard. After what seemed to be an eternity, the man finally walked outside. No sooner had he closed the door when the sneeze she'd been repressing escaped violently. Her hair pulled loose from the nail, eliciting a squeak of pain as well as the sneeze, while her eyes flew open at the simultaneous events. Max glanced up, startled at the sudden noise. Thankfully, the barn remained silent.

That was close. Relief washed over her at the thought of her narrow escape. She had to work quickly, for she could be discovered at any time. A racing stable was like a little community, bustling with grooms, stableboys, riders, and exercise jockeys. Male voices echoed outside and it was only because of the noon lunch break that the barn was empty.

Taking a deep breath to steady her nerves, she scurried out of the stall with her bag and surveyed her surroundings. The stables, she saw, were immaculate. Neatly wrapped water hoses hung on the wall, brooms were lined up in descending height order against the door, and the aisleway was clear of hay and mud. Grain bins stood at the far end of the stables, and a cart full of buckets, each identified with a horse's name and feed mix, waited for the supper hour. The stalls were lined up neatly, twenty-four of them altogether, facing each other in double rows. Every half door was numbered, with a placard overhead identifying the horse and its owner and a bridle on the door. Almost two dozen noses peeked out, and twice that many curious eyes followed her.

One stall was empty. Its door gaped open like a protesting mouth, and inside, spiders had already begun to stake their claim on the dusty space. The placard overhead read: 'DAMIEN'S CURSE,' PIERCE THORNDIKE, OWNER.

A silent thrill went through Mary Lou. As Max ran outside to do his own investigating, she withdrew a magnifying glass from her carpetbag and examined the vacant stall. Along with the cobwebs, an empty feed bucket stood in the corner with a solitary apple inside. Absently, Mary Lou put the fruit in her bag, then completed her examination. Other than the apple, there was nothing noteworthy to be found, so she ventured outside once more.

A horseshoe had been tacked up overhead as a rustic decoration. Could it be Damien's? Prying it loose was a simple matter, since the nail had rusted, and the shoe came away easily into her hand. That went into her carpetbag, along with the apple. She started to close the door to examine the bolt when she saw the empty hook on the other side.

There was no bridle. A frown crossed her face and she made a quick note, wondering if the same held true for the rest of the tack. If so, that could mean . . .

The voices outside reminded her once more that her time was limited. Mary Lou returned to the aisleway and dropped to the floor to examine the footprints. She could identify those of the groom since his were fresh, but there were dozens of others. Frustration filled her. How on earth was she to make sense of all this? She was a scientist, not a detective, but even her specialized training didn't appear to be of much help.

She was about to give up when she saw another set of square-toed tracks embedded just inside the empty stall. A layer of straw had protected them from obliteration, and the soft clay of the barn floor had preserved them remarkably well. Examining them more closely, she saw they were from a man's boots. A shiver of excitement coursed through her. Could they have been here since that fatal night? It seemed possible. While they were much more faded in the aisle, the distinctive square toes left a path she might be able to follow. Picking up her bag, she traced the faint impressions past the stalls and the tack room, and around the corner, until she came to the boots themselves.

Only gradually did she realize they were filled. Mary Lou's gasp of astonishment stuck in her throat as her gaze lifted slowly through the glass, past the perfectly creased trouser leg, up to a well-muscled thigh that was clearly visible through the fine wool. She had to swallow hard in order to continue her visual journey, but curiosity won out and her eyes swept upward to a trim waist, broad chest encased in white cotton, then to the face of the man himself.

Her mouth dropped open. He was one of the most handsome men she'd ever seen. Blazing blue eyes glared out of a face that could have graced any of Michelangelo's statues. His nose was finely formed, his cheekbones striking. His chin was firm, while dark brows made his eyes seem even more intense. Blue-black hair, perfectly straight, swept back off his face as if it had been ordered to do so, while his complexion was flushed with attractive color. Frantically, Mary Lou wondered if he was part Irish, for he had the look of a Celtic lord.

"Miss," he declared, his voice thick with emotion. "Would you mind telling me what in God's name you are doing?"

Pierce Thorndike gazed at the impudent baggage at his feet in stunned amazement. She had inspected him carefully, with a magnifying glass of all things, then finally looked directly at him. When he saw her face, he felt as if someone had punched him in the stomach.

She was stunning. Dressed in a simple cotton gown suspiciously stained with odd blue streaks, a pencil tucked behind one ear and her blonde hair falling from its knot, she nevertheless had the visage of an angel. It was the last thing he expected after interviewing a score of dowager governesses that morning, women whose faces clearly showed too many years of managing unruly children. This woman had none of their stern lines, disapproving mouths, or sharp eyes. Instead, her lips were like a cupid's bow, undeniably kissable, her nose elegant, her eyes an intense green. Her figure was a little plump, and there was a carelessness about her, but the intelligence in her eyes and her striking good looks distracted him completely.

"I'm sorry, Mr. Thorndike." The groom entered the barn with a bucket and some brushes, his face red with embarrassment when he saw Mary Lou. "I don't know how she got in here. I was helping the boy with the horses."

"Don't let it happen again." Thorndike regained his composure immediately. "I have a horse missing and a murder on my hands. I want these stables under constant surveillance. Now you, Miss," he turned the full force of his gaze onto Mary Lou. "Would you mind telling me who you are and what in God's name you are doing here?"

"Why, I . . . I'm applying for the governess job, of course." Mary Lou stammered, getting to her feet.

"Why weren't you waiting in the vestibule with the other applicants?"

"I was searching for the rear entrance to the house when I saw the stables," she said quickly, brushing awkwardly at her skirts. "I heard you had some beautiful horses, and thought I'd take a look."

"I see," Thorndike said, seeing a great deal more. Although he didn't quite believe her story, this morning's interviews hadn't been very successful. No one had suited him or his son. Thorndike frowned as he envisioned the little boy, stubbornly refusing to engage in conversation with one candidate, then sticking another with a cocklebur. One applicant tried to quiz him on his mathematical skills, and his son, who was proficient in the subject, suddenly couldn't add the simplest sums. Another attempted to play with him and had produced colored pencils, certain that like most children, he enjoyed drawing.

Unfortunately, Edward decided that the pencils made much better arrows than artistic instruments. Thorndike had found them outside, the governess shrieking and running from a well-aimed bow.

This whole endeavor was turning out to be much more tedious than he'd ever anticipated. A nagging thought entered his mind that his son had been through too many governesses in the past year, that something deeper was wrong, but he firmly pushed it aside. He himself had been a trial at Edward's age, and it was simply a matter of finding the right person.

Still, this woman appeared to be quite different from any of those he'd interviewed. He was willing to give her a chance, if she had a plausible explanation for her behavior. A glint of sunlight reflected from the glass in her hand and he frowned. "If you were simply looking at the horses, what were you doing on your knees, with that?" He indicated the magnifying glass she belatedly tried to hide behind her back.

"I . . . I lost an ear bob," she said quickly. "I think it fell off inside the stables, but I can't find it. It was rather dark in there, and I thought the glass might help."

"But Miss . . ."

"Finch," Mary Lou helpfully supplied.

"Miss Finch, you aren't wearing an ear bob."

Her hand quickly fumbled with her earlobe, then she frowned in bewilderment. "Oh dear, I must have lost both of them. How careless of me."

Her eyes met his and a slow grin came to his face. This woman obviously took him for a fool. Idly he wondered just who she really was, and what her original intention could have been. Whatever she was up to, he couldn't pass on the opportunity to see where this led.

"Do you have the required references for the position?"

"Yes, of course."

"Turn around."

"What?" It was Mary Lou's turn to look incredulous.

"Turn around." He gestured with his hand as if his request was completely reasonable.

Uncertain what to do, she slowly complied. He could see the brilliant color stain her cheeks and knew she felt like a horse at auction. Although a mantle partially covered her shoulders, the rest was clearly visible beneath his scrutiny. When she turned once more to face him, her head was held high and he saw a particularly attractive sparkle in her eyes.

"Well, sir? Did I pass inspection?"

She had pride as well as intelligence, he noted. Fighting a smile once more, he shrugged.

"Yes, I suppose you'll do. You seem sturdy enough, and don't appear to have any physical deformities. Is your education sufficient?"

Miss Finch appeared insulted. "Sir, I was an honor student at the University. I graduated with a degree."

He couldn't help his smile now, and he eyed her with a modicum of respect. "A degree? I know of no woman who pursued a degree. What on earth were you going to do with it?"

"That, sir, is my dilemma. Unfortunately, society has little use for an educated woman, as I have discovered."

She was unable to keep the pained note from her voice. Strangely enough, he felt a pang of understanding for this odd creature. She was obviously intelligent, but her gender determined that her mind would have little value to the rest of the world. He knew he was in the minority in finding this situation deplorable, for the few times he shared his opinion with his peers, they were horrified. Nevertheless, it seemed to him an extreme waste of talent to confine such women to languishing on the duvet, with nothing more exciting to occupy them than the latest novel.

Dismissing his thoughts, he turned abruptly. "I suggest you come up to the house and meet my son. Bob, search the barn and see if the mysterious ear bobs turn up. I shouldn't want them crushed by a horse, if they do exist."

She picked up a small carpetbag and followed reluctantly behind him. The path wound from the stables toward the track where the jockeys exercised the two-year-olds, past the pond and a stand of old elm trees, to the main gate. Ruffled green lawns flowed like silk from the house toward the woods beyond, while numerous trails cut through the meadows, enticing a rider to explore.

Graystone Lodge was a handsome place built just after the Civil War. Symmetrical almost to a fault, it was a two-story dwelling comprised of gray stones quarried from the nearby river—hence its name. There were three windows on the second floor, two directly below, and between them stood the front door. There were even two fireplaces, their chimneys jutting perfectly above the first floor windows. Ivy mottled the northern wall, making the house look older than its years, and a cluster of briar roses softened the corner, blurring the lines where east met west.

Normally the walk from the stables to the house took fifteen minutes. Today, it seemed quite a bit longer. Apparently Miss Finch was not in the best physical condition, as her round figure testified, and though she valiantly tried to keep up with his stride, he was forced to wait for her three times. Like most women, she was hobbled by her clothes and corset, but she obviously exercised very infrequently because she was puffing by the time they reached the house.

He glanced at her questioningly and she tried to steady her breathing. They walked through the gate, then up the main path to the door. Thorndike held it open gallantly, then led her inside, past the incredulous butler, who gave the girl an odd look, and down the main hallway.

Inside, the house was as perfectly ordered as it appeared outside. The parlor was to the right, with its gracious sofa and comfortable chairs, teak tables and polished silver tea set. Directly across was the formal dining room, the mahogany table fully extended to seat twelve people, the embroidered chairs waiting neatly against the wall like a dozen upright soldiers. Then came the sitting room, and behind that, the kitchen and library.

He didn't stop until he reached the library, and again he gestured for her to enter first. She seemed dwarfed by the walls of books, the dark green leather wing chairs, the massive fireplace, and the diamond-paned windows. Thick emerald velvet curtains were looped back with gold cord, showing off a spectacular view of the grounds. A secretary stood before the window, cluttered with journals, papers, and writing implements. But if Mary Lou was at all intimidated, she didn't show it. Instead, she simply put her magnifying glass aside and looked at him expectantly, as if waiting to see what would happen next. The woman had nerve, he thought in amusement, then reminded himself that she would need it.

"I will fetch my son. See that you don't lose anymore ear bobs in the process."

As soon as he was gone, Mary Lou collapsed into a chair with a sigh of relief. This whole situation was rapidly becoming much more complicated than she thought.

The last thing she had wanted to do was leave her comfortable home in Boston, with her laboratory and first-rate cook, and become little more than a servant in a house full of strangers. Yet she could never have predicted that disaster would strike a few weeks ago when her father risked everything, including her dowry, on a racehorse. Damien's Curse was a sure thing to win the Saratoga race, an unknown with tremendous odds against him. Upon hearing about the thoroughbred from a fellow professor who was distantly related to one of the jockeys, Rutherford Finch had invested every penny he had in the horse, confident he would make a huge profit. Yet the horse had simply vanished, his trainer found dead at the scene, and the local police were stymied.

Mary Lou wrinkled her nose impatiently. It wasn't so much her dowry that concerned her; in truth, there weren't many young men who came calling anyway. Perhaps it was because she was a trifle over-weight, unfashionably so in an era of wasp waists. She looked downward at her curved figure and instantly regretted those six poppyseed cakes she had eaten on the train. Or perhaps it was the chemical stains on her dress, the bubbling cauldrons, and the test tubes which fumigated threateningly in the parlor. When rumor circulated that she had blown up the barn, even the few admirers she did have dwindled away to nothing. Mary Lou frowned. It was the woodshed and not the barn after all, and how else was she to prove that hydrochloric acid, under the right circumstances, was combustible?

No one understood, nor would they ever. She was an oddity in a world that appreciated sameness. While her lack of suitors didn't overly concern her, for her work and her studies more than filled her life, the loss of the money was indeed a tragedy. She and her father stood to lose everything, even their home, if the horse wasn't found. Worse than that, her own future was in jeopardy. The dowry money was the only means she had to maintain her financial independence, and without it, her prospects were dim indeed. After careful analysis of the problem, Mary Lou decided there was but one thing to do: investigate the missing horse herself, and recoup her father's investment.

The idea wasn't quite as ridiculous as it sounded. Pierce Thorndike, master of Graystone Lodge and majority owner of the magnificent thoroughbred, was looking for a governess. With her university degree, Mary Lou could easily qualify for the job. And her cousin Emily, an amateur detective, offered to provide her counsel. All she had to do was get the governess position, and report back to her cousin. Even her father, an enlightened man for his time who appreciated her intelligence, reluctantly agreed it was the best possible solution.

But she hadn't fully anticipated the difficulties involved, nor had she counted on Thorndike. Besides being the handsomest man she'd ever seen, he was truly an imposing figure. Something strange seemed to happen to her in his presence, something that was difficult to quantify. Her heart fluttered, her breath caught, and an exciting emotion swelled within her. Mary Lou fanned herself, trying to regain her composure. There was nothing she would like better at the moment than to be back in her comfortable cottage, cook brewing tea on the stove, her nose firmly planted in a book and a dish of chocolates at her elbow. She had barely finished that comforting thought when a screech interrupted her.

"I don't want to see her! I want to go fishing! You promised . . ."

Startled, Mary Lou jumped up, facing the doorway, wondering what on earth to expect now. A minute later, Thorndike returned, his son standing obstinately by his side.

"This is my son, Edward. Edward, I want you to meet Miss Finch."

A boy of about eight years stood before her, dressed in good wool trousers made filthy from mud. His hair, which had been recently combed, still stuck up like a porcupine's, and freckles were sprinkled across his nose like cinnamon on custard. Edward appeared not at all happy to see her. Thorndike put his hand on his back and propelled the boy forward. Reluctantly, the boy marched toward her, and when he got within two feet, stuck out his hand. A slimy brown worm curled in his palm.

"I got this under the leaves. It's a fishing worm." He grinned mischievously.

The boy obviously expected Mary Lou to scream, or at least withdraw in horror. He gave her a look of pathetic defiance that was truly heartbreaking. Reaching for her magnifying glass, she calmly inspected the creature.

"You are quite right, that is a nice worm. It is an earthworm, an annelid. They live in damp leaves, mud, and underneath logs. I could show you some good locations to look for more."

"You could?" The boy, momentarily forgetting his desire to repel her, was instantly intrigued.

"Yes, if I decide to stay." Mary Lou straightened. "I'm not at all sure this position would suit me."

"Miss Finch," Thorndike spoke sharply. "It seems to me that you are perhaps the best suited woman I've interviewed in the past two days. Where is your uncertainty? I assure you the compensation will be generous."

"Oh, it isn't that at all," Mary Lou said blithely. "Turn around."

"I beg your pardon?"

"I need to ascertain something for myself. You don't mind, do you?"

She gave him an innocent look, as if her request

wasn't at all unusual. Thorndike looked astonished, but she could have sworn she saw a glimmer of something like amusement in those cold eyes. Complying with her request, he turned, then faced her once more.

"Yes, I suppose you will do." Mary Lou nodded, sighing in resignation. In truth, he was a brilliant specimen of a man, but he was arrogant, controlling, and a bit of a bully, traits she'd learned to deal with years ago at the University. The only way to win a man's respect was to force him to deal with her on equal terms, a lesson most didn't learn easily.

"I am very glad you are pleased," he said. There was a tone in his voice that made her feel distinctly warm and uncomfortable. Her collar suddenly felt too tight, and an odd, female awareness crept through her. Forcing her thoughts back to the business at hand, she reminded herself that the handsome, devastating Thorndike couldn't possibly be interested in her for any other reason than his son.

2

—❧—

" 'Tis hoping I am that you will find this room acceptable, Miss," Bridget Murphy, the housekeeper, said. "It faces the south, so it is very warm and sunny, and Edward's room is right next door. But perhaps you do not like sunshine? In which case, I'll be showing you the one on the northern side."

"This is mine?" Mary Lou gaped in astonishment at the lovely bedchamber. It was easily twice as large as her own room at home, and very beautiful. Cherry wood furnishings gleamed from the corners, including a bureau, night table, and washstand. A rose-colored porcelain pitcher stood waiting in a bowl, and fresh flowers filled a crystal vase on the night table. There was even a bookcase packed with classroom texts, and a writing table beside a bow window that looked out over the property. In the center of the room, a beautiful four-poster bed covered with a pretty rose quilt and plump pillows waited invitingly.

"You like it?" The housekeeper seemed absurdly pleased. "The last one didn't appreciate the sun waking her up in the morning, but I'll be thinking she just wasn't happy here. She left and returned to town. The one before that didn't care for the color. Too pink, she said. And the one before that—"

"How many were there?" Mary Lou asked in surprise.

Bridget laughed, the corners of her pale blue eyes crinkling. "More than I'd care to recall, lass. It's been hard on the master. Every time he thinks he has the situation settled, he has to rush back here and do the hiring all over again. It's enough to make the devil mad." She crossed herself quickly.

Mary Lou smiled. Bridget was as Irish as they came. Pleasantly plump with a clean white apron and a crisp manner, she had the look of a woman who had earned her own living from the time she was born, and was no stranger to work. Still, she was like a breath of fresh air in the odd household.

"He doesn't seem very friendly," Mary Lou remarked, thinking of Thorndike's cold reception. "The master, I mean."

"He's a good man," Bridget said defensively. "Not unfriendly. Reserved, you might say. He wasn't always like that. Once this house was filled with music and grand parties. But all that ended when the missus passed away."

"How did she pass?"

Bridget paused, and Mary Lou could have sworn

she shivered. But she had a bright smile when she looked up. "She caught a chill and it went to pneumonia. The doctor said her lungs were weak, and she died within days."

Something about her voice didn't encourage the conversation. Mary Lou thought it best to change the subject to one the housekeeper felt more comfortable discussing. "Why did so many governesses leave? Is Edward that bad?"

Bridget shrugged. "He has his moments, Edward does," the housekeeper explained. "But no different than other lads. And then there is the loss of his mother. Hard on a wee boy, not having his own mother to love him."

Mary Lou peered at her searchingly, but Bridget was now arranging the flowers. Casually, she gestured to the stables. "So is racing Mr. Thorndike's business?"

The lines on Bridget's face appeared to ease. "No. Master Thorndike is a businessman," she said simply. "Banking, investments; that's how the Thorndikes made their money. He's the only one of his family left now, and has to do it all himself."

"What about the horses?"

"The master isn't much of a gambler, bless him, but the horses are in his blood. He invests in only the best, trains them right, and runs them for just a few years. After that, he turns them out to pasture. He says a horse is like a man, and after doing his work, he deserves a rest. Look, you can see them there."

Mary Lou followed her finger, and saw several horses grazing in the field beyond. "Are they all retired?"

"Those are. He keeps the racers in the other field so they won't be chasing the older fellas around. Do you like horses, Miss Finch?"

"Not too much," Mary Lou admitted. "I took a fall once and broke my arm. I haven't been too keen on riding them since."

"Ah. The master will no doubt be changing that. I've never seen a man take to animals the way he does. They seem to respond to him as well. Insists that the grooms treat them right, the trainers too. Nearly broke his heart when he heard Jimmy Dwyer was killed."

"The trainer who was murdered," Mary Lou mused. When Bridget glanced at her questioningly, she shrugged. "It was in all the papers."

"I'll never forget that morning, when the stableboy found poor Jimmy lying there. A crime, all right, and no one can find as much as a hair of that horse. A beauty he was, almost pure-white from the start. But I suppose there's no point in hoping he'll be returned. You look near starved, lass, and tired. Would you care for something to eat before you retire?"

Although Mary Lou felt she should continue to question Bridget, the offer of food was too enticing for even her scientific mind to ignore. Her stomach growled, and she smiled sheepishly. "That sounds wonderful. I haven't eaten yet today."

"I'll whip something right up, that I will. I don't know what the master was thinking, not offering you tea, at least. Is that all of your bags?" The housekeeper stared at the small carpetbag on the floor.

"The rest will arrive later," Mary Lou explained. "I took the morning train yesterday from Boston and spent the night at an inn. I thought to inquire about the position first before accepting."

"I see. I don't blame you for being cautious. There aren't a lot of good jobs about for a lass on her own. It's hoping, I am, that you'll be happy here."

Mary Lou didn't bother to correct the woman's assumption that she planned to stay a long time. The less anyone at Graystone knew about her plans, the better.

Following the housekeeper into the kitchen, they proceeded past the sleepy butler to the pantry. Mary Lou's eyes widened as Bridget placed coconut cake, gooseberry jam, assorted scones, a platter of ham, some mustard, and several biscuits on a tray before her. Delighted, she began to devour the food. A fire burned cheerfully in a brick hearth, and the kitchen gleamed from beeswax and countless scrubbings. A stableboy crept in and tried to snatch a scone from the tray, and Bridget snapped a towel across his shoulders. The boy howled, but got away with the scone while the housekeeper chuckled. Instantly Mary Lou knew this would be her favorite room in the house.

"There, lass, it's nice to see someone appreciate good food," Bridget said, pouring another cup of the thick black tea. "You have a strong appetite."

"It appears I may have to increase our food allotment."

Mary Lou started as Thorndike appeared in the doorway. For a moment she thought he was teasing, but his expression was inscrutable. The stableboy took one look at him and fled, abandoning the housekeeper and Mary Lou in the face of the master's forbidding mien.

Bridget hastened to explain. "Excuse me, sir, but the wee lass came all the way from Boston with nary a bite."

"Which brings me to the question I meant to ask." One brow arched on Thorndike's face. "Is there a lack of governess positions in Boston? New York has much to recommend it, but one would think there would be a great demand for a talented female at home."

Mary Lou choked on the last piece of seed cake. "No, you are correct, there are no lack of jobs in Boston. I happen to be particular."

"In what way?" he questioned, obviously suspicious.

"A woman has to be especially careful what kind of situation she accepts," Mary Lou said, improvising quickly. "You must be aware that many governesses find themselves in jobs that turn out to be less than desirable. I do not wish to share their fate. I have heard good things about your family, and felt more comfortable applying for a job here."

Thorndike watched her closely. "What an interesting comment," he said smoothly. "I am curious to know how you obtained such knowledge. I wasn't aware governesses knew so much about the society they support."

"Ahh . . . word travels fast among our circles," Mary Lou said quickly. "We hear of families who see their governess as a slave, which families have incorrigible children, and of those husbands who feel free to prey upon an unguarded female in the house. I assure you, sir, women of my class feel it is essential to share their experiences."

That much she knew to be true. Her own childhood governess had had a surprisingly broad range of acquaintances, and seemed to know everything about everyone.

Thorndike's face lightened with understanding. "I see. I trust you will find no such problems here. If you do, you will report them to me immediately."

Her gaze met his. A shock of crisp black hair fell down to his forehead, and he tossed it back in an unconscious gesture like a colt. His shirt was open at the throat, and the muscular cords of his neck tapered down to his chest where she could glimpse a few dark hairs peeking from beneath the white linen. There was something wild about him, something dangerous and untamed, that made Mary Lou's heart pound. She was possessed of an odd desire to unbutton his shirt, to smooth her hands down that strong flesh, to feel the powerful body beneath. . . .

Good Lord, what was wrong with her? It wasn't at all like her to have musings in such a direction. Perhaps it was being away from home, or the imposing household. Or maybe it was Thorndike himself. There was something undeniably compelling about him, something that would draw any female to him like a moth to a gaslight. Whatever it was, she would have to be extremely careful not to let her biological functions rule her head. She had recently been studying the mating functions of fruit flies, and her feelings seemed all too similar to what she had been documenting. Good Lord, she was little better than an insect!

She saw his quizzical glance, and forced herself to respond to his last comment. "Thank you, sir. I will certainly endeavor to let you know if anything is wrong. Now if you'll excuse me, I must get some sleep. I want to start teaching Edward first thing in the morning. Thank you, Mrs. Murphy, for the tea. It was wonderful."

She rose, hoping that the flush she felt on her cheeks didn't show. Fruit flies indeed! She really had to get hold of herself.

Long after Mary Lou had gone to bed, Pierce sat in the library, twirling a glass of port. Bridget appeared in the doorway, drying her hands on her apron.

"Will there be anything else, sir?"

Distracted from his thoughts, he glanced up, then shook his head abruptly. "No." When the housekeeper started to leave, he stopped her.

"Mrs. Murphy, I would like to ask you your impression of the new governess."

"Miss Finch, sir?" Bridget appeared surprised. "I think she is a very bright lass, and will be good for Edward."

"Yes, she informed me she had a degree. But she certainly is different, unlike any governess I've ever seen. I have a feeling there is more to Miss Finch than meets the eye." When the housekeeper started to protest, he held up his hand. "Don't concern yourself, I fully intend to investigate her background and references. After all, she will be in charge of my son. Until I discover otherwise, I'm willing to give her a chance. The traditional governesses certainly haven't had much success with Edward. Perhaps Miss Finch, for all her eccentricities, will do better."

"I'm certain she will, sir." The housekeeper said emphatically, relief apparent in her voice. "I have a feeling about people, sir, and I think the lass will do everyone some good."

"I hope you're right. You can go now." Pierce turned away as Bridget left and stared outside the window, thinking of the mysterious Miss Finch. A smile curved his lips in spite of himself. She'd looked adorable, her hair and dress disheveled, those peculiar green eyes closed in sheer bliss as she sampled a cake. Her love of sweets was apparent, for he'd watched her for a good five minutes unobserved while she heartily enjoyed Bridget's cooking.

His smile died as he recalled a moment when something passed between them, something that could cause tremendous problems if allowed to ignite into flames. Was his attraction to her the reason he offered her the governess position? He had gone with his instinct to hire her on the spot, in spite of his suspicions. Could he have had motivations other than that she appeared to be the best candidate?

He immediately drove off the thought. Mary Lou Finch was his governess, a woman under his protection. To entertain anything else was grossly immoral.

3

—🌿—

Mary Lou awoke and gazed about her in confusion. It took a full minute for her to remember where precisely she was. Sunlight poured through the mullioned windows of the manor house, puddling onto the floor like a pool of gold. Even though she was in the governess's room, a servant's quarters, it was beautiful.

Glancing at her bag sitting on the carpet, she thought of her real reason for being here. Damien's Curse was missing, and with him, her dowry. While the dowry money wasn't a fortune, it was enough to provide for her in old age. She would be, as they said in polite society, a spinster, but a rich old spinster was in much better circumstances than a poor one. Although it wasn't the most appealing thought, Mary

Lou was practical. Someone had to look out for her best interests, and it appeared that someone was herself.

Opening her notebook, she examined her scribbled impressions and tried to make sense of them all. Someone had stolen the beautiful thoroughbred and murdered his trainer. Why? It wouldn't be easy to hide a horse like Damien's Curse. Even her father thought he would be discovered within a few days; yet two weeks had passed and no one had seen him. Taking out the folded newspaper article, she reread it for the hundredth time.

Damien's Curse, prize thoroughbred of Graystone Stables, was discovered missing this morning from his stall, and his trainer, James Dwyer, murdered. The man's body was found by the stableboy near the barn door, his head bludgeoned, as if struck with a heavy instrument. A woman's bloody handkerchief was found on the body, and the police surmise one of the servants had tried to stanch the wounds, although none of them recalled placing it there.

Damien, Graystone's entry for the Saratoga Cup, is two years old and was considered a dark horse for the race. Rumor has it that the horse is astonishingly good, in spite of the investors' attempts to keep his reputation a secret. Still, quite a bit of money has been wagered on him, and more than one person would benefit from his disappearance from the race.

Graystone's stables were guarded that night by Robert Shoemaker, the head groom. He is considered a trustworthy man, and has served Graystone for over fifteen years. Shoemaker testified that he had been on watch, but admitted he had fallen asleep. Yet he couldn't fathom how someone could have taken the horse without him awakening.

Mr. Dwyer, who lived with his wife and children in a little cottage near the property, was highly respected. A retired jockey, he had worked with horses for years and was known throughout the country for his excellence. His wife testified that he couldn't sleep that night, and left the house to investigate the stables. Since he often did this, she thought nothing of it, and was horrified to hear of his death the next morning.

The neighbors were questioned, but could add nothing of value to the investigation. Upon speaking to the townspeople, there was rumor that a discharged servant of Graystone had been asking about the horse. The police are acting upon the possibility that the man bore Mr. Pierce Thorndike, the horse's owner, a grudge. A warrant has been issued for his arrest. . . .

The rest of the article described the family's devastation, and Thorndike's loss. Putting the article back inside her bag, Mary Lou tried to envision what happened that night. Someone had entered the stables and, without rousing the groom, opened

Damien's stall and led him outside, intending to steal him. The trainer may have surprised the thief, and lost his life as a result. Or had he? Glancing again at her notes, the significance of the trainer's presence struck her fully. Was it really a coincidence that Jimmy Dwyer was there on that particular night? Did insomnia lead him to the stables, or did he have a more sinister reason?

She would have to play the role of governess until she found out. Replacing the notebook in her bag, she recalled Bridget's surprise that she only had one bag with her. She'd immediately sent for the rest of her things, although her wardrobe had always been severely limited. A smile came to her face as she envisioned Thorndike's expression when her laboratory equipment arrived. He would probably be shocked, but perhaps that was to the good. The man showed signs of unbearable stuffiness. Yet she'd have to be careful; Thorndike was suspicious of her already, and the man wasn't a fool.

He had agreed to let her dog stay, although he drew the line at letting Max sleep in her room. The little terrier wasn't too happy with his accommodations in the stable, but there wasn't much help for that. Even now, he was outside her window registering his complaints with a loud barking.

"*Shh.*" Mary Lou opened the window to quiet the dog. Leaning against the sill, she took a moment to admire the graceful lawn, the gently rolling hills, and the stately oaks. Horses dotted the fields, quietly grazing or playfully running in the cool morning air. In the mares' field, she saw the foals running in beautiful symmetry with their mothers. A few of the less ambitious babies were nursing, and their mothers stood still, allowing them to take their morning breakfast. Even though the hour was ungodly early, she could see the grooms carrying buckets, hear stableboys shouting to each other, and riders working the horses with a lunge line and a whip. It seemed incredible that someone had managed to come into the midst of all this in the middle of the night and steal a valuable horse, but that was what had happened. Damien was gone.

Max stopped barking immediately upon seeing her, and wagged his tail. Mary Lou retreated from the window, intending to fish inside her bag for a treat. She had barely opened the latch when an odd motion inside her bag caught her attention. Cautiously opening the top, she peered inside and she saw her few clothes, neatly folded if a little stained, her books, her manuals, and notes.

On top of them all, hissed a coiled-up garden snake.

Stifling a scream, Mary Lou shut the bag, her heart beating frantically. A moment later, she chided herself for her reaction. It was just a little snake, and a harmless one at that. She was well acquainted with all varieties of reptiles, and could easily identify venomous species. This one was clearly a Colubridae, a little garden predator, and wouldn't harm her at all.

Still, it was something of a shock to see it in her bag. A rueful smile came to her as she immediately understood its significance. Edward. No doubt the boy was responsible for this prank, thinking to send her fleeing in terror. Unfortunately for him, she was made of much sterner stuff. Moreover, she had a job to do, an investigation to conduct, and she wasn't about to let a contrary child or an innocuous reptile interfere with her plans.

Donning her robe, she brushed her hair up into a knot, then hoisted the snake out of her bag. The reptile squirmed at this treatment, but she held it firmly behind its head, and marched down to Edward's room. Thankfully, garden snakes didn't have fangs, so she didn't have to worry about finding them embedded in her flesh.

The boy was still sleeping, and didn't answer her knock. Undeterred, Mary Lou opened the door and marched inside, the snake twisting and squirming frantically in her grasp. Edward appeared angelic, feigning sleep under a thick quilt, but Mary Lou knew better.

"Edward, I suggest you wake up immediately. You and I need to talk."

The boy opened his eyes and stared at the governess in stunned surprise. His eyes grew even wider when she thrust the squirming snake beneath his nose.

"I had a little visitor this morning in my room. I thought maybe you'd know how it got there."

Gasping, Edward pushed himself back against the headboard as far as he could go. He couldn't take his eyes off the snake, nor the woman who held it before him like Medusa herself. His mouth opened, then he closed it, then it opened again.

"I . . . I don't know . . . "

"Tsk, tsk." Mary Lou shook her head sternly. "It won't do, boy, it simply won't do. When one and one makes two, nothing at all can change that."

His eyes lowered and he looked abashed. "I . . . I'm sorry."

"Much better." Mary Lou nodded, yet continued to position the loathsome reptile close to the mischievous youth. "As you and I both know, this is a harmless garden snake. I certainly hope you won't try something like this again, particularly with a more dangerous species."

"No!" The boy looked at her in horror. "I wouldn't—"

"I didn't think so," Mary Lou said calmly. "Now since you seem so enamored of reptiles, I suggest you dress quickly and prepare yourself for today. You will spend a good deal of time researching snakes, then writing a paper on their genus and activities. Do you understand me?"

The boy, after recovering from his initial surprise, now looked obstinate. Pushing the snake away from his face, his lower lip thrust out, and he glared defiantly. "What if I don't?"

Before she could answer, the door opened behind her. Mary Lou whirled, instinctively hiding the snake behind her back. Edward appeared horrified as he saw his father enter the room.

"What in blazes is going on here? It's barely dawn."

Pierce Thorndike was standing on the threshold, belatedly tying his satin robe around his waist. If Thorndike was impressive in his day clothes, he was twice so in his sleeping garments. Mary Lou felt a sharp tug on her senses as she took in the elegant sapphire of his smoking jacket, the smoldering blue of his eyes, and the firm set of his jaw. Disgracefully, her mind wandered to his muscled shoulders and she wondered what he wore beneath the coat, a notion too intoxicating to pursue. Good Lord, what was wrong with her?

Shaking off her thoughts, she saw that he was staring at his son suspiciously. Apparently, this wasn't the first such prank Edward had pulled. The boy's cheeks flushed red and he opened his mouth to confess, when Mary Lou interrupted quickly.

"Unfortunately, my dog woke Edward. Are you certain you won't reconsider and accommodate him in the house? He is very little trouble."

Thorndike looked astonished, then his glance went from his son to Mary Lou. She was standing against one wall, her hands determinedly behind her back. His eyes narrowed, and it was almost as if he could see through her meager clothing to the garden snake. He opened his mouth as if to demand to know what she hid there, but then seemed to think the better of it and closed it just as quickly.

Edward, who was equally surprised, stared at her pleadingly, just waiting for the moment when she would betray him. When it didn't happen, he looked even more confused, but he turned to his father and shrugged.

"I don't see why he can't sleep in her room," Edward said quickly. "It would keep him from barking."

"I do not allow mongrels in my house," Thorndike thundered. His brow darkened in suspicion. "Are you certain, Miss Finch, that there is nothing else you want to tell me?"

Mary Lou shrugged, feeling the snake curl behind

her back. "Why no, sir. I am rather forthright, as I think you have seen. Getting back to the subject at hand, I'll have you know that Max is no mongrel. He is a purebred fox terrier. But since you object so strenuously, I suppose we'll simply have to make do."

Pierce's eyes went once more from her to the boy. Edward, who looked mightily relieved, simply shrugged once more as if such matters were beyond him. The master of the house obviously didn't quite believe the story he was being fed, but acted with discretion.

"Yes, I suppose we'll all have to make adjustments. Miss Finch, would you mind getting dressed and joining us for breakfast? And Edward, you may as well rise now. I'm certain Miss Finch has a full day planned for you. "

"Why, indeed I do. We're studying snakes today, aren't we, Edward?"

Thorndike's face suddenly cleared and he cast a speculative look upon his son. Edward, seeing his father's knowing scrutiny, nodded vigorously at Mary Lou's suggestion.

"Yes, I'll be doing a paper on them. I'll get dressed right away."

He leaped from his bed as if anxious to get busy writing. Mary Lou smiled in satisfaction, then gave Thorndike a questioning look.

"Will there be anything else, sir?"

Thorndike stared at her for a long moment, and she could have sworn something stirred in the depths of those blue eyes. His glance swept lower, and Mary Lou was suddenly aware of the poor nightgown she wore, and the flimsy robe that covered it. Her generous figure, tightly corseted and laced by day, was clearly displayed beneath the cotton garments. Clothes had never been a primary concern for her, but now she felt positively naked beneath his assessing gaze. She longed to tuck her robe more closely about her, but she couldn't with the snake hidden behind her back. Her bare toes curled on the hardwood floor, and she saw him observe them. His mouth curved in amusement.

"Just your presence at breakfast. I think, Miss Finch, you are definitely an unusual addition to your trade. I am beginning to feel myself fortunate."

With that astonishing remark, he turned swiftly and walked out of the room. Edward gazed at the empty doorway in relief, then turned to the governess.

"Miss Finch . . . " The boy gazed at her sheepishly, grateful that she didn't get him in trouble. He was also obviously puzzled. The snake trick was usually more than sufficient to terrorize any governess. "I . . . "

Without waiting for his forced gratitude, Mary Lou took the snake and tossed it out the window. Turning back to the boy, she wiped her hands briskly and efficiently, as if this was all in a day's work.

"No thanks necessary, Edward. This is between us. But I want that paper done today, without any grief. And I don't want to find any more living objects in my room. If you are upset about something where I'm concerned, I expect you to come to me and we'll discuss it. Do I make myself clear?"

"Yes, Miss." The boy sighed in relief. "I will get it done."

*   *   *

While Edward was writing his paper, Mary Lou had a few moments of freedom. Excusing herself for a walk, she ambled toward the stables, trying to appear as if she had no particular destination in mind.

The place was buzzing like a hive of bees. Grooms brushed their charges, exercise jockeys galloped horses along the track at a blistering pace, and stable-boys lugged enormous bales of hay into the barn. As she watched the routine, she was struck by the fact that the racehorses were like athletes; bred for speed, they did little besides eat, sleep, and work.

One of the jockeys dismounted and took off his cap, wiping away the perspiration his furious gallop had generated. The horse behind him frothed with sweat, but otherwise looked fit and healthy, ready for another run. Seeing Mary Lou, the jockey gave her a curt nod.

"Morning, Miss. You must be the new governess."

"Yes. I'm Mary Lou Finch." She gestured to the horse. "He's a beauty."

"I'm Rudy Wiese. That's Colonel Watkin's 'Dancer'," he said, glancing at the thoroughbred. "He's getting to be an old man now, but he still likes to run. It's the young ones who need the work." He indicated a two-year-old who chafed at the cross-ties securing him in the barn aisleway.

"It must be difficult without a trainer right now," Mary Lou commented.

Rudy nodded. "Thorndike will have a tough time replacing Jimmy. Trainers like him don't grow on trees."

"Was he really that good?"

"He was more than good. Jimmy had been a jockey himself, you know. Rode in all the big races, including Saratoga. Took the three-mile dash in '85 on Susquehanna for the cup. Do you remember it?"

Mary Lou smiled and shook her head. "No, I was a bit young."

"It was a hell of a race. He rode for Lorillard, trained for him, too, before coming to Graystone. We were lucky to have him. And now . . . well, it's a hell of a thing, if you ask me."

"Why do you suppose he was here that night?" Mary Lou asked casually.

The jockey shrugged. "His wife said he thought something was wrong. I don't doubt that; I've seen the man work. He had a sixth sense about him when it came to those horses."

"But don't you think it's odd that he should show up on the same night someone steals the horse?" Mary Lou persisted. "I mean, it is a dreadful coincidence."

The jockey stared at her for a long moment, then spat onto the ground. "Jimmy was a good man," he said softly, and she could hear the outrage in his tone. "There is no way he would betray the master or try to take that horse. And no one's going to say otherwise."

"I didn't mean to imply—"

"Excuse me, Miss. I've another horse to ride."

Without another word, the jockey went into the stables. Mary Lou sighed, her shoulders slumping. Getting information appeared to be near impossible. Horsemen, apparently, were clannish, and didn't like to talk to anyone outside their world. Yet if she couldn't gain their confidence, how would she ever find out what happened to Damien?

Turning, she was about to go back to the house when she saw the curtain move in the library. A shiver went through her as she saw a man pass in front of the glass.

Thorndike had been watching her.

4

—❦—

"She's very charming, Thorndike. Watch that I don't steal her for my own children."

Pierce glanced at his friend Peter Whitesell, then followed his gaze out the window where Mary Lou was teaching Edward from a swing. He frowned as he recalled the early morning scene a few days ago.

Edward had obviously put a snake in Miss Finch's room. Instead of shrieking, shouting, pounding on doors, and then storming out of the house, Mary Lou seemed to take the incident in stride. What kind of woman was she?

It was a puzzle that Pierce couldn't quite piece together. That she was a brilliant scholar was apparent. He had received a glowing reply from one of her professors that morning in response to his telegraphed

inquiry for a reference. Yet he wasn't foolish enough
to believe that the job was her only reason for being
at Graystone. He had already observed her trying to
talk to the jockeys and grooms in between her lessons
with his son. Recalling her presence in the stables
when he'd first met her, his frown returned. Yes, she
was up to something and he was determined to find
out what.

Still, she handled herself with such aplomb that
he couldn't help being pleased. His son was doing
very well under her tutelage—even Bridget was impressed. And the memory of Mary Lou standing defiantly in his son's room with the reptile hidden behind
her back, touched him more than he would have
thought. That coupled with the fact that she had
been nearly naked, the threadbare cotton gown
barely covering her plump form, aroused him instantly. For that reason he had tried to avoid her the
past few days, but found it next to impossible.

Troubled by his own thoughts, he returned his
gaze to his friend. "Yes, she is unusual, to say the
least. Did I tell you she has a degree from the
University?"

Peter shook his head, and dropped into a chair,
helping himself to a cup of Bridget's coffee.
"Beautiful *and* brilliant! Where did you find this creature?"

"She claimed she heard about the position
through a friend," Pierce remarked thoughtfully.
"Her methods of teaching are a little peculiar, but
she's making tremendous progress with my son."

"Peculiar?" Peter asked curiously.

"She spent the morning having Edward read the

Leatherstocking Tales, then the better part of the afternoon collecting specimens of worms. Now they appear to be discussing mathematics from the swing."

"Edward seems to have accepted her much better than any of the other governesses," Peter remarked. "I remember he scared the bloomers off that sourfaced Mrs. McCarthy when he put that frog in her bed."

"I'm afraid he hasn't gone much easier on Miss Finch," Pierce said dryly. "He greeted her with a worm in his hand and a snake in her room."

"How did she react?" Peter asked curiously.

"By teaching him the Latin names of worms and assigning him a paper on snakes. Nothing Edward does seems to upset her in the least."

"Remarkable. You wouldn't blame me if I offered her double what you're paying, would you?"

"I think I'd take off your head," Pierce said seriously. "I just hope she can continue to tolerate Edward's pranks."

"Well, you can't blame the boy too much," Peter said softly. "This year must have been hard on him, with Clarissa's passing and you traveling so much." His gaze fell to Pierce's arm. "I see you no longer wear a band. Have you given up mourning?"

Pierce felt a pang of guilt rise up inside him. His tone was sharper than he intended when he replied. "Yes, I have given up mourning. It has been more than enough time, and given the circumstances . . . " He shook his head, as if wanting to forget. "But I haven't neglected my son on purpose. Unfortunately, my business and investments require travel."

"I didn't mean it that way." Peter sounded offended.

"I know," Pierce said. "I'm sorry. It's just that the subject of Clarissa has a way of bringing back memories."

"She was beautiful." Peter glanced toward the fireplace where a picture once hung over the mantel. "I see you've taken down her portrait."

"I didn't think it healthy for Edward to display it so soon after his mother's death."

"You didn't destroy it?" Peter asked, astonished.

"No, I have it in the attic. Edward may desire it when he gets older. Until then, I thought it best for all concerned to leave it where it is."

Peter sipped his coffee for a moment, then gave Thorndike a sly grin. "Well, I suppose the widow provides some consolation. How is she?"

Pierce sent him a cool look. "Mrs. Norcross and I share an interest in the horses, but that's where it ends. We are merely good friends."

"Of course you are," Peter said with a wink. As he gazed out the window at the beautiful governess, his lip curled mockingly. "It is fortunate Miss Finch is your governess and therefore completely unsuitable. It must be tempting as hell to have such a lovely woman around, knowing she is under your 'protection.'"

"What are you suggesting?" Thorndike asked, his voice thunderous.

"Nothing at all," Peter shrugged, though his eye twinkled. "Although it would be understandable for a man like yourself, alone for so long without female companionship, to find himself . . . intrigued by the possibility of a liaison with his charming servant. However, I know your scruples and such a thing is not within the realm of possibility . . . I would think."

"You are correct." Pierce tried to keep the anger out of his words. "Miss Finch is my son's governess. No one is more aware than I of the delicacy of her situation."

Peter deftly changed the subject rather than risk Thorndike's displeasure any further. "Have you learned anything about the missing thoroughbred? It seems shocking that the police haven't found a clue in all this time."

"They are checking on the whereabouts of Bill Cooke, the servant I discharged a few months ago. Seems the fellow left the area, and they are trying to locate him through relatives. He is the most likely suspect at this point."

"I suppose the man may have felt angry enough to have done such a thing," Peter concurred. "I remember him. Sullen-looking chap."

"Bad-tempered, too. It takes a great deal to upset Bridget, but he managed to do so. He swore revenge when he left my employ, but I never thought he'd stoop to murder."

Peter shook his head. "I guess you can never tell, especially with servants. It's well you got rid of him when you did." Glancing back outside, his solemn expression changed to amused disbelief. "Good Lord, what is she doing now?"

Pierce glanced outside in time to see Mary Lou topple from her seat. "It seems our brilliant governess isn't much on swings. I'd better go rescue her. Can you stay?"

"I have a meeting later, but I wouldn't miss this for the world. You're a lucky man, Thorndike, to have found such a talent."

Pierce could hear his friend's laughter behind him as he went outside to help the unfortunate Miss Finch. Edward dissolved in chuckles at the sight of his governess sitting in the dirt, although he tried to choke his mirth when his father approached. Mary Lou appeared more than a little embarrassed to be caught immersed in the mud beneath the swing, her skirts flung up to her knees, and several inches of petticoat clearly visible. Max barked excitedly, racing around the swing, while his mistress tried to adjust her dress.

"May I be of some help?" Pierce reached down to assist her, somehow managing to hide his amusement.

"Thank you." Given no choice, Mary Lou reluctantly took his hand, and he hauled her to her feet. She was heavier than most women, and he was again forcibly reminded of her round curves and enticing figure. The shock of her palm in his was another surprise, and he reacted instantly, amazed that such a harmless touch could affect him so intensely. He quickly released her, yet the soft, smooth quality of her skin against his made him long to feel her hands all over him.

To his relief, she appeared not to notice. Instead, she gave him a rueful smile, indicating her mud-stained dress, then gazed behind him at his companion.

"Miss Finch?" Peter stepped forward. "I understand you are the new governess. I am Peter Whitesell, a friend of the family."

"It's nice to meet you," Mary Lou said wryly, shaking the dirt out of her dress. "It's been a little while since I sat on a swing. It appears I'm out of practice, although it was the oddest thing. I just slid right off."

"It's only 'cause you were going too high and trying to count with me at the same time," Edward said quickly. "Miss Finch was teaching me how to multiply. If you swing frontwards thirty times, and backwards the same amount, then you've done sixty swings. Thirty times two is sixty."

Peter whistled, impressed, then glanced at Thorndike with a grin. "I see she is everything you said and more. I warned him, Miss Finch, that I may try to persuade you to enter into my employ instead. I guarantee I have a much better temper."

"I appreciate that, Mr. Whitesell," Mary Lou said softly. "But I am very happy at Graystone at the present."

"If that should ever change—"

"Aren't you going?" Thorndike asked meaningfully. "I recall you had a meeting this afternoon."

Peter chuckled, delighted to have irritated him. "Yes, I have to catch the noon train. It is a pleasure, Miss Finch, and if I can ever be of assistance, just let me know."

He walked off whistling a jaunty tune, while Thorndike scowled. Turning to his son, he folded his arms and questioned him abruptly. "So what else did you learn besides the fact that you can swing and Miss Finch cannot?"

A choked sound came from Mary Lou, but Edward, delighted in his interest, thrust out the cup for him to examine.

"We found really good worms. Night crawlers. Did you know there are lots of families of worms? There are flatworms, ribbon worms, roundworms, and segmented worms. Even leeches are worms. I remember some of their names: Platyhelminthes, Nemertea, Aschelminthes . . . "

"Anne . . . " Mary Lou coaxed him.

"Annelid!" Edward said triumphantly. "We're going to take these fishing and learn all the kinds of fish. I told Miss Finch about the bass, and we're going to try and catch him."

"So you include fishing in your talents?" Pierce turned to Mary Lou. "We used to go fishing a lot. I've tried to catch Old Sam for years now, without success. I used earthworms, night crawlers, minnows . . . just about everything. Yet the codger sees through all our tricks."

"Perhaps it just needs a more analytical approach," Mary Lou said. "I happen to know how bass live, where they eat, when they sleep. By learning all of this, Edward increases his chances to catch him. One needs to understand one's quarry in order to succeed, don't you agree?"

"That's an interesting thought." His eyes met hers and he felt again the odd, physical reaction she seemed to effortlessly generate in him. She was an amazing teacher. To hear Latin names tripping effortlessly off his son's tongue was amazing. Even more incredible was Mary Lou's patience. Glancing at the swing, he saw what he suspected: there was a sheen of wax coating the wood, enough to cause Mary Lou's tumble. His frown deepened at the sight, and when he looked back at her, he saw Mary Lou's look of comprehension.

"Edward," she said firmly. "It appears someone was careless and spilled something on this swing. No wonder I fell! I suggest you get a sponge and some hot water from the kitchen and scrub this down. Otherwise, someone could get hurt."

Pierce was about to reinforce the command when he saw his son glance shamefacedly at the swing. Without questioning her order, he nodded, put down the cup, then ran to the kitchen to do her bidding. As soon as Edward was out of earshot, Pierce spoke softly.

"I must apologize for my son's behavior, Miss Finch. I truly hope you weren't hurt, and that his pranks haven't upset you too much."

She raised her face to his and he saw that her eyes, an interesting shade of sea-green, softened, and she shrugged as if the incident mattered little. "Edward is an amazingly bright boy, Mr. Thorndike. I see his rebellion as evidence of that intelligence. I plan to channel it into his studies."

"I also think Edward just didn't like his former governesses," Pierce said thoughtfully. "They didn't seem to understand him. This past year has been difficult for him, with his mother passing, then our horse being stolen, and our trainer murdered. I'm sure you read about the incident in the papers. Edward was very close to Jimmy. I haven't had a chance to return his belongings to his family yet, but I asked the groom to put them in the storage shed. I don't want the boy upset any further."

"I understand he's been through a lot," Mary Lou said softly. "Be that as it may, he owes a teacher respect, and I will see that he gives it. Once we are past that, then I can really begin to teach him."

"I think you have been amazingly successful already," Pierce said truthfully. "But you must tell me if he persists with his pranks, for I will discipline him."

Mary Lou looked at Pierce for a moment, then smiled. "I appreciate your help, but I assure you I am not at all afraid of Edward. Furthermore, he must learn to respect me, not because you want him to, but because he does."

The wisdom of her words struck him, and he was once more amazed at the odd Miss Finch. A wisp of straw still stuck to her hair from her fall, and he reached up to remove it. Mary Lou looked startled at the gesture, her eyes widening. He smiled and tossed the straw to the ground, but didn't move away from her, noticing up close that her skin was faintly flushed. He became aware of her scent, clean and fresh, like the outdoors, and of her womanly curves just inches away from him. Perspiration gleamed on her flesh like tiny pearls, making her glow with a healthy radiance, and Pierce was aware of his own sweat beading on his forehead just from being this close to her. Thankfully, Edward ran up with his bucket and Mary Lou stepped backward.

"That's it, Edward, scrub it well," she said briskly, an odd note in her voice. Pierce glanced at her, but she was all business now with his son present. "Did you know that wax is made of animal or plant fats? It is for this reason that we have to use very hot water to break it down, or ice water in winter, which would cause it to harden. The scientific reasons for these changes are created by . . . "

Pierce walked away slowly, watching his son scrub the swing, his brow intent on his teacher's words. Yes, he'd been incredibly lucky to find Mary Lou Finch, yet he couldn't ignore what had passed between them. Whatever caused this odd compulsion he had toward her, he'd have to control it. Mary Lou Finch was a governess, his son's teacher, nothing more. It was a lesson he repeated over and over in his own mind.

Mary Lou watched Pierce leave, a shiver of desire still racing through her. Good Lord, what was wrong with her? Nothing had happened. Or had it?

The sensation of standing so close to Thorndike certainly had an affect on her. Mary Lou swore she could feel the hot blood pumping through her veins, and her skin was as sensitive as if a feather had just been traced all over it. Closing her eyes, she savored the odd experience. She felt curiously alive, and more physically aware than she could remember.

Shaking off her thoughts, she forced herself back to the matter at hand. She wasn't here to perform biological experiments with Pierce Thorndike, as enticing as the thought might be. No, she was here to investigate the missing horse, something she had found challenging since she spent so much time with Edward. Her mind wandered back to Pierce's comment about the trainer's belongings, and a quick thrill ran up her spine. She didn't want to question Edward due to the nature of the crime. But Thorndike had mentioned that Jimmy's things were still in the storage shed. Might they contain a clue, or some hint of what had happened? It was certainly worth a look.

She hadn't much time, for Pierce had made it

plain he planned to return the man's possessions. Mary Lou resolved to investigate as soon as possible. By focusing on the task at hand, she could put the handsome Pierce Thorndike and his seductive chemistry from her mind.

She hoped.

Thorndike hated it when everyone else was asleep, when the minutes became hours and the hours became eternity. Ever since Clarissa's death, this had been happening more and more. It was as if her spirit haunted him. He stared moodily at the crackling fire. He thought about having a brandy, but experience told him that liquor would only induce drowsiness, not the blessed relief of real sleep. No. Tonight, like many other nights, that refuge would not be his.

A moment later, the hair stood up on the back of his neck and he slowed his breathing, listening intently. Something was wrong. A door closed softly somewhere in the house, then silence followed. Swiftly he slipped out of the library. Could his son be up to another prank? Anger rushed through him at the thought. If that was the case, he would take matters into his own hands. Edward had to learn to respect other people, in spite of his own emotional difficulties.

Yet when he peered into his son's room, he felt a surge of relief. Edward was sleeping in his bed, his little head practically buried beneath the covers. But if it wasn't Edward, who was creeping about the house?

The wall clock told him the hour was barely three.

Snatching a gun from his room, Pierce lit a lantern and went downstairs. He searched each room, paying careful attention to the doors and windows. Everything appeared normal. Yet when he reached the kitchen, he saw that the door leading outside was not bolted.

His fingers tightened on the weapon as he thought of the stables. Could the intruder who had killed his trainer have returned? It was an unpleasant thought, but one he couldn't dismiss.

The path to the stables was dark, but clearly marked. A cold summer breeze blew through his robe as Pierce walked determinedly toward the barn, holding the gun carefully. When he reached the stables, however, he saw that the gate was firmly secured. Puzzled, he glanced back toward the house and noticed that the storage shed was open. Could someone be hiding inside? Venturing closer, he put the lantern on the ground, then quietly slipped through the door.

At first, it was hard to see. He cocked his gun, reassured by the deadly sound in the darkness. Taking another step, he saw a furtive movement near the storage trunks and a shadow fell across the floor. There was something about the figure that seemed familiar . . . Pierce lunged toward the body, successfully tackling the figure, then cursed as he wrestled it to the ground.

Mary Lou Finch struggled furiously in his arms.

5

"What in blazes?" Thorndike hauled her unceremoniously outside into the lamplight. Mary Lou tried to break free, but he clasped her arm firmly and glared at her as she stood in the dim light.

"Miss Finch?" he asked, astonished. "What are you doing out here?"

Mary Lou swallowed hard. She had just barely begun looking through Jimmy Dwyer's things when she'd heard footsteps. Her hand closed around the object she'd discovered on top of his clothes, and she secreted it in the pocket of her dress. She never expected to be caught like this. Good Lord, the man must have eyes in the back of his head! "I . . . I suppose I was sleepwalking."

His gaze narrowed, and his eyes became

impossibly bluer. Mary Lou was reminded of the
color at the base of a candle flame. Under other circumstances, she would have admired their intensity,
but that was next to impossible as his fingers tightened around her wrist.

"Sleepwalking?" he questioned. "Do you expect
me to believe that?"

"Honestly, it's true!"

"We will go up to the house and discuss this in detail," he said coldly. "I'm warning you, Miss Finch,
you had better have a good explanation."

With that, he hauled her out of the shed, pausing
only long enough to lock the door. He didn't let go of
her wrist, holding it firmly to prevent her from running away. She admired the wisdom of his action.
Given half a chance, Mary Lou considered wryly, she
would have run away.

The walk to the house seemed incredibly short.
By the time they got to the library, her heart was
pounding furiously. Thorndike closed the door and finally released her. Mary Lou skittered past him to the
far corner, putting the relative safety of a chair between them.

"Well?" He stood before her, waiting for an answer.

Mary Lou sighed. It was utterly tempting to confess everything and throw herself on his mercy, but
she couldn't do that. Everyone was a suspect at this
point, Pierce Thorndike included. She would normally deplore telling a half-truth, but tonight she had
no other choice.

"I really do have a problem," she said, crossing her

fingers behind her back in a very unscientific manner. "When my mother died, I began sleepwalking. My father thought it due to grief, because it started the night of her wake, but it has continued intermittently since, about once or twice a year."

Mary Lou didn't trouble to enlighten him that tonight wasn't one of those nights, but thankfully, Thorndike didn't ask.

"And your father knows about this?" he asked incredulously.

She nodded. "He had a doctor examine me, but he could find nothing wrong. The servants were aware of it, so they kept an eye out in case I wandered too far. So far, it hasn't happened. It is very embarrassing, however. For this reason, I was never permitted to go to boarding school, nor to spend many weekends away from home. My father feared the worst."

A shred of doubt still lingered in his eyes, but the harsh suspicion had gone. His eyes traveled down her gown to her feet, then up to her face again. "I should think your father would be most concerned, Miss Finch. I certainly would be if I had a daughter who wandered into strange places in her sleep, especially if she had the presence of mind to dress."

Mary Lou felt the color drain from her face. She had allayed one suspicion, only to rekindle another. "I often sleep in my clothes, because of the possibility of this happening."

"I see." He said, his tone telling her he didn't believe her for an instant. "I also find it most unusual for a governess to have servants. Your little problem grows more perplexing by the moment."

"My father has fallen on bad times," she improvised frantically. "For that reason I found it necessary to seek employment."

"So he sends his beautiful sleepwalking daughter into the world as a governess. I should like to meet your father at some point, Miss Finch. I imagine the conversation would be equally as interesting as the one we are having now."

Panic filled her. In truth, her father hadn't been happy about her coming here, but had only agreed when there was no other solution. Desperate, Mary Lou took refuge in high dudgeon. "If you are unhappy with my services, sir, I will look elsewhere for employment."

The gauntlet lay between them. Thorndike appeared to consider her words. "I have no objection to your performance, Miss Finch. Frankly, I am very pleased with the progress you have made within such a short time period. You've managed to reach my son, which no other governess has been able to do. No, I would be foolish indeed to complain about that."

Relief flooded through her. "Thank you, sir."

Some of the hardness left his face and he gazed past her, as if seeing into some secret part of himself that he kept hidden. "I also sympathize with your need to wander the night. I, too, am cursed with a similar affliction, although I am fully awake. It began with the death of my wife. It usually starts with the same dream, more like a nightmare, then I cannot return to sleep. I suppose there are some things the mind just can't accept."

Something caught in Mary Lou's heart. She

sensed that this proud man did not often admit a weakness to anyone.

"How did she die, sir?"

The question hung in the air. Thorndike gazed at her, his eyes smoldering with emotion. "I'd prefer not to discuss it."

Mary Lou ignored the tightening in her stomach. "You must have loved her very much," she said gently, wondering why the thought upset her.

"Do you believe in love, Miss Finch?"

Thorndike stared outside the window into the night, his striking profile framed against the glass. His black hair fell perfectly across his forehead, an astonishing contrast to his midnight-blue robe, while his sensual mouth curved in thought.

His manner was so odd that Mary Lou found herself stammering. "Yes, sir. I believe I do, sir."

"With all of your scientific knowledge? Come now, I expected a more cerebral answer from you."

He spoke sardonically, but there was a deadly serious note beneath his words. Mary Lou didn't quite know how to answer.

"I do think it exists, sir," she said slowly. "There is much documented information about it, from Byron to Freud. However, I have observed many of the rituals we associate with love among insects and animals, leading me to believe that some of it is a result of mating functions."

"Mating functions?" He turned away from the window and came to stand closely beside her. He lifted her face to his, and gazed deep into her eyes. "Then you have never been in love, Miss Finch?"

"No, I can't say that I have. . . . " Something strange was happening, some odd tension growing between them. Mary Lou sensed the change, but wasn't at all sure what to make of it.

"I find that hard to believe," Thorndike said hoarsely. "Indeed, next to impossible."

Perhaps it was the moonlight spilling into the room and bathing them in silver. Or maybe it was the warm scent of spring fueling the welter of confusing emotions that raced through her. For the wildest moment, she thought he would reach for her, take her into his embrace, and kiss her. A yearning spread through her, filling every cell in her body, making her want to hold him, to comfort the pain she sensed in him, to explore the sensuality that seemed to radiate from him.

Her mind rebelled even as the thought formed. He was her employer, not a suitor! She was behaving ridiculously. Yet she couldn't stop the sensation, nor could she quell the inexplicable longing that burned inside her.

He seemed to sense her thoughts, for he released her and took a step backward. Disappointment mingled with regret inside her, even though she found it easier to think without his disturbing presence so close.

"I think I should go to bed now," Mary Lou said softly, her voice unsteady. "It is getting very late, and I have an early day planned tomorrow."

"Miss Finch," Thorndike's voice stopped her. "Do not be deceived into thinking I believe everything you've told me. I know there is more to your story than you have chosen to reveal. However, as long as your presence does not endanger my son, I will not object to you keeping your own counsel. Bear in mind, however, that I will not see you jeopardize your own safety any more than my son's. And I will not hesitate to take action if that occurs."

Mary Lou looked back at him incredulously. How could he confide in her one moment, then be so cool and autocratic the next? "Certainly, Mr. Thorndike," she answered demurely. "I understand completely." Then she turned and fled the room.

Mary Lou had barely departed when Thorndike cursed. He'd been dangerously close to breaking the promise he'd made to himself, and the woman had been in his household less than a week. But she had looked so damned beautiful, like an unearthly fairy creature, her hair tumbling softly about her as if just roused from sleep, her voice genuinely concerned. He shook his head, disgusted with himself. She was under his protection, and he had absolutely no business befriending her, or desiring her, for that matter. She was his son's governess, and that was all.

His thoughts drifted to the shed where he'd discovered her snooping. He wasn't foolish enough to believe her story, no matter how attractive she was. Whatever she was up to, he intended to put a stop to it. Before it was too late.

Mary Lou wandered back to her room in a daze. Surely she had imagined this entire incident, and would wake in the morning to find it all just a dream.

Gazing at the closed door, she wondered what had just happened. Had the master of Graystone really spoken to her the way he had? And that one moment when it seemed he would kiss her . . . surely she was mistaken. A man like Thorndike could have any woman he wanted. Was it possible he was . . . attracted to her?

Her reflection caught her eye and she winced in embarrassment. Her body was too soft, too round . . . her breasts too large. At age thirteen, they seemed to have developed overnight, and she had become suddenly very conscious of the male eyes on her in the schoolroom. Now at age twenty with the rest of her filled out to match, those eyes were much less interested. No, a man like Thorndike couldn't possibly desire a woman like her. He was simply trying to be kind, and she had read too much into it.

Shaking her head, Mary Lou sternly reminded herself that she was here on a case, and not to moon after Thorndike, no matter how devastating he was. Slipping out of her dress, she absently reached into her pocket and withdrew the package she'd taken from Jimmy's things. Slowly, she opened the box and gazed at the contents. There, on a black velvet bed, nestled a beautiful ruby ring.

The stone winked at her in the candlelight. Mary Lou turned it, watching the sparkling prisms dance around the room. While not of the finest quality, it nevertheless was a lot of money for a trainer to spend. The receipt was still inside, and showed that it had been paid for just before Damien's disappearance. But why would the trainer have kept such a ring in the barn? If he meant to give it to his wife, wouldn't it have been safer to keep it in the cottage, where he didn't risk it being lost or stolen? Unless it wasn't for her . . .

Mary Lou took the ring out of the box and examined it more closely. There wasn't much room for an inscription, but inside the band she could make out the letters N LOVE J. What did it mean?

With every clue Mary Lou found the mystery only grew more complex. She put the ring carefully inside the box and placed it in her satchel. She would have to find out more, but it would be difficult, especially now when she had newly aroused Thorndike's suspicions.

Turning down the gas jet, she slipped into bed and pulled up the covers. Try as she might, her thoughts refused to obey her and continually returned to Thorndike. Why was she so drawn to him, a man she barely knew? How much did he know? Sleep was a long time coming, and even then she dreamed of a pair of burning blue eyes.

6

—🌿—

"Good morning, Miss. You're looking a little peaked today." Bridget quickly poured a steaming cup of coffee and placed it before Mary Lou.

"Miss Finch, perhaps I should remind you that we breakfast sharply at eight," Thorndike said, never looking up from his newspaper.

"I'm sorry, sir," Mary Lou said softly. The tension hung in the air like a Boston fog. "I woke with a slight headache. I always do the morning after . . ." she let her words trail off. She was about to say after sleepwalking, but didn't want to remind him of the night before. She was still too shaken by what had happened between them. Evidently, from the way he was acting, he didn't care to be reminded either.

"You'll not be the only one feeling a bit out of sorts this morning," Bridget said, giving Thorndike a disapproving glance. "Only Master Edward seems in good form."

Edward had finished his breakfast and was perched at the window. Mary Lou could hear Max's encouraging bark as he spotted the young boy just above him.

"Yap, yap, yap . . ."

"Miss Finch," Thorndike growled, the paper coming down an inch to reveal a penetrating blue eye. "Do you think you might silence your pet for a blessed moment? I'd like some semblance of peace."

Mary Lou and Bridget exchanged a glance. "Edward," Mary Lou said softly, hushing her own words. "Come away from the window and he'll stop barking."

"But I want to play with him—"

"Perhaps, sir, you'd prefer your breakfast in the dining room, where you usually eat?" Bridget intervened quickly, sensing a crisis. "After all, it is much quieter there."

"I should be able to eat anywhere in this house I choose without the Civil War bursting about my ears," Thorndike said harshly. "Although I can see I will get no quiet here. Bring my coffee into the dining room."

With that he stormed off, taking the newspaper with him. Bridget clucked her tongue, and gave Mary Lou an apologetic glance. "Sorry, lass. He's not usually like that. Something must have set his nerves on edge, that's for sure."

"I can't imagine what," Mary Lou said, stirring a teaspoon of sugar into her coffee. It was impossible to believe this was the same man who had spoken to her so confidingly the night before. "Edward, why don't you go outside and play with Max until lessons start? I think Bridget saved him a bone from dinner."

Edward appeared delighted with that idea. Bridget gave him the bone and he raced outside, eager to give the dog a treat. The housekeeper chuckled at the picture of the boy racing around the backyard with the dog at his heels. "I daresay, it's good to see the lad so happy. He likes the wee pup."

"Boys and dogs go together," Mary Lou said, enjoying the moment of quiet. She sipped her coffee thoughtfully, then glanced at the housekeeper. "You know, I think I'd like to pay a visit to Mrs. Dwyer. I imagine she must be feeling terrible after the loss of her husband."

"Aye, that she is." Bridget nodded. "Poor thing is heartbroken. She lives at the little cottage near the woods."

Mary Lou nodded. "Do you happen to know her given name?"

" 'Tis Grace. She came with Mr. Dwyer years ago, from his racing days in New York City. Her family had money from what I hear, and were none too happy with her marrying a horseman. But he was a good man, so they came around for all that."

"I see," Mary Lou said casually. "Did Mr. Dwyer and his wife get along?"

Bridget pursed her lips as if reluctant to speak. "As good as some. Mr. Dwyer was a handsome man, and the ladies had an eye for him. His wife wasn't happy about that, but he treated her and the little ones well, so there wasn't much to complain about."

Mary Lou thought about the ring. "N" didn't stand for Grace, that was certain. She was about to ask more when the peace was shattered by a knock on the door, followed by the butler's grave countenance.

"Miss Finch, I think you should come. Quickly."

Mary Lou heard Thorndike's voice in the parlor. She and the housekeeper rushed to the front door where a man stood with an assortment of boxes. Edward stood behind him, while Thorndike gazed at him incredulously.

"Would someone mind telling me what on earth is going on here?"

Mary Lou's eyes fell on the boxes and she brightened with glee, all thought of her headache gone. "They've come! I can't believe so quickly!" She gazed at the delivery man as if he was an angel. "Sir, you must have silver wings on your feet!"

The man at the door smiled sheepishly, then indicated the cartons. "You are Mary Lou Finch?"

"Yes, I am."

"Then these—"

"Are my laboratory supplies." Eagerly Mary Lou opened the first box, then lovingly withdrew a bundle from its depths. Gingerly, she unwrapped the package, and a microscope appeared.

"Isn't it beautiful! My father bought it for me when I was fourteen. Edward, look! We can truly begin our science studies now."

Edward and Max peered into the open box, as if

to see what other treasures lay inside. Thorndike cleared his throat threateningly, then indicated the assortment of trunks.

"Miss, do you mean to tell me all of this is your . . . equipment?"

"Oh, no, not all of it," Mary Lou said happily. "That one contains my clothes." She indicated a tiny trunk nestled alongside the cartons.

Thorndike stared at her in disbelief. "Where do you propose to keep all of this paraphernalia?"

"I was hoping to use the barn as a makeshift laboratory," Mary Lou explained. "Some of the chemicals can be dangerous, so I would not think to bring them into the house. Even an old shed will do."

His expression didn't change. "Dangerous. How very interesting." Thorndike dipped into one of the boxes and held a test tube up to the light. "Miss Finch, I forbid you to bring this equipment anywhere near my stables. You may not be aware that some of my horses are worth more than this house."

"But I must set up my laboratory. I am in the middle of several studies that I have to complete. And it will be very informative for Edward. He will be able to do real experiments," Mary Lou argued desperately. Surely he wouldn't forbid her . . .

"Do you mean I can use all this, too?" Edward pulled out a specimen jar and peered inside.

Thorndike sighed, giving in against his better judgment. "There is a small cottage at the end of the garden path that you may use. It is made of stone, so if you decide to incinerate yourself, the building will be preserved."

A rush of relief sped through her and she gave him a grateful glance. "Thank you, sir."

"You are welcome," he replied. The tension in the room seemed to fade, and his eyes met Mary Lou's, one brow arched mockingly. "You truly are a woman of learning, aren't you?"

"Yes, sir, to a small degree anyway."

"Incredible. I meant what I said to you last night, however. Do not cause injury with these things. Otherwise, I will change my mind."

"You have nothing to fear," she said, keeping the barn-burning story to herself. "I have had extensive experience with chemistry. It is a particular hobby of mine."

"So I recall. Biology, too."

Mary Lou suddenly realized he was referring to her mating comments the previous night. She felt the color rise to her face, and only hoped it didn't show.

Thankfully, Thorndike seemed preoccupied. "Beecham, would you mind seeing that Miss Finch's things are settled? I would like to know that she is, indeed, blowing up the cottage instead of the house."

The butler's eyes widened, but he turned quickly to the delivery man outside the door. "I believe you heard the master, sir. Please take these . . . things into the garden house. I'll take care of the clothing."

As they lugged her cartons away, Bridget spoke quickly. "Will you be needing anything else, sir?"

"No," Thorndike said. "I have to go into town today. Make sure you keep everything locked up securely. I thought I heard fairies wandering around last night."

Mary Lou refused to look at him, while the house-keeper threw up her hands in disbelief. "Fairies! 'Tis joking you are, Mr. Thorndike. I never heard such nonsense."

"Nor I," Thorndike said softly.

Mary Lou ventured outside with Edward, enthusiastically setting up the laboratory. "We'll set the test tubes up here, the gas burners there, the microscope on this table. I'll put the pestle and mortar on this shelf. Edward, why don't you put the slides in beside the microscope, and I'll put the petri dishes in this cabinet. These are the very latest development in scientific investigation."

"What are they for?" Edward asked, perplexed at the sight of the small, shallow dishes.

"They are used to grow bacteria cultures," Mary Lou patiently explained. "There are all kinds of living creatures that we cannot see with the naked eye. Some of them are good bacteria that keep us healthy, but others cause illness. Scientists grow them in order to learn how they live and how we can best control them."

"Do you mean," Edward's nose wrinkled, "that little bugs are on us now?" He gazed at his arm.

Mary Lou laughed. "Yes, I suppose you can think of them that way. There are thousands of bacteria living harmlessly in your nose and mouth. They are on surfaces we touch and spread between people."

Edward made a disgusted face as he examined his hand. "I can't see anything."

"That's why we use the microscope. Come, we'll

take a few drops of water from the pond and we'll examine it under a slide. You'll then be able to see the other world through the glass."

That intrigued the boy, and he eagerly assisted Mary Lou with setting up the rest of the equipment. When they were finished, she stood back and eyed it proudly. If anything, her laboratory looked even better here than it did in her woodshed back in Boston. Test tubes glinted in the morning light, while the gas burners gleamed enticingly. Gaping bookshelves now groaned under the weight of her own texts. Neatly labeled jars of chemicals waited beside measuring tools, and a small scale stood at the edge of the counter. The cottage had been kept in immaculate condition, and she barely felt it necessary to run a dust cloth over the surfaces. It was the laboratory she'd always dreamed of.

"Can we go now?" Edward eyed the microscope longingly.

"After we've finished your sums. Mathematics is a very important part of chemistry, you know."

"No! Let's go now!" Edward got to his feet and began racing around the table. "Can we? Can we go?" Rounding the corner, he accidentally banged into the counter. The microscope tumbled to the floor with a loud crash.

"Oh no." Edward stared at the broken glass in horror. Moisture welled up in his eyes and he looked at Mary Lou in abject shame and terror. "I didn't mean it! I really didn't!"

Mary Lou sighed. "It's all right, it was an accident."

"Really, I didn't mean to do it! Honest, it just fell!"

The boy burst into tears and plastered himself against Mary Lou's skirts.

Mary Lou patted his head in compassion. Edward's reaction was exaggerated for what had happened, and she wondered why he seemed so terrified. Had one of his governesses been excessively harsh with him? She was certain Thorndike never reprimanded the boy unduly.

"There, there, Edward, don't carry on so. The only things broken are the slides, and we can replace them. Why don't you help me. Fetch that carton from the shelf there and we'll patch it right up."

The boy lifted his red face, his eyes brimming with relief. "Can you truly fix it?"

"Yes, I am certain." Mary Lou smiled reassuringly.

The boy rushed to get the box, and Mary Lou picked up the microscope. It was just as she thought. The lenses were all intact, and only the thin slides had shattered. Carefully, she picked out the glass, then took a new slide from Edward's hand.

"There we are. Good as new. See?" She showed him the instrument.

Edward grinned, the tears still sparkling on his freckled cheeks. "Are you sure it will work?" The worried look returned.

"We'll find out, won't we? Now why don't you sweep up the glass and I'll fetch the dustbin so no one gets cut."

The boy appeared genuinely happy, and rushed to get the broom. Mary Lou watched as he swept carefully, cleaning up the shattered glass better than any Dutch housewife. She scooped up the pile of glass shards and tossed them in the dustbin, then brushed her hands in satisfaction.

"There now. Let's go to the pond and fetch some samples. You take the jars, and I'll bring the notebooks. Put them in that bag." She indicated a burlap sack.

Edward eyed the gleaming jars uncertainly. "What if I drop them?"

"You won't," Mary Lou said. "I know you can do it."

Edward held his head high, taking the burlap sack and gripping it tightly. He carried it as if it contained treasure, his little fingers knotted tightly in the rough material. Mary Lou smiled. It obviously meant a lot to the boy to let him carry the jars, and proved her trust in him. Edward wasn't a bad child, he was just emotional and confused. His attention span wasn't as great as other children she'd seen, but that, Mary Lou was certain, could improve. She only needed to find ways in which he could shine, and build his confidence and patience. The rest would come when he was ready.

Later that night, after Edward had gone to bed, Mary Lou went downstairs. Carrying the carpetbag in one hand and her candle in the other, she ventured out to the cottage.

The door was locked, but Thorndike had given her the key and it took only moments to open the bolt. Inside, everything was just as she left it. The test tubes gleamed in the dim light, the shiny metal pans and glass dishes waited on the counter. She had set out all of the tools she needed, and saw that the knives, razor, stain, and slides were still neatly positioned beside the microscope.

Placing the satchel on the table, she withdrew the apple she had found in Damien's stall. The past week had left it even more shriveled, but that couldn't be helped. She needed her equipment in order to run the right tests. Thankfully, Thorndike hadn't returned, so she had a golden opportunity to sleuth.

After cutting the apple in half, she sniffed the fruit, and detected a bitter odor. A thrill of excitement shot through her and she took the razor and peeled a thin strip of the skin, then put it in the test tube. After adding several chemicals, she drew off the remaining mixture and tested it. Observing the results, her expression grew grim.

Arsenic. Quite a lot of it, even in the small sample. Using a copper apparatus, she repeated the test with a piece of the core. This time, the results were even more impressive. Without a doubt, someone had intended to drug Damien. This high a concentration was probably meant to kill him; if not, he would never race again. Mary Lou thought of the rats she'd seen after ingesting this drug and shuddered. It was a terrible death.

Mary Lou studied the test tube thoughtfully. When she had seen the apple laying in the feed bucket, she had thought it odd. Most horses, especially racehorses who worked constantly, would no more leave an apple than she would a slice of chocolate cake. She'd thought perhaps the apple was the enticement the thief used to gain the horse's confidence, but it seemed he had a much more sinister motive in mind.

Sitting back in her chair, she made some notations in her notebook. So, whoever had stolen the horse perhaps intended to drug him instead. But something must have gone very wrong. Had Jimmy Dwyer walked in on someone trying to feed the prize horse a drug-laced fruit? Or could something else, equally peculiar, have taken place?

"Well, well, Miss Finch. Would you mind telling me what you're doing?"

Thorndike stood at the door.

7

❧

Mary Lou swallowed hard. He'd caught her again!
He must have just returned from town. Calming her
shattered nerves, she reminded herself that he
couldn't possibly know what she was really doing.

"A simple experiment," she said bravely. "After I
set up the equipment I thought I'd make sure everything was in good working order."

"Miss Finch, I thought I made it clear that I didn't
want you endangering yourself by becoming involved
in any investigations."

Mary Lou could feel the color drain from her
face. "But I wasn't . . . "

Thorndike didn't reply, but simply picked up the
piece of apple. "I recognize a test for drugs when I

see one. What did you find?" He sniffed the apple. "Arsenic, I would think."

Her mouth hung open, absolutely refusing her silent command to close. "How did you know—"

"Do you take me for a fool, Miss Finch?" He put down the fruit and faced her, his eyes hard and glittering.

He was furious, Mary Lou realized a moment later, deadly furious. She swallowed hard. "But I only wanted to see—"

"If your theory was correct." He grabbed her shoulders, his fingers tight. "And now you know. So what have you gained from your knowledge, except that should it become known, you would endanger yourself? What do you think would happen to you if the party responsible for Damien's disappearance were to discover your investigation? I have no intention of finding your body the way my trainer was found! Do you understand me?"

His voice was thunderous, and he gave her a quick shake, as if determined to get through to her. "Yes, sir," Mary Lou managed, more frightened than she cared to admit. Thorndike's temper was unnerving, to say the least. She had never been alone with a man in such a situation, with this kind of outrage directed at her. She was within his employ, and no one would rush to her rescue, no matter what he did. But why was he so determined that she not investigate? What did he have to hide?

She didn't dare ask, but held her breath, waiting to see what would happen next. He could easily dismiss her, order her out of his house, and then where would she be?

She attempted to smile, trying to ease the tension between them, but saw no answer on his implacable face. "I'm sorry, sir. I didn't mean to upset anyone."

It took a moment, but her meek response finally seemed to register, as did her capitulation. She saw the tightness in his jaw soften.

"Good." His grip eased, yet he continued to hold her. Thankfully, the anger seemed to leave him. Mary Lou felt his touch become almost a caress as his hands slid down her arms. That strange sensuality she'd experienced in his presence asserted itself once more, and she became so physically aware of him it almost hurt. Looking up, she saw the same longing, the same unbearable desire in his eyes. He seemed to be fighting something within himself, and she wasn't at all certain which side she wanted to win. Yet he released her as quickly as he'd touched her, and turned on his heel. When he reached the door, he paused, then turned back to face her.

"I apologize for my outburst. I am simply concerned that no one else in my care be injured."

"I understand," Mary Lou exhaled, surprised to discover that she'd been holding her breath.

His gaze captured hers and the look in them made her weak. She thought for one terrifying second that he was going to say something about the strange attraction between them or even do something about it. Instead, he departed quickly, leaving her alone in the cottage.

Mary Lou collapsed onto a chair, gazing at the little glass tube before her. Her body felt as if it was on fire. Why? He had only touched her shoulders, hadn't done anything improper. Yet she could still feel the electricity in the air, and knew her own restraint was no thicker than the chocolate on an eclair. What was happening between them? What did Pierce Thorndike want from her?

And, more importantly, what did she want from him?

Thorndike returned to the stables, cursing his own desires. Peter had been right; it had been too long since he'd been with a woman in the physical sense. The thought of seducing his governess was completely unacceptable, yet this woman had a way of getting under his skin. That she was brilliant was obvious; no one else thought to test an old apple lying in the barn for poison. But her intelligence could only lead to danger. He had to keep her out of trouble, yet it seemed whenever he was within ten feet of her, all he could think about was seducing her. Somehow he had to regain control, prove to himself that he could behave in a noble manner. Perhaps it was time to focus his attentions elsewhere.

"Saddle up Blackwatch, Bobby," he called to the sleepy stableboy.

"Are you going out, sir?" The boy looked at the dark sky.

"Yes. I'm going to visit the Widow Norcross."

"Pierce! What a nice surprise!" Vivian Norcross stood on her porch and held the door graciously open. "Won't you come in?"

Thorndike entered the comfortable home and

sank down into a seat in silent appreciation. The widow was a striking woman of about thirty-five years, with auburn hair and a firm figure from riding. She sat across from him and ordered tea for herself, brandy for Pierce. A servant deposited the tray and quickly departed.

"Your usual," she said, leaning forward with a smile to hand Thorndike his drink. "I swear my maid thinks you and I are having a scandalous affair. She always leaves so quickly when you're here."

Pierce drank deeply from the brandy glass and gazed out the window to the rich pasture beyond. "How are things at the stables?"

"Very good. Would you like to see?" She rose as if to accompany him.

"No, don't trouble yourself. I'll look before I leave." This wasn't going as he expected. Somehow Pierce had hoped that upon seeing the beautiful widow, his inappropriate desire for his governess might somehow dissipate. Instead, he struggled for conversation. "How is the new colt?"

"Boston Blue is wonderful," the widow smiled fondly. "He's all legs and full of himself. Pocos, his mother, doesn't know quite what to make of him, but I think he'll do just fine. Pierce, we don't have to do this, you know."

"Do what?"

"Make small talk. We've known each other far too long for that."

"I know. It's just . . . " Thorndike struggled with the words. "I'm sorry, Vivian, I shouldn't have come. It's terribly late, and I've just realized how tired I am."

"Please, don't say that. You are welcome here any time." Vivian stood before him and took the glass, her fingers closing around his. For a moment they touched, her slender hand covering his, and their eyes met in silent communication. She looked beautiful in the moonlight, her eyes wide and luminous, her mouth curved in a sultry smile. "You could even stay the night if you are too tired to ride."

Her voice contained a clear invitation. Thorndike shook his head. "I don't think that's a good idea. I have to go to town tomorrow. But thank you."

He stepped back and stood before the window. Vivian flushed in embarrassment and disappointment, then covered it quickly by finishing the last of his brandy. Thorndike didn't seem to notice. Instead, he gazed at the moonlit stables, as if engrossed in his own thoughts. The widow watched him for a moment, her eyes narrowing, then she came to stand beside him and rested her hand possessively on his shoulder.

"So tell me about your new governess. I hear she's a beauty."

Pierce startled, then glanced down at her, his dark brow knotted. "I wouldn't have taken you for a gossip, Vivian."

"It's just neighborhood talk, that's all. But as a woman, I am curious. Tell me about her."

"She is beautiful," Pierce admitted, watching a shadow cross the woman's face. "Also brilliant, and wonderful with Edward. I've never met anyone quite like her. One minute she's analytical, the next she's an innocent, brimming with passion. But she is Edward's governess."

"Meaning . . . "

"Meaning exactly that."

The widow gazed at him for a moment, then smiled. "She sounds interesting. Perhaps I should make her acquaintance."

"I wouldn't advise it," Thorndike said dryly. "Miss Finch isn't exactly your type. She's quite the scholar, interested in chemistry and biology. She may consider you a subject for an experiment, and I couldn't guarantee your safety. But I do very much admire Miss Finch and hope—"

"Yes?" The widow interjected expectantly.

Thorndike smiled. "Hope that she will stay, for Edward's sake. Now if you'll excuse me, I'd better be getting home."

"Of course." Looping her arm through his, the widow indicated the door. "I can see why this conversation would make you uncomfortable. Fear not, good friend. Your little secret is safe with me. All of them are."

Mary Lou returned to her room, still shaking from her encounter with Thorndike. Why was he so upset? Was he truly afraid for her, or what she might find? How much did Thorndike know?

It didn't make sense that he was involved in the theft of his own horse . . . did it? Of everyone involved, his loss was the greatest. Why then, was he so mysterious? Could he be protecting someone else?

Mary Lou shook her head. It was all too difficult to fathom. Then she thought of his hands on her and her breath caught. What was it about the man that made her react so physically to him? She didn't understand it at all. One minute he was yelling at her, the next . . . She closed her eyes, imagining him taking her into his arms, kissing her with the same kind of passion she'd just seen in his eyes. . . .

Mary Lou shook herself, forcing the embarrassing thoughts away. She was his governess, and could never be anything else. A man like Thorndike wouldn't marry a servant. And she certainly didn't see herself as a mistress! That made her wonder if he had one at all, and immediately the vision of his mysterious business trips came to mind. Was Thorndike involved with a woman, some wealthy, sophisticated lady who enjoyed everything his hard-muscled body had to offer?

The thought was painful, but very likely. Pierce was a man of great passions—she had seen that already. And his wife was dead. A mistress would be the logical choice; such situations were tolerated as indulgences by married men, and for a widower, completely understandable. Why then, did the idea make Mary Lou so wretched?

She returned to her notes, forcing herself to concentrate on the case. That was, after all, why she was here, not to contemplate the seductive Pierce Thorndike and his liaisons. When she finished her notes for the night, she was about to place her book on the nighttable when she paused.

She didn't want to leave her notes out in the open. It would be a simple matter for Thorndike or even Bridget to find them. Her gaze was drawn back to her dresser, and she remembered that one drawer was locked. Sinking back on her heels, she took out the keys Bridget had given her and tried them one at a time. Finally, the last one fit and she felt a sense of satisfaction as the lock turned.

Inside, there were some books, a few articles of clothing, and some letters. Puzzled, Mary Lou picked up a letter and realized it must have belonged to the former governess. She was about to pile all the things together to give them to Bridget when the name on the envelope caught her attention.

Miss Nancy Gettings.

"N" for Nancy.

Mary Lou sat down on the floor and toyed with the letter. Of course, it would be an invasion of privacy to open it. Yet she was supposed to be investigating a crime. Curiosity overwhelmed her and, after a moment's contrition, she slid her finger beneath the seal.

It was a love letter. Mary Lou squirmed as she read the message, professing everlasting devotion. Passing over the sentiments with barely one eye, she felt as guilty as if she was seeing this man and woman naked before her. Flipping the letter over to the other side, her breath caught when she saw the signature.

All my love, Jimmy

Thorndike's trainer had been involved with the governess. Clearly, no good had come of it, for the woman had departed so quickly she hadn't even taken all of her personal belongings, including these letters, which once must have meant everything to her. Putting the note back, Mary Lou closed the drawer and locked it once more, feeling as if she'd unforgivably invaded the woman's secrets.

Yet another piece of the puzzle had snapped into place. Jimmy Dwyer had been seeing Nancy Gettings. Could the barn have been their trysting place? Or had Jimmy Dwyer been there for a less romantic reason? Mistresses cost money, especially ones with a taste for ruby rings. Could the loyal Jimmy have betrayed his master for a price?

Mary Lou thought of Pierce's reaction if her theory turned out to be true. He obviously placed enormous trust in his trainer, and to discover that the man meant to kill his horse would devastate him. Perhaps that was why Thorndike didn't want the case investigated. While such a truth could no longer hurt Jimmy, it would have a terrible effect on his family and even Pierce's own son if it came to light.

It was just a theory, but the best one she'd come up with yet.

8

Beecham entered the cottage the following morning, holding a silver tray with an envelope. "Miss, I believe this is for you."

"It must be from my cousin Emily! Edward, finish your work and I'll be with you in a moment." Tearing the envelope open, Mary Lou ignored the butler's inquisitive glance and hurried to the gaslight to read the letter.

> *My Dear Mary Lou,*
>
> *I am so glad you decided to investigate the missing horse yourself! I really feel you are doing the right thing. After all, you must secure your future, for the world is not a*

friendly place for an unmarried woman. I
have every confidence you will succeed.

You must obtain more data. Go to the local
police and get their report. Ask for Officer
Merrimack. Check with the coroner and verify
cause of death. Meet neighbors and friends.
See if any of them have financial trouble or
wish Thorndike harm. Fear not—it is, as
Holmes would say, only the first step that
costs. Good luck, Emily Hall.

Crumpling the letter into her pocket, Mary Lou felt the weight of the world on her shoulders. How on earth was she to obtain such information? Digging around the stables at Graystone was one thing, calling on coroners and policemen quite another. And if Thorndike found out . . .

She couldn't let that happen. Deep in thought, she picked up a test tube when Bridget tapped lightly on the door.

"Excuse me, Miss, but there's someone here to see Master Edward . . ."

"Grandmother!" Edward immediately ceased his experiment and raced across the stone floor. "We're cutting up grasshoppers. Come look!"

Mary Lou glanced up curiously from the laboratory table as a silver-haired woman swept into the room. Dressed in the height of fashion, with a monstrous hat draped in black, she opened her arms to the little boy and gave him a hug.

"Why Edward, look at you! You are filthy! You rather take my breath away! And what is all this about cutting up bugs?" The woman withdrew a bit from the boy and quickly assessed her gown for damage.

"Miss Finch is teaching me . . . anatomy," Edward said proudly, pleased to have gotten the difficult word right. "Look, my grasshopper is right there, and you can see the mouth and the crop, even the rectum!"

"Edward!" The woman withdrew to her full five feet, two inches. "We do not say 'rectum'! Perhaps you should say something more like 'disposal system.'"

Mary Lou gritted a smile, then extended her hand. "Hello, I am Edward's governess, Miss Finch. Rectum, unfortunately, is the correct word for that part of the gastrointestinal system. I would really prefer the boy to be accurate for his test."

"I see." The elegant woman's gaze met Mary Lou's for the first time, incredulous that a governess would speak to her at all. She was a very striking woman, in spite of the black mourning garb she wore. Luminous blue eyes gazed out of a face that resembled a Madonna, and her features were patrician, finely sculpted like a carved ivory brooch. No wonder Thorndike had fallen in love with her daughter, Mary Lou mused; this woman must have also been lovely in her youth. A disturbing pang went through her at the thought, which she quickly dismissed as ridiculous. Why should it bother her that Thorndike's dead wife had been beautiful?

"I am Mrs. Doisneau, Edward's maternal grandmother," the woman said coolly, ignoring Mary Lou's hand. "Most of the previous help didn't work out for Edward. Naturally, I am concerned with his education. The boy is very bright, and I want to make sure he is well taken care of." She glanced around the room and shuddered at the collection of test tubes, microscope, and razor blades, then covered her mouth at the sight of the grasshoppers jumping around in a bowl. "Good heavens, it appears I arrived just in time. What on earth is going on here?"

"It's our laboratory," Edward explained. "Miss Finch is teaching me science and biology. Sometimes we experiment with chemicals. Today we are learning about animal's . . . "

"Digestive systems," Mary Lou supplied helpfully.

"I see." The woman's gaze turned icy and she stared at Mary Lou as if wanting to dissect her. "Is my son-in-law aware of this?"

"Yes," Mary Lou smiled. "My equipment arrived just last week. He very generously allowed me use of the cottage so I can teach Edward."

"I should think a classroom environment suffi-cient for teaching, without all of this . . . ghastly dis-play," she continued coldly. "I shall have to speak to Mr. Thorndike immediately. Is he at home?"

"He returned last evening," Bridget replied from the doorway. "But he went out again this morning."

"He certainly is away a lot. I don't suppose the Widow Norcross has anything to do with that?" Without waiting for a response, she turned to Bridget and asked, "Mrs. Murphy, would you have my bags brought in? I will take the yellow bedchamber."

"Of course," Bridget said, but without her cus-tomary cheer. Mary Lou could have sworn she heard the housekeeper mutter something under her breath.

"Oh, and Edward, I plan to take you on an outing this afternoon," Mrs. Doisneau said. "After tea, of course."

Mary Lou forced a smile. "Edward, why don't you wash your hands and go visit with your grandmother? I'll clean up here."

"But I haven't finished." Edward looked regretfully at his dissected grasshopper.

"I'll put your assignment aside for tomorrow. I think we'll then advance to a crayfish," she said, picking up her scalpel and turning it in the gaslight. "Or perhaps a rat. You will enjoy seeing the inside of one of those, I daresay."

A choking sound came from behind the door. Everyone looked at Bridget, but she appeared the picture of innocence. As Edward reluctantly followed his grandmother, Bridget turned to Mary Lou with a reassuring smile.

"Don't fret, lass. One day won't hurt his schooling," the housekeeper sighed. "I'm sure the master will set things right when he returns. I have to go into town meself to pick up a few things at the market, and thought you might like to join me. You've not been out of the house since you've come here."

Mary Lou nodded immediately. With Thorndike out of the way and Edward taken care of, she would have a golden opportunity to see the police and question Edward's former governess. It seemed for once, the fates had been kind. "I have a few errands to run. I'll get ready right away."

The town center was a short distance from Graystone. Bridget disembarked at the market, her basket tucked under her arm, while Mary Lou set off for Nancy Getting's house.

It was just on the fringe of town, Bridget had told her nervously. Mary Lou was amused. Apparently Bridget was afraid she would hear horror stories about Edward, and had tried to talk her out of the visit. But Mary Lou wasn't dissuaded and insisted she just wanted to return her things.

The cottage was exactly where Bridget described. Mary Lou knocked on the door, but no one answered. After waiting a moment, she glanced into the back-yard.

A woman sat on a chair facing an easel, com-pletely unaware she had a visitor. She was tall, at least five feet eight inches, and slender as a reed. Her dark hair flowed about her shoulders like a cape, and she frowned intently, studying the painting before her with dissatisfaction.

She was pretty, yet at second glance, something wasn't quite right. Mary Lou saw a hardness about her eyes, a set to her jaw that indicated this woman had a temper. Her theory was proven a moment later when, disgusted with her work, she threw up her hands in exasperation, then turned to walk back to the house.

She stopped abruptly when she saw Mary Lou. Her confusion changed to a frown as she took in Mary Lou's dowdy dress, the chemical stains, and the bag under her arm. "I'm sorry," she said in a dismiss-ing voice, obviously thinking Mary Lou an eccentric society woman collecting for the poor. "I have already donated to the orphanage."

"No, I'm not here for that," Mary Lou said, disliking the woman on sight. "I'm Mary Lou Finch, the new governess at Graystone. You must be Miss Nancy Gettings."

"Yes." The woman gazed at her with interest, then a sneer came to her face. "I suppose you have your hands quite full with Master Edward. Is that what you came to see me about? Because I won't return, no matter what. That child is a terrible brat, and nothing can induce me to put up with him again."

"I don't find him so at all," Mary Lou said loyally. "Edward is extremely intelligent and just needs a different teaching approach."

"I see." Nancy smiled brittlely. "Then it all worked out for the best." She started to go into the house when Mary Lou held out her bundle.

"I found some of your things in my room. Clothes. Jewelry. Correspondence. I thought you might want them . . . especially the letters."

Silence hung between them like a curtain. Nancy stared at the parcel, then at Mary Lou. She could see the play of emotions on her face. Fear? Guilt? She forced a smile and indicated the house.

"Won't you come in? I was about to make tea."

Mary Lou followed her into the kitchen, where tins of paint lay open and multicolored cloths were tossed into the sink. Nancy prepared tea, then reluctantly set out the cups. Mary Lou saw her hands tremble, then, after pouring the liquid into the pot, took a seat beside her.

"I don't know where my manners are. I guess I was just frustrated by the painting." She waved her hand toward the door.

"No matter," Mary Lou said. She reached for her

bag and withdrew the ring, then placed it on the table between them. "I think Mr. Dwyer meant this for you. I thought it best if you took it, especially now."

The woman stared at Mary Lou as if trying to gauge how much she knew. "You read my letters?" She ventured cautiously, but already knew the answer.

"Just one," Mary Lou admitted. She decided to try a direct approach. "Tell me, Miss Gettings, was it hard to love a man who lived so close by with his wife and children? And did you hope to marry him?"

"I had hoped, but it became apparent he would never leave her!" The woman cried, then gasped as if afraid she'd already said too much. Picking up her tea, she drank it quickly. "There is no sense in hiding anything," she said softly, her shoulders drooping in resignation. "You read the letters; you know. I loved Jimmy Dwyer. And he loved me."

"Enough to steal a horse? To try and get money to buy you the things you desired?" Mary Lou questioned softly.

The woman shook her head furiously. "Jimmy would never have done that. He would have had nothing to do with stealing that horse. He loved them more than he loved anything else—including me." She gave Mary Lou a wry smile. "I know that sounds odd, but it was true."

"Why was he there that night?" Mary Lou persisted. "He had gone home. Why did he return to Graystone?"

"I saw him that afternoon." Nancy rose and stared out the window. "I told him I was leaving. He begged me to see him one more time. Perhaps he thought to persuade me, but I couldn't continue on in that way any more. He showed me the ring." She gestured to the box. "I said I didn't want it."

"What happened?"

"I agreed to meet him that night. When I arrived at the stables, I found him there, dead. I nearly lost my mind. You cannot imagine what it is like to see the man you love, lying there on the floor. I tried at first to stop his bleeding with my handkerchief, but then I ran out. I couldn't let anyone find me there, I couldn't explain . . . I didn't know what had happened until I heard the next day."

"Did you see or hear anything?" Mary Lou questioned, her heart sinking. If Nancy's story was true, she had discovered nothing other than a tawdry love affair, which was no one's business. And the handkerchief seemed to confirm the tale. She remembered its mention in the newspaper account of Dwyer's murder.

Nancy paused, then shrugged as if hesitant to speak. "I'm not sure, but I thought I heard the blacksmith, Will Starkey, arguing with the groom. They both sounded as if they'd been drinking."

"What were they arguing about?" Mary Lou asked, trying to quell her excitement.

"I heard the groom say something about Thorndike; he was afraid he'd be caught in his cups. Willy told him not to be concerned, he'd take care of Thorndike himself. I remember thinking it was odd Willy was there so late. He normally does his work on Saturday mornings, unless there is an emergency. But I left before I saw him. I could be mistaken."

Mary Lou nodded. It was a lead. A weak lead, but

one all the same. She rose, intending to leave, when Nancy gave her a speculative look.

"So you're really staying on as governess? Frankly, I don't know what Jimmy saw in Edward. I thought that child a holy terror. No matter what happened between Jimmy and myself, there was no way I would have stayed at Graystone."

Mary Lou smiled softly. "Perhaps Jimmy saw the potential in Edward, the same way he would a troubled horse. In any case, yes, I am staying. Graystone holds considerable attraction for me at the moment."

"I can well imagine." When Mary Lou gave her a blank look, Nancy grinned. "The master of Graystone is very handsome, is he not? But you know as well as I that he could never marry a governess. Take my advice, Miss Finch, and be careful how high you set your sights."

"I have no idea what you are talking about," Mary Lou said coolly. "Thank you for the tea. Good day." Departing, she closed the door and could have sworn she heard laughter behind her.

The heat in her face gradually dissipated as she walked down the dusty town road. Could Nancy Gettings have somehow divined the attraction she felt for Thorndike? Of course not, she thought quickly. She didn't even know the woman. Yet her words rankled, and she pushed them firmly from her mind.

Mary Lou walked thoughtfully toward the police station, her conversation with the governess still fresh in her mind. It was right next to the barber shop, sandwiched between that and the bakery.

She paused at the door, unable to decide if the

lime water or the freshly baked doughnuts smelled better. After a moment's thought, she decided it was definitely the doughnuts. Ignoring the quizzical stares of the men in their barber chairs, she raced up the stairs to the station and walked inside.

Two of the police officers sat at their desks, obviously just passing time, while the clerk was busy filing. When Mary Lou entered, one of them put his feet down from where they'd been resting on top of his desk and reluctantly removed his hat.

"Can I help you, Miss?" He gave her stained dress a puzzled glance.

"I'm looking for Officer Merrimack," Mary Lou said, ignoring the discomfort she felt. She would much rather be munching on one of those doughnuts next door than interrogating a policeman about a murder.

The second man rose reluctantly, and stepped around his desk. "I'm Officer Merrimack. What can I do for you?"

Mary Lou smiled in relief. Maybe this would be easier than she thought. "I'm looking for information about a missing horse. Damien's Curse. I believe he was stolen from Graystone Manor, and his trainer found murdered."

The policeman spat out the coffee he'd been drinking. "What have you got to do with that?" he asked incredulously.

Mary Lou shrugged. "I happen to be acquainted with the owner of the house and have taken a personal interest in the matter. I would like to see a copy of the police report, and understand where your investigation has led."

If she suddenly grew two heads, she didn't think the man could look any more astonished. "A copy of our report . . . now see here, Miss. I don't know who you are or what you have to do with all this, but I don't like it. I don't like it one bit."

The police chief came to stand before him, sharing the same glare. Mary Lou swallowed hard. Somehow, she didn't think she'd manage well in jail. Backing toward the door, she smiled. "Well, I guess that's it, then. I suppose this was a bad idea. It was just that my cousin, Emily Hall, thought that as you were a personal acquaintance, you might be willing to help me. But—"

Instantly, the policemen's expressions changed. "Are you talking about Miss Emily Potter?" Officer Merrimack asked, his tone now reverent.

"Why, yes," Mary Lou said in bemusement. "My cousin is Mrs. Hall now. Emily suggested I contact you—"

"You should have said that when you first came in! Emily Potter's cousin! Please have a seat. Brilliant woman, Miss Potter is. Solved a real tough case for us once, a blackmailer who'd made more than a dozen lives a misery. Refused to take any of the credit after. She said the success was reward enough in itself."

Mary Lou took a seat, unable to believe her ears. The police chief nodded in agreement with everything his colleague said, and even added a few words of his own.

"Real smart woman, Miss Emily. I hate to admit it, but once in a while, when I'm really stuck, I've been known to telegraph her for advice. She always puts me right on track. Amazing. Do you share her talent?" Both men looked at her with renewed respect.

"Oh, no," Mary Lou said hastily. "That is, I am more developed in the sciences. However, I have a personal interest in the Thorndike case—"

"Damned bewildering, that one." Merrimack shook his head and offered Mary Lou a cup of coffee. "We've searched high and low and can't find a hair of that horse. Amazing."

"How in the devil could a horse like that disappear?" The police chief shook his head. "White as snow, with just a touch of gray. Beautiful colt. You'd think someone would have seen him."

"Then there have been no reports at all?" Mary Lou said, opening her notebook and scribbling furiously.

"None," Merrimack said. "We honestly didn't search too much the first few days. We kept thinking someone would see him. Even Thorndike didn't press us—he must have thought the same thing. But as days became weeks, we realized trouble was afoot in more ways than one."

Mary Lou peered at the man inquisitively. "What is your opinion of what happened?"

Merrimack glanced at the police chief. The older man rummaged in a cabinet, then handed a file to Mary Lou.

"The report is all in there. We were called in by one of the servants, a Mrs. Murphy, to be precise. The poor woman was so upset she could hardly talk. A man had been killed, and the racehorse stolen. Unbelievable."

"So you went out there—"

"Yes. Sure enough, poor Jimmy Dwyer lay dead, the colt gone. We figured Dwyer was bludgeoned to death, although we didn't find a murder weapon. The stableboy got sick when he saw his old friend, and the groom was dead drunk. He and the blacksmith had gone out drinking earlier in the evening, and they came back the worse for wear. Yet it was all very odd."

Mary Lou glanced up from her scribbling. "What makes you say that?"

"The alarm wasn't given until the stableboy found the man dead the next morning. The coroner thought he'd been killed some time during the night, and his body lay there all that time. Apparently, no one heard anything."

"Interesting." Mary Lou chewed her pencil thoughtfully. "Did you see the coroner's report?"

"It's in the file," the police chief nodded. "Concussion to the back of the head. He was facing away from the horse's stall. Probably trying to defend the poor brute."

"Have you any suspects?" Mary Lou questioned.

"The most promising one we have is a servant by the name of Bill Cooke. Has relatives up in Boston. Say they don't know his whereabouts, but he'll turn up sooner or later."

"How about the neighbors?" Mary Lou asked. "It seems they have access, and may have learned about the horse's potential."

"There's Whittaker next door. Seems he and Thorndike had a falling out. We searched his stables, but the horse was nowhere in sight. The closest neighbor after that is a good five miles away, and that's the Widow Norcross."

"Have you looked into the background of the blacksmith?"

The officers looked at each other and burst into laughter. "Old Willy?" Merrimack asked in astonishment. "He's been around for ages. Why on earth would old Willy want to become a horse thief?"

"He had access, and he knew the value of the horse," Mary Lou pointed out. "You yourself said he was there that night. I think it might be well to establish where he was later, after the groom passed out," Mary Lou said firmly. "Also to discover if he's ever been implicated in something like this, and if he's a betting man."

"Yes, Miss." The two policemen began to make notes. Merrimack glanced up a moment later. "It should be easy to verify his whereabouts. We hadn't really taken him off our list, you know. Everyone at this point is suspect, even Mr. Thorndike himself."

Mary Lou looked at the man, feeling her stomach tighten. "Why would Thorndike kill his trainer and steal his own horse? Both were invaluable to him."

"I didn't say it was likely, I'm just saying he's a suspect. I have nothing personal against the man, although the gossip spread like wildfire after his wife passed away."

"Do you know how she died?" Mary Lou couldn't keep the thrill from her voice.

The policeman shrugged. "Seems she had run out into the night during a storm. No one went after her. When they found her in the morning, she was frozen and shivering, barely conscious. She caught pneumonia and passed on a few days later. We thought it looked mighty suspicious."

Mary Lou's heart beat faster. Thorndike a murderer? It seemed impossible, and yet . . .

"Do you have reason to think Mr. Thorndike wanted his wife dead?" Mary Lou couldn't help but ask.

The two officers exchanged glances, and it was the chief who answered. "Mrs. Thorndike was a very beautiful woman, and received a lot of attention wherever she went. Rumor has it that she wanted to leave him. A man like Thorndike wouldn't take kindly to that."

"Divorce?" Mary Lou asked incredulously. No one in society ever divorced. Women went to Europe to escape tedious husbands, while their mates found refuge in the arms of a willing woman. Many a New York shopgirl wore diamonds given to her by a rich uncle, and the uncles themselves changed nieces with amazing regularity. But there were no divorces. "Was he . . . involved with anyone else?" She thought of the Widow Norcross, the mysterious woman Mrs. Doisneau had mentioned.

"Not that we've seen. If anyone had admirers, it was her. And you know how gossip is. There's your side, my side, and the truth somewhere in between."

Mary Lou nodded and returned to her notes. "I see in the report that you interviewed the neighbors."

"Yes, we're still questioning them." Merrimack stood beside her and closed the file. When Mary Lou glanced up, he gave her a wink. "Do you suppose Miss Potter might be interested in giving this case a little look-see? The newspapers are relentless that we haven't been able to find the killer, let alone the horse. Any light she could shed on the matter would be greatly appreciated."

"I imagine copies of the reports would be helpful?" Merrimack grinned, his eyes skimming over Mary Lou's curvaceous form. "I was just going next door for some chocolate doughnuts. Perhaps you would like a few while our clerk takes care of everything?"

Mary Lou's stomach rumbled in answer. "I think that sounds like a fine idea," she said enthusiastically.

The officer returned a few minutes later with a paper sack, and the three of them indulged in chocolate ecstasy while the grumbling clerk painstakingly made copies of the documents in the file. It took more than an hour to copy them all, but within that time period Mary Lou had her hunger satisfied, and a crisp, clean file of all the reports Emily had requested in her hand. Bidding the men a cheerful good-bye, she ventured out into the street and ran straight into Pierce Thorndike.

9

❧

"Miss Finch. What a pleasant surprise."

Thorndike's tone was filled with suspicion as Mary Lou felt all the color leave her face. He glanced up at the police station, then down at her. His gaze centered on the thick file she held, and a cool smile curved his mouth.

"Did you have business with the local authorities?" he questioned.

Mary Lou swallowed hard. The policeman's story about Thorndike's wife haunted her, and she instinctively took a step back. He was, in their minds, a suspect. Could he have been involved with her death? The missing horse?

"Miss Finch?" His gaze seemed to measure the distance between them and his eyes narrowed.

Mary Lou tried to appear bewildered, which under the circumstances, wasn't that difficult. The last thing she wanted to do was to give away her suspicions. "I . . . Good heavens, this is the police station! I was looking for the telegraph office and wandered in here by mistake. How utterly silly of me."

Thorndike appeared to consider her seriously. "Miss Finch, there isn't a telegraph office here in Milltown. You must go to New Hope."

"Well then that explains why I haven't found it." Mary Lou gave him a charming smile. "If you'll excuse me, I will be on my way . . . "

She attempted to hide the file under one arm and stride past him down the steps. Unfortunately, the folder slipped to the ground, the papers spilling out. Mary Lou scrambled to pick them up, aware of Thorndike's daunting expression. When she rose, his eyes met hers with a penetrating stare.

"Interesting. I wasn't aware you included police reports in your scholarly reading material. A more suspicious man might think you weren't being entirely honest with me."

Something stirred in those elusive blue eyes and Mary Lou was forced to look away. She toyed with the folder, nervously running a finger along the edge. When Thorndike continued to wait patiently, she sighed, knowing she had to provide an answer.

"I have found, sir, that like many other so-called virtues, honesty isn't always the best policy."

"I see," Thorndike said. "Then you do not consider yourself a virtuous woman?"

His tone made her face snap up toward his. Coming from another man, she would have thought his words a double entendre, but this was Thorndike. "Of course I do," Mary Lou replied, knowing she had to tread carefully. Pierce Thorndike was no fool, and she could tell he wasn't in the pleasantest mood as it was. "But sometimes, silence is more prudent than truth."

After a long pause, he finally spoke. "I find I have to agree with you, on one count anyway. Truth can cause distress, but sometimes, so can silence." He signaled to his driver, then glanced down at her once more. "How did you get here? Did you travel alone?"

"I came with Mrs. Murphy," Mary Lou said. "She offered to let me accompany her into town. Mrs. Doisneau arrived for a visit, and Edward is with her. I didn't think you'd mind."

"In that case, I suggest that you return with me. I would like to speak to you. I will have my driver inform Mrs. Murphy of the change of plans. Kindly wait here."

Mary Lou nodded, but her heart sank. His meaning was clear. He didn't believe her for a moment, and meant to confront her. Surely he wouldn't dismiss her! Yet if he thought she'd been prying into his personal business, he might well be inclined to send her on her way. How on earth was she to get out of this mess?

Thorndike entered the police station, firmly closing the door behind him. Although she strained to listen, she couldn't hear much more than the low tones of the clerk, and the rumble of one of the officers. Curiosity overwhelmed her and she wondered why Thorndike was here. Was he investigating the missing horse himself? Or was he here on some other business? Were the police correct in their suspicions of him? What kind of man *was* Pierce Thorndike?

She heard footsteps and barely had time to step away from the door before Thorndike emerged. Noting her close proximity to the keyhole, she saw the corner of his mouth twitch as if suppressing a smile. He made no comment, however, but simply gestured toward his carriage, indicating that she should enter.

"I really don't mind returning with Bridget," Mary Lou began. "It's no trouble. I'm sure you have other things to do."

"Not at all. I'm looking forward to spending a few moments conversing with you. I have a feeling it will be most enlightening, particularly since Bridget told me of your travels. Did you find Miss Gettings in good health?"

There was nothing for her to do but heave a sigh and enter the carriage. To her dismay, she saw that he had taken the brougham, with its narrow seat that encouraged intimacy. Placing the file beneath her, she slid as far to the opposite side as possible. She heard Thorndike say something to the driver, then he opened the door and climbed in.

The carriage bumped to a start, and Mary Lou felt the tension rise as Thorndike slowly removed his gloves before turning to her. He looked imposing and powerful and unbearably handsome, dressed in a dark business suit with a clean white shirt beneath a form-fitting vest. She flinched in response to each idle slap of his gloves against his thigh.

He gave her the same mocking look as before.

"Why, Miss Finch, you seem rather jumpy. Is there something you'd like to confess?"

"Noooo," Mary Lou swallowed hard. Thorndike had a presence that was unnerving under general conditions, let alone as judge and inquisitioner.

"Well then maybe I can assist you. Why don't you start by telling me the true reason you were at the police station, and why you went to visit Miss Gettings."

"But I did!" Mary Lou said indignantly. "I told you—"

"Yes, I know what you said." He cut her off quickly, as if running out of patience. Settling back into the carriage, he stared out the window and began speaking softly.

"Miss Finch, I want to tell you about the night Damien disappeared."

A quick chill raced up Mary Lou's spine. Was he going to confess something, or solve the mystery himself? "Yes, sir," she said, trying to keep the eagerness out of her voice.

"I had just come home from a business trip and had retired for the evening. Damien had been with us for almost a year. His training was going well, and there was very little publicity about him. His lineage was unremarkable, as was his build. Yet that horse could *run*. Only a few people knew it, since none of us were sure how he'd do in an actual race, but he showed tremendous promise. Jimmy Dwyer said he'd never seen a colt like him.

"So we had no reason to think anyone would try to steal the thoroughbred. He wasn't a winner, had no glowing reputation like Golden Heels or High Stakes.

He was just an unknown horse with the instinct to run and a heart to back it up."

Mary Lou saw his face soften when he mentioned the horse, and realized Damien was much more than just a stake to Thorndike. He continued in the same tone.

"A stableboy found Jimmy Dwyer's body the following morning, and Mrs. Murphy called for help. Have you ever seen a corpse that's been dead for several hours?"

"No," Mary Lou admitted softly. "That must have been terrible."

"It was. He was already stiff, and his eyes stared up into the heavens, eyes that will never look upon his wife and children again." Thorndike's gaze came back and met hers squarely. "Do you understand what I'm saying?"

Mary Lou choked. "Yes, I believe I do, sir."

"I was very fond of Jimmy. He was an excellent man with the horses, good to everyone, including my son. I know why he was at the stable that night, and it is no one's concern but his own. I am acquainted with his family, and could imagine their grief if the truth came out, particularly so soon after losing him. Do you understand?"

"I have no intention of telling anyone about Miss Gettings, sir."

"Good. That would be unforgivable. The worst part of all is that this attack had nothing to do with him. Someone was trying to steal my horse, and Jimmy lost his life because of it."

Mary Lou lowered her gaze to her lap. She could

feel the file rustle beneath her, and she forced herself to sit completely still.

Thorndike continued inexorably, his voice now stern.

"I am determined that no one else get hurt, and I do not care to what extent I must go to protect my household. The monster who killed Jimmy is still at large. While I suffer over the loss of my horse, the loss of the man means much more to me, as does everyone under my protection. I will not tolerate anyone putting himself at risk, no matter how seemingly noble the cause. Do I make myself clear?"

"But—" Mary Lou tried.

Thorndike glared at her in outrage. "Stay out of my business, Miss Finch! I am trying to warn you that this situation is dangerous, something best left in the hands of the police and not an inquisitive schoolmarm!"

She drew back indignantly at that. The carriage rumbled on, the minutes stretching into eternity. Mary Lou stole a glance at Thorndike, and saw the firm set of his jaw, one of the few visible signs of his mood. He was still angry with her. Clearly, he felt she was needlessly poking her nose into something that didn't concern her. But she couldn't explain or defend her position without revealing everything.

What was his role in all this? Why did he become so upset whenever he thought she was getting close to the truth? Were his motives truly as innocent as he'd have her believe?

So he knew about the affair between Nancy Gettings and his trainer. Was her hypothesis right, that he wanted to keep things hidden to avoid a possible scandal? What about his nighttime wanderings, his secretive nature, his cold fury at her meddling? Who was Pierce Thorndike, after all?

He could be kind; she'd seen that already in his treatment of his servants and his son. He was also very intelligent, capable, and had a presence that made people bend to his will. He could also be charming. But she sensed there was much more beneath his dark, handsome exterior, more than he wanted anyone to know.

The tension hummed between them and Mary Lou sighed. If she was going to stay on at Graystone, she didn't want him angry with her. It would only make him more concerned with what she did, and more determined to prevent her sleuthing. That is, if he didn't dismiss her first. And if any of her suspicions were founded, his anger would only make her situation more precarious. No, somehow she had to smooth things over between them.

"Sir," she ventured, pausing when he turned his cold gaze on her. "I am sorry to have upset you. I understand how you must feel. Finding your trainer had been murdered must have been terrible. I apologize for my intrusion."

She took his hand in a gesture of sincerity. His fingers stirred in her grasp, but he did not attempt to remove his hand. An agonizing moment later he looked up, and to her utter gratitude, the fury of minutes ago had abated.

"Thank you, Miss Finch," he said gently.

Mary Lou smiled, relief rushing through her. She had penetrated his armor, and he had responded. Yet as the minutes ticked by and he continued to hold her hand, the intimacy of the gesture began to affect her. What on earth was wrong with her? He was only holding her hand. Yet she wondered wildly if he could feel the pounding of her pulse.

He suddenly seemed to realize what was happening, for he released her hand quickly, murmuring something that sounded like an apology. Immediately, she clasped her palms together as if trying to erase the sensual imprint he'd made, but it didn't help. Her starched lace collar seemed suddenly too tight, and her dress, a simple cotton shirtwaist, rubbed in all the wrong places. Her heart pounded. Did their touch have the same devastating effect on him?

It was a long ride back to Graystone.

When Mary Lou descended from the carriage, Thorndike thankfully said nothing. Her emotions were roiling, and she was grateful that he walked with her in silence toward the house.

As they approached, Mrs. Doisneau stood at the door, her foot tapping impatiently as if she'd been waiting forever. "I'd heard that you returned. I demand to see you immediately. I feel the matter is urgent." She gave Mary Lou a disparaging glance.

"I have no doubt that you do, Madam," Thorndike said. "If you don't mind, Miss Finch and I were about to have tea. I will join you afterward. I find it difficult to think without sustenance, don't you, Miss Finch?"

Mary Lou looked at him in surprise. She could almost swear she heard a hint of amusement in his voice. "Yes, I do."

"Then it's all settled. Madam, I will meet with you shortly when I've been fortified with scones and some of Mrs. Murphy's excellent jam." He gave Edward's grandmother a polite nod, then walked into the kitchen, gesturing for Mary Lou to precede him. Mrs. Doisneau gaped in consternation, but Thorndike closed the door behind Mary Lou and heated the water. Bridget had laid out a full tea, and he ate as if he had all the time in the world. Mary Lou sighed inwardly. She would never understand him.

"You wished to see me, Mrs. Doisneau?" Pierce entered the parlor where Edward's grandmother sat with her needlepoint. The plunk of the needle through the fabric, which sounded like a gunshot in the quiet room, instantly telegraphed her mood. Her lips were drawn tightly together in a thin line of disapproval, and when she finally lifted her face, condemnation blazed in her eyes.

"Mr. Thorndike," she began, her voice icy. "I arrived here for a visit with my grandson, and have been very upset by what I have observed. Edward is an intelligent and sensitive child, and I disapprove of the way he is being raised, most extremely this new governess you've employed. . . ."

"Madam, I understand how this must appear—" Pierce attempted, but she interrupted him with a look as sharp as her needle.

"Please hear me out, sir. Edward, after all, is still a blood relative, even though my daughter is . . . no longer with us."

Thorndike sighed and dropped into the chair across from her. "Proceed, Madam," he said calmly.

"Thank you. I am very concerned by what is going

on here. I found Edward in some sort of makeshift laboratory, chopping up insects. I understand Miss Finch allows him to keep ridiculous hours, even permitting him out in the evening air to look at the stars! This situation must be rectified immediately."

"Mrs. Doisneau, I appreciate your concern for Edward, I truly do. And I agree he is a bright little boy in need of direction. But I disagree with you about Miss Finch. I think she's made tremendous progress with Edward in a relatively short time, and I am very pleased with her teaching methods, unconventional as they might be. Edward responds well to her, and has learned much already."

Instead of being reassured, the woman looked deeply offended. "Obviously, nothing I think matters to you at all. Now that Clarissa is no longer with us, I suppose you mean to cut off the rest of the family from Edward."

"I have no such intention, Madam, as you well know. I merely happen to disagree with you. Edward has been through a succession of tutors, the process of which you haven't witnessed. I have. Let me assure you that I, too, have my son's best interests at heart, and if I thought for a minute that he wasn't in the best of care, I wouldn't hesitate to do something about it. But I am very pleased with his education. Miss Finch has exposed him to advanced science and mathematics, as well as English and history. She's even taught him the Latin names of the insects, trees, and ponds nearby. Are you aware she has a degree from the University?"

Mrs. Doisneau stared at him as if not comprehending. "A degree?"

"Yes. And I've received glowing reports from her professors. The woman is extremely talented, and seems to genuinely like Edward. It would be foolish of me indeed to dismiss her, when she appears to be the best thing that has ever happened to him."

"I see." Her eyes narrowed thoughtfully. "Mr. Thorndike, are you sure your . . . admiration for this woman is only on Edward's behalf?"

Thorndike's expression grew thunderous and he met the woman's stare with an equally blazing one of his own. "Madam, what are you suggesting?"

"She *is* pretty, in a common sort of way," she continued. "And one might consider her interesting, due to her intelligence. You've been alone a long time, and I understand loneliness. I'm just wondering if perhaps there is some other reason you seem so determined to be her champion."

Thorndike rose and took a step toward her, fighting the surge of outrage her words engendered. Mrs. Doisneau wisely held her tongue, but she lifted her head with as much dignity as she could muster.

"I understand you are still grieving for your daughter, so I will overlook that remark. Let me once again assure you that you are welcome here at any time, and that I appreciate your interest in my son. If there is nothing more, Madam, I must return to my work."

She quailed in her seat, but that was the only sign she even heard him. Instead she gazed out the window, her sewing tossed aside, her arms folded. When she spoke, her voice sounded far away.

"It did not take you long to forget my daughter, did it Mr. Thorndike? You made her desperately unhappy, you know. For that I shall never forgive you."

He strode out of the room without looking back.

Outside, Thorndike walked down to the stables to saddle his horse. The walk helped cool his anger, yet he knew that part of the reason he'd reacted the way he did to her words was the grain of truth in her assertions. He was deeply attracted to the governess.

His pace slowed as he recalled their carriage ride. When she'd innocently taken his hand, he was overwhelmed by the urge to pull her into his arms and kiss her until she swooned. Just the slightest contact with her gave him a rush of sexual awareness that made his loins throb unbearably.

And it wasn't just physical attraction, though he felt that in spades. Mary Lou's unfashionable gowns, her disheveled hair, and the lushness of her figure seemed more charming to him than the thin, polished ladies with whom he normally associated. She really was an extraordinarily handsome woman, which even his mother-in-law had noticed. But more than her golden beauty, it was her mind that fascinated him. He was also deeply touched by the affection she displayed toward his son.

Yes, he would be insane to get rid of her, regardless of what Edward's grandmother thought. Taking up the reins, he led Blackwatch out to the clearing, then, swinging up into the saddle, rode off into the darkness.

Mary Lou heard hoofbeats and glanced out the window, seeing Thorndike and his magnificent thoroughbred melt into the darkness. Sitting down before her dresser, she brushed her hair thoughtfully.

Where did Thorndike go at night? Why was he so secretive? Was he seeing a woman? She thought back to her earlier conjecture that Thorndike had a mistress, and her heart sank. Then she recalled that moment in the carriage when he'd held her hand, and something had passed between them. Could Thorndike feel the same way about her? Did he think of her, look forward to seeing her the way she did him, feel that little flutter in his chest when she smiled?

Of course not, she chided herself. She was reading too much into all this. He had never done anything to suggest a personal interest in her. She was Edward's governess, nothing more. It was time she remembered who she was and why she was here, and stopped entertaining daydreams of the handsome master of Graystone.

10

— 🌿 —

"Miss Finch?"

A discreet knock on the door caused Mary Lou to look up in surprise as an elegantly dressed woman entered the cottage.

"Please," the woman said, her voice like velvet. "Don't let me interrupt. I just thought I'd stop by and introduce myself. Mrs. Doisneau told me I'd find you here."

Mary Lou grew more puzzled by the moment. "That's perfectly all right, Miss . . ."

"Mrs." The woman said, a smile curving her beautiful face. "Mrs. Norcross."

Mary Lou's heart skipped a beat. So this was the mysterious Widow Norcross! Somehow she managed a polite smile. "Mrs. Norcross, I'm pleased to meet you. Do you mind if we step outside? The smell of the chemicals can be very unpleasant if you aren't used to it."

"No, not at all." The widow turned and exited, leaving a scent of rose water behind.

After putting her notes aside, she followed the woman out the door. An Arabian mare waited patiently by the fence, obviously recently dismounted, and Mary Lou recalled Bridget's comment that the widow loved horses. An odd trepidation grew inside her, and she wondered at the meaning of this visit.

"I thought I'd come and say hello," The woman said softly. "It can get quite lonely out here, away from the excitement of the city, and I wanted to let you know you are welcome to visit me any time." She glanced at the fields and trees, then back at the house with an expression of appreciation. "What a beautiful place Graystone is! I can understand why Pierce is so attached to it."

"Mrs. Norcross," Mary Lou said slowly. "I appreciate your kind thoughts, but you must be aware that I am the governess here. Wouldn't your invitation be more appropriate for Edward's grandmother, or perhaps Mr. Thorndike himself?"

The widow appeared startled for a moment, then broke into laughter. Mary Lou silently admitted she'd never seen a more handsome woman. Auburn hair swept up beneath a hat that was cocked rakishly to one side, drawing attention to a face of carved perfection. Her dark blue riding habit was enhanced by a snowy-white blouse beneath, and seemed to exactly match her eyes. Mary Lou felt her heart sinking.

"I suppose this must seem strange to you, but

Pierce has spoken of you so fondly that I feel as if I know you already." The widow extended her hand. "I was truly hoping we could be friends. Please forgive any presumption on my part."

"No offense taken." Mary Lou accepted the hand-clasp, but continued to study the woman thoroughly, wondering what Thorndike had said to her. "You must have seen him rather recently, as I've only been employed here at Graystone a short while."

"Oh, I see him quite often. Last night he was telling me of the tremendous progress you've made with Edward. His son is everything to him, you know."

Mary Lou's cheeks heated at the remembrance of Thorndike's late-night rides. Apparently, he'd been having a secret rendezvous with this woman. Reminding herself it was not at all her business, she managed to shrug as if it concerned her little.

"That's very kind of you to say. If you don't mind, I must be getting back. Edward should return from his riding lesson at any moment. He is a bright boy, but he needs constant stimulation."

"Like father, like son," the widow said brightly. Giving Mary Lou a pat on the cheek with a kid-gloved hand, she cocked her head appraisingly as if admiring a work of art. "You are very pretty, my dear. I can understand the attraction the men at Graystone must feel for you. It must be quite difficult to have a fresh young thing like yourself within reach, and yet be unable to do anything more than admire. I dare-say, I can understand Pierce's dilemma."

Mary Lou gazed at the woman in astonishment. Mrs. Norcross turned and walked toward the horse, then slipped gracefully onto her mount to gallop across the fields. A sickness started within her belly and Mary Lou fought the churning acid with a hard swallow. The widow was Pierce Thorndike's friend, and apparently, lover. It was just as she'd surmised.

Why then, did she feel so ill?

Mary Lou returned to the cottage, deep in thought. She had to stop thinking of Thorndike in romantic terms. It seemed even the widow was suspicious of their relationship, and Mary Lou blushed at her implications. One thing was perfectly clear. It was time to get on with the case, and stop making a total fool of herself.

While waiting for Edward's return, she picked up her bag and took out the horseshoe. A theory had come to her after talking to the police, one she wanted to test. If Dwyer's presence had been innocent, then he was surely trying to protect Damien. But from whom? Her thoughts went back to Miss Gettings' statement, that she'd heard the blacksmith that night. Could the blacksmith, having gotten the groom drunk, have returned with him and sought to poison Damien? Perhaps he'd been seen by the trainer before the apple could do its deadly work. In the scuffle that ensued, might the horse, sensing danger, have bolted?

There was one way to find out. Mary Lou replaced the shoe in her satchel. She would investigate the neighboring properties at the first opportunity.

After supper, Mary Lou held out her hand to Edward. "Let's clean up, then it is time for your bath and bed."

"But I want to go back to the laboratory!" Edward said plaintively. "It's still light out!"

"Not enough for our dissection. We will finish tomorrow. Perhaps instead, we can study a few of the stars tonight?" Mary Lou grinned as the boy's sullen expression immediately brightened. "If you bathe quickly and put on your nightclothes, I will take you outside for a few minutes and let you find the Big Dipper."

"I don't think it wise to take the boy into the night air," Mrs. Doisneau said disapprovingly. "He'll catch a chill."

Mary Lou forced a smile. "I appreciate your concern, Madam, but the weather is very balmy. And I shan't keep him out long. But you must agree the best way to study astronomy is to see the stars themselves! It is very clear tonight."

"I don't agree. The weather—"

"Miss Finch is right," Thorndike said, interrupting her. "I see no difficulty in letting Edward onto the porch for a few minutes. You won't keep him long?" He glanced at Mary Lou.

"Not at all," she said, grateful for his support.

"Good. Then it's settled." Thorndike disappeared behind his newspaper once more, while Mrs. Doisneau rose, scraping her chair loudly on the wooden floor. The woman's lips pursed so tightly Mary Lou thought her face would be sucked inside out. Lifting her head high, she brushed past Mary Lou and swept from the room. Sighing, Mary Lou realized that she had somehow offended her, which didn't bode well for her own position at Graystone.

Returning to the house a short time later, she let

Thorndike take Edward to bed. Bridget brought in a light snack of warm milk and cookies, and Mary Lou accepted the treat with a smile of thanks.

Thorndike reentered the room and Mary Lou rose, prepared to leave him in peace and head for her own bed. But as she started to pick up her milk, he stopped her, putting a hand on her shoulder.

"Miss Finch, please don't go on my account."

"I wasn't," Mary Lou said quickly, although that was exactly why she was leaving. "It is getting late, and I am a little tired."

"Please, stay a while. I find that the silence of this house is sometimes oppressive."

Mary Lou gazed at him in surprise. Admitting such a thing did not seem to be in Thorndike's character at all. She put down her glass and stood before him. "Very well, sir. What would you like me to do?"

"It doesn't matter. Do whatever you would normally do. Read a book. Write a letter. Whatever."

Mary Lou nodded, then sat rigidly in a chair. The fire snapped in the grate and a log collapsed, sending a shower of sparks into the air. Waiting quietly, she was certain Thorndike wanted to talk to her, perhaps scold her again for investigating his case. But he said nothing. Instead, he simply began reading, first some kind of business reports and then some figures in a ledger.

Yawning, Mary Lou began to relax. There was something comforting about his presence, something oddly reassuring in spite of the sexual chemistry that lingered between them. She watched him, grateful for the moment to observe him without being observed herself. He really was extraordinarily handsome. His dark hair gleamed in the firelight like a crow's wing, and his thick black lashes were downcast, intent on his work. He had removed his jacket and his white shirt was immaculate and pressed to perfection. It was open at the throat, revealing his Adam's apple and Mary Lou could make out a small triangle of ebony hair curling below it. Dark trousers clung to his thighs, well-muscled from riding, and his stride as he rose to remove another book from the shelf was purposeful.

A prince from a fairy tale. Yet this prince had a troubled child, a meddlesome mother-in-law, a wicked widow as a lover, and an enemy who'd made off with a prize steed. A smile came to her face as she imagined him the hero of a story, but the idea didn't seem so far-fetched. Snuggling into the chair, Mary Lou allowed her eyes to close, dreaming of castles and knights in shining armor.

Thorndike put his pencil aside and watched her sleep. The fire warmed her cheeks, making them pink, and her hair fell around her in charming disarray. The glow from the candles caught the blonde threads of her curls, which gleamed in the dim light like spun gold.

It was selfish, he knew that, but he hadn't wanted to be alone this night. Although no one in the house except Mrs. Doisneau remembered, today had been his wedding anniversary. It was still hard to believe that Clarissa was gone. He glanced at the place where her portrait had hung, and studied the landscape that now graced the same spot.

She still haunted them all. Pierce thought back to the conversation with his mother-in-law. Although he didn't agree with her about Mary Lou, she was right to be concerned about Edward. Was it simply because of his mother's death that he had become so difficult, or was there more to it? While the boy was improving scholastically, Pierce wasn't so sure about his emotions. He wanted to help, but didn't know where to start. Perhaps Miss Finch, for all her eccentricities, could enlighten him.

Rising from his desk, he poured himself a brandy, then returned his gaze to Mary Lou, drinking in the sight of her as he would a healing potion. She was the picture of innocence, which was not entirely accurate, he thought dryly as he recalled her visit to the police. Yet her gesture in the carriage touched him deeply, and he could still feel the powerful sensual urge her slightest touch engendered. But more than that was her underlying concern. It had been a long time since a woman truly cared what he thought, and as he watched her sleep, he knew that was dangerous.

Even more dangerous than the desire he felt for her.

Dawn broke, and Mary Lou awakened slowly, sunlight barely brightening the window. She was still in the library, a quilt drawn up over her shoulders. Thorndike. She remembered watching him before the fire, and must have fallen asleep. An odd warmth filled her at the memory, and she wondered once more at the master of Graystone.

Rising, she realized she was up before the servants. Even Max was still asleep. Regretfully, she thought of Bridget's scones, but she wanted to survey the grounds. And with Thorndike present, the more precautions she took, the better.

Tiptoeing upstairs to get her bag, she slipped out of the house and followed the path toward the lush green pasture at the end of the property. Glancing at the barn, she noticed that the fields to the east of it were secured with a fence. Beyond that was thick woods. Whether the horse bolted or someone led him, there was but one way to go.

The path led to a brook which laughed and chuckled like the voices of a dozen children, tripping over smooth white-granite stones and winding around a huge oak tree. There was a small footbridge over the water. Mary Lou crossed it to the opposite side, where she supposed the next property began. The grounds on this side of the stream weren't nearly as well cared for, and the weathered barn was badly in need of paint. The main house had a shuttered look, and scarcely a pansy or petunia softened the empty porch. A few horses watched her inquisitively from a paddock, and she could see a sign out front that read WHITE PINE STABLES.

A garden stretched before her, and Mary Lou smiled, picturing Edward scrambling between the lettuce plants. Stepping carefully around it, she approached the pasture, which was unfenced and open. If Damien had run, surely he would have come here, where grass and water beckoned. . . .

No sooner had she formed the thought when her pulse quickened. On this side of the bank lay a patch of thick dirt, right where the stream was most narrow.

There, in the middle of the clay, was the clear imprint of a horseshoe!

Excited, Mary Lou crouched down to examine the mark more fully. The edges were just beginning to erode in the wind, but the moisture of the stream and the lack of rainfall had kept the track mostly intact. Taking the shoe she had pried from Damien's stall out of the bag, she placed it in the clay to compare the marks.

They were identical. Mary Lou had noticed that Damien's shoe was more heavily worn on the left side, and the print revealed the same thing. She also noticed that the front of the shoe cut more deeply into the mud than the back. That seemed consistent with a jump, for surely the horse would land in a forward position.

Jotting down her impressions, she smiled in satisfaction. It appeared entirely possible that her supposition was correct, that the horse either came this way or was led this way . . . eagerly, she scanned the ground for a man's track.

"Hey! What are you doing there? This is private property! Damned gypsies!"

Startled, Mary Lou nearly dropped her pencil. Glancing up at the huge frame-house, she saw the shutters open, and an ill-tempered man shaking his fist at her through the open glass.

"Hello!" Mary Lou waved her hand in what she hoped was a friendly gesture. "I'm your neighbor!"

"Neighbor!" The man waved his hand at her. "Liar! No woman lives at Graystone except the housekeeper. Now get off my property!"

"But—"

"I'll fetch my shotgun, by God I will!"

Mary Lou grimaced, but hastened back toward the house. Edward was right. Mr. Whittaker wasn't exactly a friendly sort, and the last thing she needed was to get him riled. But surely he was just threatening . . . to her astonishment, a shot rang out. The man was really trying to kill her!

Frightened out of her wits, Mary Lou hiked up her skirt and leaped over the brook. Cold water splashed up to her thighs, forcing a gasp from her, but she didn't look back. Instead, as she reached Thorndike's property, a sigh of relief swept through her. Pausing for a breath, she felt her heart pounding as if it would come through her chest, and her lungs ached. Once more she was not at all certain she was cut out for this. No, she should be at home in her comfortable cottage, a lemon cake at her elbow, and a test tube bubbling merrily. . . .

The sounds of hoofbeats broke her thoughts. Mr. Whittaker couldn't have followed her on horseback . . . could he? Her heart was in her throat as she turned, half expecting to see a loaded shotgun in her face. Instead, she saw the master of the house, astride a beautiful black thoroughbred.

"Little fool," he said harshly, his blue eyes glittering furiously. "What the hell were you doing up there?"

11

—❧—

Mary Lou swallowed hard. She didn't like confrontations at the best of times, and before breakfast was completely unacceptable. Yet somehow she didn't think it wise to inform Thorndike of that. He swung down from the horse in one fluid motion, and the glossy animal stood stock-still, his large liquid eyes gazing at her in what seemed to be shared disapproval. Dressed in riding clothes, Thorndike looked unbearably handsome, yet she could feel the anger emanating from him.

"I thought . . . you weren't up yet." She cringed as she heard her own voice squeak, and involuntarily took a step back. Dimly she wondered if he'd gotten up early, or had gone during the night.

"I am not here to discuss my schedule. How do you explain yourself?"

He advanced another step and Mary Lou backed up until she was pressed against the trunk of a tree. Panicking, she turned to run, but he must have read her thoughts for he braced one hand on the tree just beside her head and leaned in close. Deciding to brazen it out, she spoke defiantly, unwilling to let him know how much his nearness affected her.

"I woke early and went for a walk. It is a beautiful morning. Surely you don't have any objection to that?"

His eyes met hers, measuring, weighing her answer. It was obvious he didn't believe her. When she tried to break away from the hypnotic hold of his stare, he lifted her chin and gazed deeply into her eyes.

"Does a morning stroll include invading another man's property, and nearly getting shot in the process? Miss Finch, do you realize what could have happened?"

There was an odd touch of emotion in his voice, rendering Mary Lou unable to think. "No," she answered honestly.

"If he hadn't missed you, I would certainly have had to call him out, and I most likely would have been arrested for murder. Whittaker is a cantankerous old man, but I have no desire to kill him."

Mary Lou stared at him in astonishment. Surely he didn't really mean he would go to such lengths to avenge her, when she was just his son's governess?

"I didn't know," she said softly. "I was following

the brook, and crossed the bridge. By then he saw me."

His black expression seemed to lighten a bit. His eyes fell to her plump figure, her chest still heaving slightly from exertion. Mary Lou was suddenly aware of their close proximity, and that he had her trapped in his arms. The situation didn't appear to disturb Thorndike in the least, while her own blood pounded heavily in her veins. A cool smile curved his mouth and Mary Lou wished she had just a fraction of his control.

"Physical exercise doesn't seem to be your natural state, yet I constantly seem to be finding you engaged in it." When Mary Lou started to protest, he shook his head. "I thought we had an understanding. Should you decide on another stroll, I shall accompany you. If I am not here, ask the groom or one of the stableboys to come with you. But I don't want you wandering the grounds by yourself, nor do I want you questioning people who could possibly be dangerous. By the way, Whittaker is innocent of any involvement with the missing horse. You have my word on that. His quarrel with me is related to something entirely different."

Mary Lou's mouth fell open, then she closed it quickly. "I am sorry, sir."

"Very well. Come with me to the barn while I untack Blackwatch. I want to discuss something with you."

Mary Lou frowned at his strange request, but felt herself in no position to question him. Instead, she did as he suggested and followed him into the barn.

The stables were warm and the scent of hay filled

the air. The groom, Bob Shoemaker, yawned sleepily, then his eyes widened with surprise when he saw Thorndike enter with his horse. Glancing at the empty stall, he shrugged sheepishly.

"I didn't know you'd come, sir."

"So I see." Thorndike removed the saddle and handed it to the groom, then gave Mary Lou the reins. "I left strict instructions that these stables were to be guarded at all times. I came out early this morning and was able to remove my horse, saddle him, and ride out of here without seeing a soul. It is little wonder we've had one incident already."

"I'm terribly sorry, sir," Bob said softly. "It won't happen again."

"I'd like to see you in the tack room, please."

Mary Lou gazed at the floor, embarrassed for the man. Apparently, there was hell to pay. But she really couldn't blame Thorndike. Shoemaker had obviously left the stables unguarded, which was dangerous for everyone.

She could hear the voices in the tack room, Thorndike's cool and firm, Shoemaker's more emotional. Blackwatch stood perfectly still before her, his dark eyes questioning. Mary Lou petted his nose, admiring the horse's beauty. Some of the words drifted out to her and she wished she was anywhere but here.

". . . too much whiskey. You are an excellent groom . . . I understand your weakness. I'm not here to criticize . . . will not allow anyone in my household to be in danger . . ."

Mary Lou tried not to openly listen, but her mind churned furiously. Graystone's head groom had a habitual problem with alcohol. Was it coincidence that the blacksmith took him drinking on the night the horse disappeared?

It was an abashed groom that appeared shortly after. He refused to meet Mary Lou's eyes, but instead shouted for the stableboy and began to turn out the remaining horses.

Thorndike unbridled Blackwatch himself, talking to him softly, then put on his halter. After picking up a brush, he began to groom the thoroughbred, taking care to curry out the sweat marks accumulated from the saddle.

"So Miss Finch, I want to ask you something. Why do you think my son is so rebellious?"

The question seemed to come out of nowhere. Mary Lou shrugged. "Partly it's his age. I also think because he's active, he naturally revolts against sitting still for too long. But I also think . . ." her voice trailed off as she carefully framed her answer.

"Yes, Miss Finch? Don't turn shy now," Thorndike said solemnly. "I can take whatever you have to say."

"I think he's afraid of being abandoned," Mary Lou said quickly. When Pierce looked at her strangely, she felt her face getting warm. "I am no alienist, sir, but I think I understand how he feels. He's lost his mother and a series of governesses have left him. I think he rebels in order to precipitate the very thing he fears."

Thorndike appeared surprised for a moment, as if her observation had never occurred to him. Picking up another brush, he came around to her side of the horse.

"You know, Miss Finch, you may be on to something." He indicated the stallion. "Blackwatch here was completely unmanageable, or so his trainer thought. Turns out he was abused by his former owner. What his trainer saw as belligerence was simply fear. Jimmy Dwyer took this horse in hand and taught him how to use that energy."

"Did it work?" Mary Lou asked.

Thorndike smiled. "He's won some of the biggest purses in the country. I don't race him now, but he still likes to show off. Galloped across the fields this morning and scarcely broke a sweat."

As if knowing they were talking about him, the horse nuzzled Pierce affectionately.

Mary Lou smiled. "He seems to like you."

"We understand each other." Thorndike picked up a cloth and began to rub him down. Odd sensations stirred within Mary Lou as she watched the man with the magnificent horse. Something about them was exactly matched—a wild streak that would never totally be tamed.

Pierce rose and patted the black stallion thoughtfully. "Miss Finch, you have wisdom beyond your years. I don't know if I've told you, but I am very pleased with your work."

Mary Lou flushed with pleasure. She would never have thought those few words would mean so much, but coming from him, they did. Thorndike put the horse into his stall, and firmly closed the door. When he finished, he returned to her.

"Shall we go?"

He held out his arm, and Mary Lou took it,

smiling up at him. Never would she understand him. One minute he was cold and demanding, the next minute, warm and generous.

They had just reached the barn door when a crash sounded from outside. Mary Lou heard several men's voices, followed by the shrill whinny of a mare. Thorndike immediately headed through the middle of the barn to the mare's stall on the opposite side.

The groom was there, as were several other men. Mary Lou recognized the new trainer, along with a well-dressed man who simply nodded in Thorndike's direction. Another man was clinging to a glossy chestnut stallion, who snorted and champed, evidently well aware he was on the ladies' side.

"Mr. Woodhill." Thorndike extended a hand, which the gentleman took. "I didn't hear you arrive."

"I just got here. Seems Chance wasn't one for waiting. He almost busted out of the cart when he scented your mare." He indicated the row of stalls just inside the barn.

"Are you ready to breed him now?" Thorndike asked.

"The sooner the better. Old Chance here is chomping at the bit. This is his first time, so he's liable to be a little confused."

Mary Lou saw what he said was true. The poor stallion reared and snorted, uncertain of what was going on, but somehow knew he had a part to play in all of it.

"Fine. Do you need help?"

It was Bob Shoemaker who answered. "It might be a good idea for you to remain, sir. Especially since this is the lad's first breeding."

Thorndike nodded, then stripped off his coat and draped it over the fence. He turned to Mary Lou, giving her an apologetic smile. "I'm sorry. I shall see you at breakfast."

"Sir, do you mind if I stay?" Mary Lou asked quietly. When Thorndike gave her an odd look, she shrugged. "For a scientist, this is irresistible."

"I see. In that case, I suppose it's all right, but stay hidden in the back. I don't want the men distracted, and stallions are unpredictable, especially when they're young. More than one has killed a mare, or been killed itself if things don't go right."

Mary Lou's eyes widened, but she nodded in understanding, then slipped unnoticed behind the breeding shed. One of the stableboys had brought a pile of ropes, while the others gathered around, some out of curiosity, the more experienced out of a desire to help.

Woodhill's groom waited outside while Shoemaker prepared the mare. Mary Lou glimpsed the mare's name, Amanda's Toy, on her door, as the groom led her to the breeding shed. The beautiful chocolate-colored horse gazed at him affectionately, and nudged him as he positioned her in the center of the shed. When Shoemaker slipped the ropes around her legs, effectively hobbling her, she barely looked up but munched on some hay as if this was all in a day's work.

"She's ready!" Thorndike called.

A moment later, it seemed the horse from hell had come upon them. Mary Lou gasped in astonishment as the stallion, smelling the mare, kicked and reared furiously. The men tried to restrain him, but the mating urge caused the horse to plunge recklessly forward, his nostrils extended, his eyes wild and excited. Moving even farther back, she could still see the horse as he surged past the men and leaped toward the shed.

Unfortunately, the door was only part way open and poor Chance found himself mating with it instead of the mare. The men roared with laughter, even as they tried to restrain him, while Amanda glanced backward and seemed to roll her eyes in disgust. She turned her liquid gaze to Pierce as if plainly asking him, "Was this the best you could do?"

Even Thorndike broke into laughter, petting the mare and trying to reassure her. She seemed much more matter-of-fact about the whole endeavor, and waited patiently for the men to drag Chance away from the door.

When they finally managed to get the stall door open, the colt bolted inside. Amanda, already uncertain about this untried youth, broke free of her ropes and turned to face him. Thorndike shouted to the groom and together they tried once more to tether her, while Chance, in his frenzied excitement, attempted to mount her head. Once more the men roared with mirth, until they finally got the horses properly positioned.

This time, Chance proceeded in a proper fashion. Needing no urging, he mounted the mare. Amanda kicked and bucked, in spite of the restraints, her powerful hooves connecting solidly with the colt. Mary Lou gasped as she saw blood trickle down the horse's leg, but the stallion seemed oblivious to anything except sexual pleasure. He slid his engorged penis inside her, bit her neck, and the mare shrieked in pain and fury.

Mary Lou's mouth went dry and her stomach tightened. There was something incredibly primitive about their coupling. Flushed, she looked up and found Thorndike's eyes on her. The moment was electric, all the more because the other men didn't know she was there. Embarrassed, she dropped her eyes to the floor, almost grateful when Bob hauled the colt away once more.

"Is he hurt?" One of the men asked the groom.

"Chance? Nah, they all go through that. He got lucky, though. If one of those hooves connected a little higher, it would have done some real damage."

He took the colt outside to tend to his injuries, while Thorndike removed the ropes from the mare. Mary Lou heard him speaking quietly to the horse, who trembled, her eyes wild.

"Easy, girl. You've done good. Good mare."

Amanda calmed quickly, accepting his hand as he petted her. All of the nervous tension seemed to leave the mare with Thorndike's voice, and she visibly gentled at his touch, glancing about in bewilderment.

Thorndike smiled, petting her nose. "Isn't much in it for you, is there? Poor Chance, doesn't have enough experience yet."

His meaning became clear and Mary Lou colored violently. Slipping out of the stall unnoticed, she walked back up to the house, swallowing hard. She felt curiously alive, and her blood seemed to throb in her veins. She closed her eyes, but her body still shivered at the memory of his eyes when they'd connected with hers during the breeding.

*   *   *

Later that afternoon, the butler entered the laboratory carrying a small silver tray. "Miss Finch, a letter for you."

Mary Lou took the envelope from the butler and glimpsed her cousin Emily's address in the corner. Turning to Edward, she said, "Why don't you finish writing the report from our experiment? Afterward we can review it, then head to the pond. We can study the algae bloom and take Max for a walk."

Edward eagerly dug into his work, and Mary Lou took the letter to the gaslight. Opening the missive, her heart beat proudly when she read Emily's opening lines.

> *Have received your reports. Excellent work, Mary Lou, I could not have done better myself. You certainly underestimated your talents for sleuthing. The reports are very complete and contain numerous leads. I can envision myself consulting with you in the future.*
>
> *I have some information for you. The Boston police have taken Bill Cooke into custody. He has a record, and is considered a bad sort, so he may very well be our man. But there are other threads here. I can find nothing on Willy Starkey, although the local police have agreed to question him and will forward their results to me. I, too, find it interesting that he was there the night of the murder.*
>
> *Proceed with care, Mary Lou, and know that I am but a telegram away, should you*

*need help. I've also telegraphed Merrimack
and asked him to assist you in any way possible.—EH*

Mary Lou folded the note and thoughtfully replaced it in the envelope. She was so preoccupied
that she didn't see her hair fall from its knot and slide
over her shoulder into the flickering blue flame of the
Bunsen burner. Edward glanced up from his report
and gasped in shock.

"Miss Finch!" he shrieked, his eyes like popped
umbrellas. He pointed to her hair. "You're on fire!"

12

—❧—

"Fire!" Edward's cry had obviously been heard by someone up at the house, as what looked like every member of the household staff rushed to Mary Lou's assistance. Mary Lou frantically tamped out the flames eating her long blonde hair, while Max barked excitedly, circling his mistress, and Edward climbed on a bench to help smother the flames with a towel. It was Thorndike himself who tossed a full bucket of water at Mary Lou, effectively putting out any remaining sparks.

"Good heavens!" Bridget said in alarm as Mary Lou sputtered furiously. "What on earth happened?"

"She leaned over the Bunsen burner," Edward said, his voice trembling with excitement. "Her hair just lit up like one big giant torch!"

"I shouldn't say I'm surprised," Mrs. Doisneau said deprecatingly. "This equipment is obviously dangerous. It was simply a matter of time before someone got hurt. Thank God it wasn't Edward."

Thorndike scowled, and pushed past the woman to the governess. Mary Lou attempted to shake off the water, while trying in vain to improve her appearance. When she glanced up, Thorndike was standing before her, his eyes full of concern.

"Are you all right, Miss Finch?"

"Yes," she answered, mortified and dripping like a wet cat. "I am perfectly fine. Edward was correct in his synopsis. I had no idea my hair would fall out of its knot and light up like that. I shall certainly be more careful in the future."

Glancing at Edward, Mary Lou saw that he still held the towel he'd used to help her. Giving him a smile, she patted his head. "You are my hero, Edward. I think you saved my life, your father's help notwithstanding."

The little boy flushed with pleasure. "I did! I ran right up to her and used the towel to put out the fire!"

If he had saved Tammany Hall, Edward couldn't have looked prouder. Even Thorndike smiled and he solemnly shook the boy's hand.

"I'm proud of you, son. That's what makes a real gentleman. You came to a lady's assistance when she desperately needed it. You've done well today."

Edward grinned from ear to ear. Even his grandmother had to smile as the boy blushed, clearly pleased with his father's praise. Bridget patted him fondly, then came to Mary Lou.

"Why don't you clean up, lass, and come for tea. I'll take the boy with me."

"Thank you," Mary Lou whispered, grateful that Bridget seemed to read her mind. While Mrs. Doisneau still preached about the dangers of scientific equipment, Mary Lou went to her room and quietly closed the door. Pouring water into a pitcher, she glanced into the mirror over the washstand and burst into tears.

Her blonde hair, her one real beauty, lay in a snarled, charred mess around her shoulders.

Stunned at her appearance, she attempted to use the hairbrush, but it seemed to make matters worse. More hair fell out, and what remained looked ghastly. Worse than that was the smell. Mary Lou thought she'd never forget that peculiar odor as long as she lived.

It was foolish, silly and utterly feminine, but the sight of those frizzled locks did what Whittaker's gunshots couldn't accomplish. Mary Lou gave in to despair and allowed herself the luxury of a good long cry. Flinging herself on the bed, she sobbed not just for her hair, but for all of the pain she'd felt in the last few years; the rejection of suitors, the lack of use for her degree, the brave front she'd put on at college, the loss of her comfortable home . . . it seemed that nothing in the world could induce her to stop crying.

She felt utterly foolish, but how could she not, especially when she started to think of her future? By taking the governess job at Graystone, she had jeopardized even that. If she was exposed as an impostor, no one would ever hire her as a real governess. What was left? Factory work? If she didn't recover her dowry, what was to become of her?

A knock sounded on the door. Startled, Mary Lou

sat up and quickly wiped her face. She didn't want to concern anyone or to frighten Edward any more than she already had. "Come in," she called, her voice hoarse.

"Miss Finch." To her surprise, Thorndike entered the room, carrying a tea tray. After putting it on the nighttable, he turned to her, his expression grave. "Mrs. Murphy thought you might prefer your tea here."

"Thank you." Embarrassed that he should see her like this, Mary Lou turned away and faced the window. "That was very kind of you both."

For a long moment, he said nothing, but simply stood by her bed awkwardly, uncertain of how to help her. Mary Lou struggled to hold back her emotions, but it became impossible as she once more caught sight of her reflection. Fresh tears spilled forth, and she covered her face in her hands.

Thorndike stood there for a moment, then he took her in his arms and held her like a child. His embrace felt warm and strong, his scent clean and masculine, and Mary Lou allowed him to hold her. Trying desperately to quell her sobs, she gestured to his shirt.

"I'm getting you all wet," she said in a choked whisper.

"That's all right." For once Thorndike didn't seem at all distant or formal. Instead, a warm smile curved his face and his eyes seemed like the twin blue flames of a candle. Mary Lou started to smile in response, but tears bubbled forth again. Thorndike handed her his handkerchief, and she mopped her face.

The heat of his embrace seemed to penetrate her damp clothes, and her cheek pressed against his shirt felt wonderful. He smoothed her hair from her face, and took the handkerchief from her, then dried her tears himself.

"I must look a fright," she whispered into his chest, refusing to look at him.

"You look beautiful," he said earnestly.

Something in his voice sounded entirely too sincere and she gazed up at him in surprise.

A warmth burned in his eyes, different from the compassion she'd seen there before—something much more complicated than simply caring for a servant. Mesmerized, she watched him kiss her burned hair as if in homage to her pain. A thousand emotions exploded within her at once like a storm of shooting stars, and when he bent down to kiss her lips, it seemed the most natural thing in the world.

All thoughts of her charred hair were forgotten as Mary Lou surrendered to the devastation of his kiss. She had secretly wondered for so long, and wanted him so desperately. But it was even better than just physical desire, although that was beginning to pound through her veins like liquid fire. No, the tenderness and caring, the comfort and friendship, these made the kiss an unearthly kind of torture.

Suddenly he stopped, as if just realizing what he had done. Mary Lou felt a rush of disappointment as he straightened, and Thorndike looked as though he wanted to be anywhere but here in her room.

"Forgive me, Miss Finch," he said softly, the words coming hard. "I apologize for my actions. They were inexcusable. If you feel you must seek employment elsewhere after this, I completely understand."

She stared at him for a long moment. Her body shivered from the loss of his warmth and she put her arms around herself to stop the trembling. He had just kissed her senseless and now he was sorry?

Pride came to her rescue, and she managed to speak in a calm tone. "That won't be necessary, Mr. Thorndike. What just happened is as much my fault as yours. Please do not concern yourself."

"Miss Finch—"

Mary Lou gave him a frosty stare. "Please don't make this any more embarrassing than it is. If you don't mind, I'd like to be alone for a few minutes."

He rose, stood in the doorway for a moment watching her, then sighed.

"Take as long as you need. I will see you at supper." Then he was gone.

Mary Lou gazed at the closed door, wondering what had just happened. She touched her fingers to her lips, still feeling there the tingle of Thorndike's kiss. Yet the meaning of his apology was unmistakable. Embarrassment surged through her. He was simply trying to be kind, and she had read too much into it. The only hope for her was to act as if nothing had happened.

Tucking his handkerchief carefully beneath her pillow, she dipped her flannel into the water bowl and pressed it to her face. The cool cloth made the swelling in her eyes more bearable. Next she removed the last remnants of ruined hair with her brush, then leaned over the bowl, pouring the water into her damaged tresses. Using the bar of soap nearby, she lathered her hair several times, then rinsed it completely and wrapped it up in a towel. Determined, she opened her bag and withdrew a pair of scissors.

Removing the towel, she let her long blonde mane fall to her waist. Critically, she assessed the damage and realized the only thing she could do was cut her hair to even out the curls. Grimacing, she slid the blades beneath the damaged tresses and snipped each lock of hair, the trimmings tumbling onto the towel beneath her. It took the better part of an hour, but finally, she could gaze into the mirror and not react with shock.

Her hair was much shorter, and she looked regretfully at the shorn curls that had taken years to grow. But the new style wasn't completely awful. Tendrils were already framing her face as her hair dried, and she'd managed to cut off all the burned ends. Braiding the rest, she secured it firmly behind her neck, then changed her dress, putting on her best blue cotton tarlatan. She even slipped on pearl earrings, a gift from her father that had always made her feel special. Thus fortified, she ventured down the stairs for supper.

Thorndike's voice came from the dining room. Breathing a sigh of relief, she entered the kitchen where Bridget bustled around. Mary Lou took a seat near the fireplace, while the housekeeper glanced at her in surprise.

"You'll be looking very nice, Miss. Clipped your hair, did you? It's even bonnier than before."

"Thank you," Mary Lou said, convinced the woman was lying through her teeth.

Bridget gave her a fond glance. "Are you going to

join them in the dining room? Mrs. Norcross and Mr. Cornwall are with us tonight."

"No!" Mary Lou said emphatically, recalling the beautiful widow and her self assurance. She was still raw from her embarrassing episode with Thorndike. There was no way she wanted to endure Mrs. Doisneau's jibes and the widow's arched smiles.

At Bridget's curious look, she hastened to explain. "I don't feel up to company."

"Ah." Bridget nodded at the wisdom of her words. "I suppose not. Then you'll have supper with me. I've baked a special lemon cake, the kind you like. I thought it might pick up your spirits."

Mary Lou smiled, feeling instantly better. There was something about Bridget's cheerfulness that refused to allow any gloom to remain. Smiling, she helped herself to the savory roast beef when the door burst open and Thorndike walked in.

"Miss Finch, I thought I had asked you to join us."

Mary Lou sputtered while Bridget seemed busy cutting the cake. "Why I . . . I assumed . . . you have company . . ."

"Miss Finch, when I issue an invitation, I expect you to comply. I don't think it's too much of an inconvenience to ask you to endure my company at meals. Do you find it so?"

"Well, no," Mary Lou said, completely taken aback.

"Good. From now on, you are to take all your meals with the family. Is that understood?"

"Yes, sir." Regretfully, she eyed the cake. Pierce saw where her attention was, and one side of his mouth quirked.

"Do not be concerned, Miss Finch, I will ensure that you have enough to eat. Shall I escort you?"

Mary Lou burned furiously, but could do nothing but accept his arm. This man! she thought in outrage. One minute he acted as though she didn't exist, the next he was seducing her until her toes curled, then he was peremptorily ordering her around. It wasn't to be born!

But at least she didn't have to worry about him harboring any misgivings about what had transpired between them. Apparently, he'd completely wiped it from his memory. No, he was his normal, forbidding self, and she felt none of the embarrassment she'd expected facing him. When she entered the dining room, Mrs. Doisneau gave her the expected look of disapproval, while the widow gave her a false smile. Edward said "Hello," then looked away, distracted by his food. Only Robert Cornwall rose and greeted her with any genuine enthusiasm, after introducing himself as Thorndike's lawyer.

"I insisted Miss Finch join us," Thorndike said as the women's brows arched. "She is after all, a member of this household."

"How nice," the widow said blandly. Her eyes went from Pierce to the governess, then back again. As ridiculous as the notion was, Mary Lou swore the woman read her thoughts, for her brows lifted even higher and her color, beautiful to begin with, deepened into an apricot-rose. Mary Lou could feel her own color rising, but Thorndike buttered his bread as if nothing unusual had occurred, as if he hadn't kissed her senseless only hours before. . . .

"Well, Miss Finch, I see that you've improved

your appearance," Edward's grandmother said. "Those new short cuts are very much in vogue, I assure you."

"Thank you," Mary Lou managed, aware that Robert was looking at her curiously.

"Your hair looks real pretty," Edward said generously. "You can't even see where it burned up."

"Miss Finch had a little accident today with her burner," Thorndike explained.

The widow looked at Mary Lou with pity. "How awful! You must have been terrified, poor dear. I certainly hope the science was worth the loss of that beautiful hair."

Robert flinched, and even Thorndike gave her a sharp look. Her arrow struck deeply, and Mary Lou struggled to keep her voice even. "It was an unusual mishap, and entirely my fault. I was distracted, which for a scientist, is inexcusable."

"Yes, but to have your hair catch fire! I couldn't imagine such a thing! I would have been devastated." She shook her head sympathetically, then turned to Thorndike and laid a beautifully manicured hand on his coat. "Do let me give you a few scarves for her next time you visit," she implored, practically purring. "I have ever so many, including the ones you've given me as gifts over the years. I've treasured them all, you know."

Mary Lou looked at the widow, seeing her sparkling white blouse, emerald-green riding coat, and perfectly coiffed hair. A garnet glimmered darkly at her throat, emphasizing a face that needed no additional attention. This was the kind of woman who should be with Thorndike, she thought, her heart

sinking. Glancing from her to the master of
Graystone, she saw that they made a striking couple.
They were both elegant and handsome people,
shared a love of horses, while she . . . she was an eccentric, a lowly governess who set her own hair
aflame.

Something stuck in her throat and she gulped her
tea, surprised at the pain she felt. She was even more
surprised to see Robert give her a sympathetic look
before he turned to the widow and snapped, "Miss
Finch is beautiful without any borrowed adorn-
ments," Robert said quickly. "But I am sure she appreciates the thought. Your generosity, my dear, is
overwhelming."

Thorndike's lawyer gazed at the widow fiercely.
Why, he cares for her, Mary Lou thought in amazement. Yet all of the widow's attentions were devoted
to Thorndike. Even now she practically purred as she
extended her glass to be refilled, resting her fingers
on his other arm as he did. Thorndike, her gestures
so eloquently indicated, was hers.

Sighing, Mary Lou reached for the dessert, often
her only solace in times of trouble. But tonight, there
wasn't enough cake in the world to ease the ache in
her heart.

13

When Mary Lou excused herself right after dessert, Robert turned to Vivian. "You know, I've never seen you be truly unkind before. What in the devil possessed you to make those remarks about Miss Finch's hair?"

"I was only trying to be nice," Vivian said defensively.

"You picked an odd way of showing it," Robert said sternly. "I'm certain that's why she left so quickly after dinner."

Vivian's mouth tightened as she saw Pierce staring at the door that Mary Lou had just shut. He appeared distracted, and not at all happy with what had transpired. Even Edward was upset.

Forcing a false smile, the widow sighed. "Isn't it

interesting that Miss Finch has so many champions? I
suppose some women just fit the role of damsel in
distress."

Thorndike gave her a frosty glance, and Robert
sputtered furiously. Before they could continue the
argument, Pierce rose and indicated the library.

"Why don't we have coffee in there? I feel a defi-
nite chill in the air, and it is past Edward's bedtime.
Mrs. Norcross, if you and Robert could pass the
evening without continued speculation about my governess, I think we would all find it more enjoyable."

Vivian flushed, but said nothing. Instead she rose
and, giving Edward a kiss on the cheek, followed
Robert into the adjoining room.

She was here only because of the case, Mary Lou reminded herself the following afternoon. The widow's
visit made it abundantly clear it was she who enjoyed
Thorndike's affections, and to think anything else was
not only embarrassing, but ludicrous. It was time
she started thinking logically, and that meant seeing everyone objectively, including the master of
Graystone.

She had to admit that his part in all this seemed
more confusing than ever. Recalling the policeman's
statement, she wondered again about Thorndike's
wife. Was there more to her death than a simple illness? Had he been seeing the widow before that fatal
night? From her comments, Vivian seemed to imply
that they had been involved for a long time. Was that
why he was so determined that she, Mary Lou, stay

out of his business? Was he really worried about her, or was it because he didn't want her to learn the truth?

Returning her attention to her notes, she forced herself to focus on the data she had collected thus far. The trainer had been innocent, if Nancy's testimony could be believed, and Mary Lou didn't doubt her.

Then there was Bill Cooke. She just couldn't convince herself that he had masterminded all this. The disgruntled servant theory just seemed a bit too convenient.

What about the blacksmith? Mary Lou reviewed her notes about him. Willy Starkey more than likely needed money. The grooms spoke of his betting habits, which, over the past year, had become more extravagant. He also had opportunity. He was at Graystone regularly, knew the horses, and worked closely enough with them to establish trust.

Gazing at the notebook, she underlined the fact that Starkey had taken the groom drinking. There was something here, niggling at her . . .

"Edward," she turned to the boy, who was supposed to be doing an essay, but was instead watching the mares and foals frolic in the paddocks outside.

"Yes, Miss?" He turned away from the window, his face red at being caught.

"How are the stables guarded? Does the same man watch each night?"

The boy shook his head. "No, they take turns. Sometimes a few of the stableboys watch, sometimes the grooms. They each have a set night."

Mary Lou nodded, excitement growing within her. Willy Starkey would have known the schedule. It would have been an easy matter to entice Bob Shoemaker to indulge in a few ales, then return with him on the night he was to poison the horse. For Willy, the coast would then have been clear. He could have easily given Damien the apple, but his plan was interrupted by the untoward appearance of Jimmy Dwyer. Did Thorndike suspect the same thing? Why then wasn't he actively pursuing the case? What *was* his role in all this?

Glancing up once more, she saw Edward still staring outside. "Edward, you're supposed to be writing. What is it?"

The boy flushed, but gestured outside. "I was just watching Donna."

"Donna?" Mary Lou followed his gaze, grateful for the distraction after the widow's visit. Outside, the groom patiently walked a very pregnant mare in a circle. The mare waddled awkwardly, her belly swaying with every stride.

Mary Lou joined him at the window. "Why is he walking her like that?"

"They won't let her out in the field 'cause she'll run and hurt herself. Papa said that foal is too big. Blackwatch is the sire, but he isn't known to produce real big foals. Until now."

The mare did appear extraordinarily large, even to Mary Lou's eyes. "What is he doing now?"

The groom tied the mare to a fence, then brought out a bucket of water. He emptied the bucket over the horse, then returned to the well for another. The mare didn't appear at all unhappy with this treatment. She raised her head, seeming to luxuriate in the feel of the cool water running down her sides.

"He's just giving her a bath, trying to make her comfortable. Papa said she'll go at any time now since her milk is in."

"Shouldn't he call the veterinarian?" Mary Lou questioned.

"No, she could go on like that for a few hours yet. The good thing is Papa won't leave now until the foal comes. Donna was one of his first horses and he will stay to help her."

There was a note of satisfaction in Edward's voice that made Mary Lou smile. The boy missed his father dreadfully when he left on business. Her gaze went back to the window. "But it looks like your father is out," Mary Lou remarked. "The carriage is gone."

"He just went to town for supplies. He said he wanted to talk to the police about Damien, to see if they found out anything yet. But he'll be back."

"Well, I can see we won't get a lot done today," Mary Lou said pragmatically, her own nerves frayed. "Why don't we finish this chapter, then take a walk to the barn so you can see how Donna's doing?"

Edward's eyes lit up. "We could? Really?"

"Yes, really. But we have to get some work done first. The sooner we get through this, the sooner we can go up."

As expected, Edward fell immediately to his task with the promise of a reprieve ahead. A few moments later, a shout came from the yard. Both Mary Lou and Edward raced to the window in time to see Bob Shoemaker lead the horse toward the barn. The boy pointed with excitement.

"Something must have happened! She must be starting! Let's go see!"

"All right," Mary Lou said. "Perhaps we can help. But you must stay out of the way and obey everyone. Is that agreed?"

"Yes," Edward said happily. Taking Mary Lou's hand, he began tugging her toward the barn. "I wanted to see Donna the last time she foaled, but Papa said I was too little. I'm bigger now."

Mary Lou gave him a smile, then ventured to the barn. Already the place was in chaos. The stableboys rushed around, the groom barked orders, and the blacksmith had begun rolling up his sleeves. Max watched cautiously, staying far away from the horse's hooves, but close enough to see the action. The mare was in her stall, which Mary Lou saw was layered thick with straw. She paced restlessly, her eyes wide and alarmed.

"The sac's appeared," Shoemaker shouted to the blacksmith. He then turned to one of the boys. "Timmy, fetch the vet. I think she's going to have a tough time here. If you see the master in town, let him know the mare's time has come. I could use a drink."

The groom glanced up as Mary Lou entered the barn, and his frown became a scowl. "I don't think—"

"We'll stay well out of the way," Mary Lou said softly. "Edward wants to see."

The groom didn't appear too happy with this development, but he simply shrugged in annoyance. "He can stay if you keep him in the loft. I don't want anyone in the way, and I want to be able to get water and supplies in here. Willy, do you have a couple of ropes?"

Mary Lou turned quickly to see the man who had occupied much of her thoughts the past few days. Willy Starkey was an older man with gnarled hands and a strong back. His face was lined from exposure to the elements, and she could see a racing paper protruding from his back pocket. He gave Mary Lou a look not much friendlier than the one she gave him, then turned his back, tossing a few of the ropes toward the stall. "Yes, right here."

Mary Lou took Edward up into the loft, and they settled in a good position above the stall. Thankfully, the groom appeared entirely sober, and more than mentally prepared for what was to come. The blacksmith moved behind the horse, examining the sac that protruded from her womb. They spoke in dire tones, and Mary Lou wondered if it was the right thing to do to allow Edward to observe. If something went wrong . . .

"What's going on?" Edward propped himself up on two elbows and peered down.

"The mare is having contractions," Mary Lou explained. "Just like when humans have a baby, the uterus shrinks to push the baby out."

"Then why isn't he coming out?"

That was the question indeed. As the minutes passed, the mare's signs of pain began to increase. Her eyes grew more and more agitated as she paced the stall, straining every few minutes, then shuddering as the contraction rent its way through her. The blacksmith and the groom appeared anything but happy as they watched the horse, trying to let nature take its course, but it soon became obvious that the mare was in trouble.

"We don't seem to be getting anywhere," Willy examined the mare once more. Sweat covered her flanks, and she began to show signs of deep labor. Her knees buckled as she awkwardly lowered herself to the stall floor.

"The master won't be too happy if he comes back and finds the mare dead," the groom said, wiping his brow. "First Damien, now this."

"Dead?" Edward turned to Mary Lou in panic. "Is Donna going to die?"

Old Willy sent a foul look upward. The mare flared her nostrils, seized with a fresh contraction, but quickly resumed straining as she struggled to deliver the foal.

"Edward, perhaps we should wait at the house," Mary Lou began, but just as she spoke, they heard the sound of hooves outside. "Maybe the vet has come," she whispered hopefully.

It was Thorndike who entered the barn, not the vet, but at once Mary Lou felt the effect of his presence. The groom and the blacksmith both stepped back respectfully, and the blacksmith explained the lack of progress with the delivery. Thorndike appeared concerned, but immediately began to take charge, tossing his jacket aside and stripping off his shirt.

"I passed the veterinarian in town. He said to get started, he's got another job and won't be here for a while. There, Donna, good mare." Thorndike stroked the horse. At once the mare quieted, although it was apparent to everyone that she was in enormous pain. Speaking a few more words of reassurance, he walked behind her and examined her with the blacksmith. The sac protruded slightly more than before. Willy held up a lantern while Thorndike fell to his knees.

"I can see the hoof," he said solemnly. "Bob, have you ever seen anything like that?"

Mary Lou and Edward strained to watch. The groom stepped behind the horse, then gave a low whistle. "That's not a horse, that's a baby moose she's trying to deliver! Good God, no wonder she can't expel him!"

Thorndike nodded. "We're going to have to pull it out. Bob, sit on her head. Willy, give me a hand."

Mary Lou swallowed hard as Thorndike laid down on the ground behind the horse. She could tell by his voice that he was concerned, and that could only mean one thing: while the delivery of a foal would have been a good biology lesson for Edward, watching the mare die would not.

Edward stared, transfixed on the drama happening below. "Look!" He pointed below.

Mary Lou glanced down. Shoemaker was seated on the mare's head to keep her still. Thorndike lay behind her, his hand inserted deep into the mare. Apparently, he had managed to grip the foal's hoof and struggled to hold on while the powerful contractions gripped down on his arm. They watched in fascination as he yanked as hard as he could when the pressure eased, trying to wrench the foal to freedom. He strained against the horse as the uterus contracted again, making extraction even more difficult.

"There, he moved!" Thorndike shouted. "Bob, make sure she stays still, for God's sake, don't let her get up! Willy, keep her feet out of the way! The shoulders are huge!"

Willy knelt beside him with the ropes and tried to assist, but Thorndike was in such a position that he wasn't able to do much. Mary Lou's mouth went dry as Thorndike struggled. Fluid and blood from the mare's body covered him, and she could see every muscle in his back straining as he tried to turn the foal. Moment by moment passed, and she found herself praying, wishing the vet would arrive, hoping against hope that everything would be all right.

"We may have to cut her," Willy spoke softly. "The foal might drown in the fluid if we don't. The mare's in a lot of pain. I can't see her going on like this."

"No!" Edward cried out, scrambling to his feet. Thorndike glanced up and saw his son and his governess in the loft. His eyes blazed in anger, and Mary Lou cringed to think of what would happen later. Somehow she managed to get Edward settled, knowing that none of the men could afford a distraction now.

"I don't want to cut her unless we have no other choice. I don't think she's given up yet . . . There! I've got it! That last contraction helped, the foal moved. Thank God. Willy, get ready to pull. . . . "

The blacksmith crawled beside Thorndike on the ground and grabbed the second hoof that appeared. Pierce's arm was invisible up to the elbow as he struggled to turn the foal's shoulders. Bracing his feet against the horse's rump, he yanked the foal toward him. Mary Lou and Edward gasped in astonishment as first one shoulder slipped out, then the other. Finally, the entire foal seemed to effortlessly follow, sliding to the stable floor in a steaming fluid rush.

"Look at the size of him!" Willy said in astonishment as the foal looked around him in bewilderment. "I've never in my life seen one that big! It has to be a colt!"

"It is," Thorndike said dryly as he sat up from the floor. He flexed the stiffness from his arm, barely aware that he was soaked in blood and birth fluid. "He's the biggest that Blackwatch has ever sired. Good God, what is it now?"

Before Mary Lou could sigh in relief, the mare began to roll wildly. The groom lost his seat on the horse's head as she threw herself violently against the wall.

"Quick! The foal!" Thorndike shouted, coming to his feet in a jump. "She's colicking!"

Stunned, Mary Lou and Edward watched openmouthed as Willy pulled the foal out of harm's way. The mare, weak from the birth and filled with pain, threw herself around the stall in a blind effort to rid herself of whatever was torturing her now. Thorndike narrowly escaped being slammed against the wall as the nine-hundred-pound mare continued to writhe. Forcing a rope over her neck, Bob urged her to her feet and managed to gain some control over her before she could fling herself about once more. Gradually, the spasms passed, and the mare stood shaking in the center of the stall as if a nightmare had come and gone.

"Is everyone all right?" Bob called out. He was standing with the foal in the farthest corner of the stall. The foal, still covered with fluid from the birth sac, appeared bewildered, and gazed about as if not at all certain he wanted to stay in this crazy world.

"Yes, I think we're fine," Thorndike said. "Bring the foal over and let's see if she responds to him. She might still be in too much pain."

Bob hauled the huge, wet foal toward the mare, who trembled with pain and fear. As the groom placed the damp bundle beneath her, the mare paused, then looked down as if puzzled. She smelled the little horse, lifted her head questioningly, then finally seemed to understand what had happened. Excitement filled her and she licked the foal, then she glanced at Thorndike as if to say, so this is what this was all about!

In spite of everything, Thorndike started to laugh, as did Willy and Bob. Patting the horse, he watched as she bonded with her foal. Max stepped forward and sniffed the odd creature, as if trying to decide whether this truly was a horse after all. Edward, sensing it was all right to come down now, scrambled to the stall for a closer look. Mary Lou followed a moment later, thankful that Thorndike seemed preoccupied with the horse. Only Old Willy sent her a scowl, which she ignored.

"Will you look at that! The little bugger's too big to get up!"

Bob spoke softly, but Mary Lou saw that it was true. The foal tried to get to his feet, but they seemed far too large for his body and he slid right back down to the hay. Donna pushed at him, encouraging him once more, and the foal tried again. This time he managed to get his two front feet on the ground, and was just trying for the third when they all gave way and he landed in the straw once more.

The foal looked around with such an expression of exasperation that everyone laughed out loud. The odd human sound startled him, and he tried once again to scramble to his feet. This time, in a maneuver that would have made an acrobat envious, he managed to gather all four feet under him at once, and pull them together in synchronization. His body seemed to fly upward, and he finally stood erect, gazing about him in wonder.

Mary Lou felt a tear come to her eye as the mare reached out to her foal. It had to be just the tension and excitement, she thought, as a thousand emotions filled her. Yet her gaze met Thorndike's and she saw her own feelings reflected there. Wordlessly they shared the beauty of the moment and the kind of experience one never forgot: the wonder of life and the miracle of birth. He gave her a boyish smile, as if embarrassed at being caught. His expression was so different from his normally stern demeanor that she felt her heart breaking. . . .

"Good afternoon! Looks like I got here just in time! You folks seemed to have managed just fine!"

Mary Lou heard the cheerful whistle of Dan Forester, the veterinarian, and turned in time to see him stepping jauntily toward the stall. Thorndike rolled his eyes heavenward, then accepted the towel that Bob handed him. Turning her gaze away from him, she suddenly realized he was standing within three feet of her, half-naked. Even covered with the stains of sweat and the mare's blood, he was magnificent. His shoulders were truly as broad as she would have guessed, and his chest, she tried not to notice, was bare except for the slightest feathering of black curls. She followed them down past a washboard-hard stomach, to the waistband of his trousers, where they disappeared somewhere beneath.

Mary Lou forced her attention back to the mare. This was no time to be entertaining such thoughts about Thorndike. She was treading on dangerous ground as it was. From the corner of her eye she saw him dip the towel into a bucket of water, then scrub the blood from his arms and chest

"I don't think we're out of the water yet," Thorndike warned as the vet appeared happy to have missed the drama. "Check her thoroughly. She had a tough time with that foal, and colicked afterward. She may hemorrhage yet."

"Good God, what a creature!" Dan said in astonishment when he saw the foal. "You say you managed to deliver her of this? I would think you'd have had to put her down."

"Donna's been with me a long time, and we've been through worse before." Thorndike spoke softly. The horse seemed to know he was discussing her, for she gave him a soft, liquid glance, then returned to nuzzling the foal.

Dr. Forester chuckled. "She seems happy enough now. Probably glad to have gotten that one out of her. I'm sure that within a few days, she'll be right as rain. Right as rain!"

Mary Lou discreetly took Edward's hand to lead

him back to the house. Thorndike gave the vet a look displaying his lack of appreciation for his jaunty mood, before his eyes met hers once more, this time as if sharing in the joke. Thorndike, she realized, was even more of a mystery than the missing racehorse.

14

When they returned to the house, Mrs. Doisneau clucked with disapproval at the straw clinging to Edward's head. "Don't tell me you were in that dirty barn," she scolded, brushing him with a gloved hand.

"Donna had her baby! I mean foal! You have to go see! He's so cute . . . " Edward beamed, bursting with the news.

His grandmother looked aghast. "You didn't watch, did you?"

"Yes, he did," Mary Lou answered quickly. "It was very informative for Edward. I think it taught him more about the biology of a horse than ten books would have."

"I see." The woman gave Mary Lou another sour

look. "I will discuss this matter with his father. I think it most improper for a young man to be exposed to such a thing. Why in my day, no real gentleman would . . . "

Before she could finish, Thorndike entered the house, his shirt tossed over one shoulder, his torso still bare and his trousers stained from sweat and blood. Mary Lou squelched a giggle as Mrs. Doisneau gasped, then averted her eyes at the sight of his nakedness.

"What were you saying, Madam?" Thorndike asked, his voice rich with amusement.

The woman sputtered. "I was just . . . I think I'll go for a walk," she answered, then walked past them all into the hallway, her nose pointed high in the air.

He watched her go, then burst into a chuckle. "I suppose real gentlemen think horses come from cabbage patches," Thorndike said dryly.

Edward grinned, then tugged on his hand. "I saw it all! I saw the foal born! Can I name him?"

His father considered this seriously for a moment, then nodded. "Yes, I think that's appropriate since you witnessed the event. What sort of name would you like?"

"How about Willow, since he is as skinny as our tree, and just as big?"

"Willow it is," Thorndike said, smiling. His eyes met Mary Lou's and once more that odd tension passed between them, an almost electrical charge. Her mind returned to the kiss they had shared, and she could tell by his expression that he was thinking the same thing.

"You were magnificent, sir," she whispered,

unable to suppress her depth of awe. "You saved both horses' lives."

Thorndike shook his head, although she could tell her words pleased him. "It was in God's hands. I only helped. Mrs. Doisneau is right, however. Anything could go wrong at a foaling, and it is no place for a child or a woman." Before Mary Lou could protest, he held up his hand. "But I'm glad you were there."

With that remark, he headed upstairs, shouting for Bridget to bring him hot water. Mary Lou watched him go, a rush of warmth flooding through her. Emily's warnings came back to her, but Mary Lou realized that it was entirely too late. Thorndike had become much more than an element in the case.

It was much later that evening when Mary Lou finally fell asleep. The excitement of the foaling, the emotional highs and lows, the visit from the widow, and her experience with Thorndike all managed to keep her awake long into the night. As she tossed and turned in bed, Mary Lou couldn't help but compare the last few weeks with her life before Graystone. It seemed as if she'd been living in black and white, and suddenly, someone had poured color over her entire existence. Even more telling, she hadn't been at all aware of the lack before.

Yet one day it would be over. She would return home to her laboratory. There would be no more Edward, no more teaching, no more Thorndike . . . a surprising sadness filled her. Sternly she tried to remind herself of her true purpose, but she couldn't help feeling that her life had become much more meaningful here at Graystone than it had ever been in Boston.

Mary Lou fell into a fitful slumber, awakened a short time later by a sound somewhere in the house. Gradually, she could make out footsteps. They were deliberately soft, as if someone was taking great care not to awaken the household. The front door squeaked open, followed by muffled voices. Who could be calling at this hour?

Bravely, she got to her feet and ventured downstairs. The house was quiet, all of the rooms dark except for the library. Following the light to the door, she heard someone whispering. She could easily identify Thorndike's low timbre, but the second voice came to her a moment later. It was the veterinarian's.

Puzzled, Mary Lou's eyes fell on the keyhole. It would be the grossest impropriety to listen; the doctor probably just wanted to confer with Thorndike about the mare. Yet the lateness of the hour and the furtiveness of the meeting aroused her sleuthish instincts. Something was going on, something that Thorndike wanted no one else to know about.

Her conscience battled her curiosity, and regrettably, curiosity won. Mary Lou bent down to the keyhole.

". . . poultice for the leg. It looks much better, but I can't say what the long term effect will be . . . "

Mary Lou propped herself against the door, her ear pressed to the keyhole. What were they talking about? She could hear the vet's voice from the far end of the room, and Thorndike's low rumble in response. Suddenly the door creaked under her weight, and Mary Lou froze. There was a long pause in the voices and for a moment she thought they'd heard her, then Thorndike resumed talking.

"I'd like to check on Donna. That foal was so large it had to have caused her internal damage. She could hemorrhage anytime after the birth. . . . "

Mary Lou barely had time to spring away before the door flew open and Thorndike stood facing her.

"Good evening, Miss Finch. Not another incident of sleepwalking?" His brow raised mockingly, and Mary Lou knew he had guessed she'd been listening.

"No, sir." Somehow she managed to remain calm, even as the veterinarian looked at her quizzically. "I couldn't sleep, so I thought I'd fetch a book."

"I see." Something burned in Thorndike's eyes, and his gaze swept over her. Mary Lou suddenly became aware of the nightclothes she wore. Pulling her robe more closely about her, she tried to conceal her lush figure, but the thin fabric was entirely too revealing. Even the doctor seemed interested, for he stared at her before catching himself and looking quickly away, earning a frown from Thorndike.

"I find it exceedingly puzzling that you seek one of my volumes when you have such a vast collection yourself," Thorndike continued. "I've seen your books, and I would think you have more than enough to occupy you through a restless night."

"Yes, but I've read them all," Mary Lou said, aware that his eyes still lingered on her barely concealed form. "And you have a very nice selection, sir, if I do say so myself."

"Well then, help yourself. Mr. Forester and I are going to the stables to check on Donna. Please remain here, Miss Finch. I'd like to have a word with you when I return."

Mary Lou nodded, though her heart sank. He obviously meant to give her another well-deserved scolding when he came back. After withdrawing a book from the shelves, she flopped down into a chair to await the executioner. Beside her on the table lay an invoice of some sort that had been folded in half. Curious, Mary Lou opened it and saw it was a bill from the veterinarian, for the sum of two hundred dollars. The bill didn't disclose what the money was for, but it had been marked paid.

Frowning, Mary Lou turned the document over, looking for any more clues. What would warrant such a sum? Two hundred dollars was a vast amount of money, and there weren't many equestrian procedures that would cost that much. The vet couldn't have charged for the foal's delivery, since he hadn't been there. Yet none of the other horses appeared to be ill. Carefully, she replaced the document, folding it again so that no one would know she had looked at it.

The door slammed and Mary Lou's heart jumped. Thorndike was back. His footsteps sounded in the hall, then she heard him quietly discussing something with Beecham. Her nerves grew more tense by the moment. What would he do when he confronted her? He could be harsh and implacable when angered, that she knew. She didn't relish the idea of being on the receiving end of his fury again, nor did she want him questioning her motives too closely. He was already as suspicious of her as she was of him, and her explanations were thinner than the chiffon on a lemon pie.

Finally, he appeared. To her dismay, he closed the door behind him and poured himself a brandy. Evidently, this wasn't going to be a quick meeting.

"How is the mare?" Mary Lou asked, hoping to distract him.

Thorndike dashed back his drink, then poured himself another. Somehow Mary Lou sensed it hadn't been the first of the evening. "She's all right now," he said after a moment. "She had started to bleed, so it's well that we checked on her."

"Good Lord!" Mary Lou said, sitting upright. "If you hadn't gone down—"

"She might have died during the night," Pierce nodded in affirmation.

"Then how did you know?"

He shrugged his broad shoulders. "I don't honestly know how to explain it. I could tell something wasn't right, so I asked Dan to come back. It was the look in her eye, something about the way she moved, a stiffness that was unnatural . . . " He looked at Mary Lou and smiled softly.

"I think that's amazing," she said sincerely. "She seemed perfectly fine to me."

"It's something you acquire after years of working with horses. It's almost like a parent with a child, when you start to know by a look that they are unwell, troubled, or lying to you."

The last words dropped with all the subtlety of a blacksmith's hammer. Mary Lou swallowed hard, then got to her feet. "I'm quite tired now, really. I think I'll get some sleep . . . " She tried to walk past him, but he stepped before the door, effectively blocking her escape.

"Sit down, Miss Finch."

Mary Lou obeyed him, frightened by his tone and the look in his eyes. He took the book from her hands and read the title out loud.

"*The Encyclopedia Britannica*. Very entertaining, I would think."

Mary Lou drew in a quick breath. "I thought it might make me sleepy."

"I should think it would induce a coma," Thorndike said dryly. "But then again, there isn't much in the library that can compare with the excitement of listening at keyholes."

She was caught. He wasn't about to fall back on his gentlemanly training and pretend the incident never happened, or give her a polite warning. Cornered, Mary Lou lifted her head in defiance.

"I heard voices and I didn't want to interrupt."

"And knocking wouldn't have been appropriate?"

"I didn't think—"

"Miss Finch," Thorndike cut her off. "I understand that as a woman of science, you are naturally curious. And I know this house and its inhabitants are new to you. With a mind like yours, you are probably imagining all sorts of wild schemes, and investigating them seems the logical thing to do. But I will not allow any intrusion on my privacy, which includes listening at doors. Do I make myself clear?"

His voice was hard. Feeling like a child who'd just been taken to the woodshed by the schoolmaster, she nodded.

"Yes. I didn't think to upset anyone. It won't happen again."

He gazed at her for a moment as if measuring her

words, then tossed back the second drink. "I must admit I am disappointed," he continued softly, examining the glass as if it was of the utmost importance. When Mary Lou looked at him in surprise, he shrugged. "I didn't think I'd still be on your list of suspects. I thought we had a different relationship."

"But there is so much I don't understand!" Mary Lou cried out, unable to stop herself. "There has been a murder here, a prize horse stolen, yet no one seems to care! You are gone so much, and this house is large and frightening . . . I feel that I'm caught in the middle of some spider's web, with all these curious threads around me and none of them makes sense!"

She'd blurted out far more than she intended. Thorndike's face softened and some of the anger seemed to have left him. He put his glass aside and turned her face up to his.

"Would it help if I reassured you that you have nothing to worry about? That whatever appears to be happening will not endanger you or cause you concern?"

"I don't know," Mary Lou said, her eyes meeting his. He smelled good, of brandy and horses, but she had never seen him like this. "I want to believe you, but I don't understand you. What secret are you hiding? Where do you go at night? What do you know about the horse, and why hasn't he been found? And the Widow Norcross . . . who is that woman, and what does she mean to you?"

"You seem extraordinarily interested in my doings," he said softly, amusement flashing in the depths of his blue eyes. "I am beginning to think I should be flattered by your attentions."

Something had subtly changed in the atmosphere between them. Mary Lou recognized the shift, and her body reacted with strong arousal. There was a predatory gleam in his eye, a heated speculation that she found almost hypnotic. Her mouth went dry and it was suddenly difficult to talk.

"Why . . . I don't know what you mean . . . "

"It isn't too hard to surmise. Most of my other governesses took no notice of my presence or absence, for that matter. They certainly weren't following me around, or going out of their way to obtain my attention. And when you spoke of the widow just now, I could swear you almost sounded jealous."

Mary Lou was appalled. "You aren't saying—"

"I only mean to suggest that any man would wonder at the real motive for these late night rendezvous, particularly with a woman as beautiful as yourself, and half-dressed as well. It might make him think that perhaps you wished to discuss more than a missing racehorse, that perhaps you wanted something else entirely. I made a promise to protect you, but a man's restraint can only go so far . . . "

Before she could reply, she was in his arms. Mary Lou gasped as he embraced her, then his mouth took hers in a kiss that curled her bare toes against the carpet. Startled, she parted her lips to protest, but he deftly took advantage of her surprise. His tongue slipped inside, softly touching hers, coaxing a response from the depths of her soul.

Need, white-hot and penetrating, filled every cell

of her body. Mary Lou had little time to think of biology or mating functions, only that her blood was pounding thickly and her skin suddenly seemed overly sensitive. Every brush of his body against hers made her tingle, while his mouth utterly devastated her. Sensing her surrender, he deepened the kiss, turning her in his arms, seducing her until she was left panting and senseless. For a moment she thought she would swoon, so intense were the emotions between them, but he eased his mouth from hers and began feathering kisses along her neck and throat.

"Pierce," she whispered, unaware that she had called him by his first name. "Please."

She didn't know what she begged for, only that it continue. He seemed to understand what she was experiencing, for he touched her ear with his lips, sending a multitude of sensations through her, and whispered thickly.

"You are so sweet."

No man had ever held her like this, or kissed her like this before. And no man had ever called her sweet. She'd been reluctantly praised for her brains, for her studies, experiments and scholarly ideas, but never for herself. Like a woman dying of thirst, she drank in every part of it, from the blush of pleasure that heated her cheeks, to the dangerous ache that throbbed through her body and cumulated shockingly between her legs. . . .

"You are the most sensual woman I have ever known," he said softly. "Do you know what you've done to me . . . what you're doing to me?"

Mary Lou gasped as Pierce's hand slid down the front of her nightgown, a gasp that became a sob as he undid each button with agonizing slowness. Cool air struck her heated body as the gown slipped from her shoulders and puddled around her ankles.

She stood before him, naked. Slowly, she opened her eyes and a flush of embarrassment washed over her. Her body was too full, too round, her curves too opulent. Self-conscious, she tried to cover herself, but he took her hands away and shook his head.

"Don't. Please. I want to see you. My God, you are so beautiful."

His expression took her breath away. He stood back, drinking in the sight of her, his eyes touching every inch of her and setting her skin on fire. When his gaze met hers, she spoke softly.

"You don't have to say that." At his puzzled look, she continued shyly. "About my being beautiful. I know that I'm not. I'm round and plump and not at all fashionable. But it is very nice to hear."

Thorndike gazed at her in disbelief. "Mary Lou, let me assure you that you are indeed, beautiful." His voice was harsh, surprising her with its intensity. "Stunningly beautiful. My God, don't you think I wish it weren't the case? A thousand times I've wished you old and ugly, that maybe I wouldn't be tempted so, but I don't think it would matter. The way you care for my son, the depth of emotion you show to me . . . you could be the witch in any fairy tale and I'd still die to have you."

He stepped closer, and lifted her face to his. "I will be your mirror. Look into my eyes and see that you are indeed beautiful."

Her throat tightened and she found it difficult to breathe. Yet what he said was true. All self-consciousness left her, all of the years of feeling that she was too round, too developed, too soft. Instead, for the first time in her life, Mary Lou Finch was beautiful.

Pierce turned up the lamp, his admiring gaze lingering on her like some kind of exquisite torture. It was the most erotic sensation she could ever imagine, to be thoroughly worshipped by a man's eyes. Everywhere he looked it was as if he had caressed her, and her body tingled in response. She felt like a dew-drenched rose just opening under the warm sun, blossoming into life, filling the air with its presence and scent. Yet he smiled sadly, then reached out to trace the outline of her profile. Mary Lou's heart nearly broke at the anguished pain on his face.

"You have no idea what it is to have you within my reach, so soft, so beautiful, so sensual," he whispered. "But I have no desire to hurt you, or to cause you pain. It is the ultimate irony that as your protector, I cannot protect you from me."

He reached down and gathered up her nightgown, and pulled it up around her shoulders. He didn't button it, only wrapped her in his arms and kissed her hard on the mouth. Mary Lou's arms crept up around his neck and she felt the thunderous throbbing of his body, and knew how desperately he wanted her. She felt him shudder, and his hand slipped into her hair, drinking from her, prolonging the moment as if he couldn't get enough of her. Reluctantly, he released her, took a ragged breath, then picked her up as if she was a doll and carried her to her bed. He was gone a moment later.

Mary Lou lay there trembling, her nightgown still

unbuttoned, her entire being awakened and throbbing with passion. Joy filled her, along with regret, and a sense of loss. She couldn't believe what had just happened, yet she knew it wasn't a dream.

Pierce Thorndike had taken a magic wand and made her beautiful. Somehow Mary Lou knew she'd never be the same.

15

—❧—

"Where's Papa?" Edward cried the following morning as he raced into the dining room. "He was supposed to go riding with me today."

Mary Lou pretended to be absorbed in her eggs and toast, but she desperately wanted to know the same thing.

Bridget placed Edward's breakfast before him. "Your father had to go out of town again. Something came up suddenly. Now eat your eggs and don't be running like that. You'll upset your stomach."

"My gastrointestinal system," Edward said brightly, munching on a piece of toast and standing at the window waving to Max, while the terrier barked outside in greeting.

"Did he say how long he'd be gone this time?"

Mary Lou questioned softly, saving a piece of bacon for the dog.

"No," Bridget shook her head. "He just left his hotel address in New York in case of emergency. 'Tis a queer thing that he had to leave like that. Usually he gets more notice. Now Edward, sit down. I'll not be telling you again."

Mary Lou studied her eggs, wondering if she knew why Thorndike had to leave so quickly. Her face felt hot as she recalled what had passed between them the previous night. Surely he hadn't left on her account? Or worse yet, gone with the widow?

Biting into another piece of toast, she gratefully accepted a cup of coffee from the housekeeper. It didn't escape her notice that Thorndike had deftly evaded her questions the night before. An uneasiness filled her as she realized his seduction could have been meant to throw her off guard. . . .

"Miss Finch, are you coming down with a fever?" Bridget asked anxiously. "You look a bit flushed."

Startled, Mary Lou forced a smile. "No, not at all. I think I just forgot to open my window last night. It was very close."

"Yes, I did the same thing. I'll open them all today, and give your room a good airing. There is nothing like a nice breeze to cool things off, don't you think?"

Recalling the previous evening, Mary Lou smiled. "I entirely agree."

That night, as Mary Lou was getting ready to retire, she remembered her conversation with Bridget when she saw that the windows were open wide, allowing a wave of night air to pour into the room. She would have little trouble sleeping, she thought wryly, for it was the master of the house that gave her restless nights, and not the temperature.

Leaning against the window frame, she enjoyed the scenery. The moon was a silver crescent that dipped behind lacy clouds. Horses in silhouette moved ghost-like across the pasture, and the pond glittered, reflecting the starlight. It was all so peaceful and still . . .

A furtive movement below her window caught her attention, and Mary Lou frowned. Surely it was just her imagination . . . but at that moment, Max began barking violently and she saw a shadow flit across the field toward Whittaker's place. A prowler! Cold fear took hold of her, but she ran down the stairs to give the alarm.

By the time she reached the door, the groom and stableboys had awakened. The groom gave chase across the lawn, Max at his heels, but the intruder had vanished into the thick woods lining the property. Bridget joined her, fearfully wrapping a shawl around her as if girding herself for battle. Within a half hour, the groom returned, announcing that it was a false alarm, no one was about. Bridget and Mary Lou exchanged glances, then Mary Lou returned to her room. Filled with unease, she lay awake for hours, listening for any possible sound and wondering why it seemed a black cloud hung over Graystone Lodge.

My Dear Emily, Mary Lou wrote the next day after supper.

*I do wish you could come down. There was
a prowler on the property last night. Bob
Shoemaker gave chase, but the man disappeared. I have no idea if he intended harm, or
perhaps was plotting another attempt against
the horses. In any case, everyone at Graystone
is anxious today.*

    *Worse, I fear my growing feelings for Mr.
Thorndike are affecting my judgment. He is
the strangest man; honorable, sophisticated,
yet mysterious and evasive. He is an enigma,
the burning core at the center of this crime,
and yet I cannot fathom his motives. More
than that, I find I am thinking of him entirely
too much, and not just as an element in the
case . . .*

Mary Lou studied the neat handwriting before
her, then crumbled the last paragraph and tossed it
into the wastebasket along with a dozen others. She
couldn't possibly admit such foolishness to anyone,
especially her cousin. Emily had the strictest ideas
about detecting, and would surely frown on any hint
of involvement with one of the key suspects in the
case.

Her mind went back to the torrid scene she'd
shared with Pierce just before he left. He had almost
suggested that *she* was trying to seduce *him.* Was he
right? While Mary Lou consoled herself with the
knowledge that he was a suspect, and therefore in
need of a particular amount of attention, could she
also have ulterior motives?

Her toes curled to think of it. Yet she was getting

frustrated with the case. There were clues all around her. If she could just tie them all together, they might somehow make sense, yet the solution eluded her. For the first time in her life she had reason to doubt her own intelligence, which now seemed hopelessly clouded with emotion.

"Miss Finch!" Mary Lou put down the pen as she heard Mrs. Murphy's brogue down the hall. "Miss Finch! There you'll be." The housekeeper burst into her room.

"What is it?" Mary Lou rose quickly. "Is something wrong? Edward . . . ?"

"No, nothing like that. Most unusual business, most unusual." Bridget fluttered a telegram in front of her. "Mr. Thorndike sent a wire. He wants us all to join him at Coney Island for the races. Can you think of that? The entire household!"

"Has he ever done this before?" Mary Lou questioned, taking the telegram from the housekeeper's hands and examining it herself.

"No, never. He will sometimes have Edward join him at Saratoga, but not the other races. He seldom attends those himself unless he's in town for business, but it appears he means to go this time. And he wants us there in twenty-four hours. Would you think it was because of the prowler? I telegraphed him about last night's events."

"Of course," Mary Lou said, firmly squelching the tiny flutter of her heart. Surely Thorndike's unusual gesture didn't have anything to do with her—it would be the height of conceit to think such a thing. He was most likely worried about the safety of his son.

"We'd best get ready to leave then," Mary Lou

said practically. "I don't have much to pack, and I can help Edward. The stableboy can see to Max. I suppose Mrs. Doisneau may need help? Or will she remain here?"

Bridget tried to hide a giggle without much success. "She is very disgruntled with these plans and means to speak to Mr. Thorndike immediately. But she will accompany us to the island, where she has other friends to visit." She frowned, catching sight of Edward's schoolbooks. "Will this trip interfere with the lad's schooling?"

"Not necessarily," Mary Lou said thoughtfully. "We can continue with just a few texts. And the trip may do him good. He misses his father terribly when he's gone."

The housekeeper nodded and disappeared. A moment later, Mary Lou could hear Mrs. Doisneau's voice rising in complaint. Grinning, she quickly finished her packing, tossing a few articles into her trunk. Returning to her pen and paper, she scribbled a few hasty lines.

Thorndike has ordered us all to Coney Island Races. Will write to you from there.
Love, Mary Lou

As she folded the letter, her hopes began rising once more. She was waiting to hear back from her inquiry to the police about Willy's debts. If the gossip she heard was right, the man owed a considerable amount of money to various bookies. That would have made him susceptible to a bribe to hurt or steal Damien.

Moreover, Emily had wanted her to investigate Thorndike's friends. Even though she doubted their involvement, her chances of being able to do so had now grown tenfold. The Belmonts, the Astors, the Mitchells—all of them went to the Coney Island Races, which were held before the Saratoga meeting. And she would be with Thorndike. An unreasonable pleasure filled her at that prospect, one which she quickly attempted to quash.

When she descended with her trunk in the morning, she met Bridget at the bottom of the stairs. "Which train are we taking?" Mary Lou asked.

Mrs. Murphy looked at her strangely. "We won't be taking the train, lass. We'll take a ship down the river."

"A ship?" Mary Lou couldn't keep the dismay from her voice.

"Aye. 'Tis much faster than the train. Why, is something wrong?"

"I . . . get seasick," Mary Lou blurted out in embarrassment.

Bridget waved her hand dismissingly. "Is that all? Don't be worrying about that. I'll bring some bicarbonate of soda and you'll be fine. Besides, this isn't some wee dinghy."

Mary Lou forced a smile, but she followed the housekeeper to the carriage in dread. She had been on a boat once, during a fishing excursion with her father, and she'd been violently ill almost as soon as they'd left shore. Maybe it had just been that one incident. Maybe the sea had been rough. Maybe . . .

A few hours later, Mary Lou knew that her foreboding had been based in certainty. While it was true that the *Narraganset* was a magnificent ship and beautifully made, she could appreciate very little of it with her head permanently planted in a bucket. Every pitch, every ripple of the water, set her stomach into a new wave of convulsions. When she wasn't vomiting, she was nauseous, which was almost as bad. Bridget clucked over her, the crew brought her cold cloths and fresh buckets, and even Edward was solicitous, but nothing helped. Mary Lou was never so grateful in her life to set her feet on firm ground.

When they reached the resort area, Bridget had to help her stagger off the boat. Even Mrs. Doisneau gave her a sympathetic glance. When they arrived at the Manhattan Beach Hotel, Mary Lou couldn't appreciate the charming place with its shaded verandahs, lavish restaurants, ballroom, or shops. When she reached her room, all she could do was fall into bed, and even then the ceiling and floor seemed to rise and fall with the waves.

Passing on supper, she slept through the night, and by morning felt entirely refreshed. Her stomach rumbled, this time with a healthy hunger, and she ventured downstairs to the huge dining room to look for Edward.

"There you are, Miss Finch."

Mary Lou groaned when she saw Thorndike waiting for her in the lobby with Edward and Mrs. Doisneau.

"I understand you had a rough voyage," Thorndike continued sympathetically.

"She threw up buckets and buckets!" Edward

exclaimed enthusiastically. "They kept bringing her new ones, and she just kept filling them up—her entire gastrointestinal system threw up!"

"Edward." Mary Lou struggled to maintain some kind of dignity. She felt awkward enough seeing Thorndike after what had transpired between them, without further humiliation. "I don't think your father needs any more description than that. I appreciate your concern, and am fine this morning."

She saw the twinkle in Thorndike's eye and wanted to swat the man. She was only grateful that it was his son and not he who witnessed her humiliation.

Edward's grandmother sighed. "I don't suppose you've had much experience with ships. Sea legs are acquired over time, I suppose."

"Actually, they aren't," Thorndike said. "Some men never acquire them. The mere sight of a ship, even from shore, is enough to make them queasy. I can see we're having the same effect on you, Miss Finch. Perhaps we should continue this conversation after breakfast."

Mary Lou started to leave for the servant's dining room when Thorndike stopped her. "Is our company unacceptable, Miss Finch? I promise I won't make any sailor jokes."

Mary Lou held her head as high as she could manage. "I don't think it's proper for me to join you in the public dining room," she said softly. "I will find Bridget."

Mrs. Doisneau nodded in agreement, but Thorndike refused to release her. "I thought we'd discussed all this before. You are to dine with us."

When she started to protest, he held up his hand. "Besides, I may need you to look after Edward."

There was something in his tone that brooked no disagreement. Mary Lou nodded, ignoring the older woman's indignant glance, and followed him into the dining room.

The room was magnificent, the tables covered with snowy linens, the china first quality. Fresh rosebuds peeked out of crystal vases, and the silverware gleamed. The tangy smell of the ocean filled the room, although after her voyage, Mary Lou swore she'd never feel romantic about the sea again. Even as Thorndike ordered an immense quantity of food, she wasn't at all certain she wanted to test her stomach, but at the first bite of buttered scone, she was immediately starving. Devouring the eggs, bacon, stewed tomatoes and catfish, she ignored his smirk and sighed, sipping a second cup of delicious coffee.

"I'm glad to see your appetite's back," Pierce said, observing her with amusement. "One would think you hadn't eaten in a week."

"In my day, young ladies never displayed their appetite," Mrs. Doisneau said. "It was considered unseemly."

"I disagree," Thorndike said. "I like to see a woman enjoy her food. Too many of those ladies faint halfway through a ball due to tight lacings and lack of sustenance. Ridiculous, I've always thought. By the way, Miss Finch, I had a note from the Vanderbilts. We should see them at dinner tonight, after the races."

Mary Lou glanced at him questioningly. Surely he didn't intend to present her in public . . . Mrs.

Doisneau must have had the same thought, for she gave Pierce a frown. "I am surprised that you thought to bring your servants on holiday. I would think you'd prefer to give them a rest when you retreat."

"That is my intention," Pierce said. "Mrs. Murphy has my leave to enjoy the sun and the sea. I made the same offer to Beecham, but he prefers to remain home. Frankly, after the murder, and the prowler on the property, I am only too grateful that he does."

There was a long pause following his words. Mary Lou was aware that Pierce seldom mentioned the missing horse or the trainer's killing. Even Mrs. Doisneau seemed taken aback, for she nodded slowly in agreement.

"Who's racing tomorrow?" Edward asked, breaking the silence.

"We're running Pippin in the fifth. Vanderbilt's racing King Lear, and the Martins have their new filly. Brady is running Golden Heels in the ninth."

"That's the horse that's always winning," Edward explained to Mary Lou between mouthfuls of fish. "Papa said Damien could have beaten him easily."

A hush followed Edward's words, and Thorndike lightly fingered his fork. "Yes, he could beat him. He's about the only horse this year with a chance."

"Hopefully, he will turn up in time for the Saratoga Race," Mary Lou said softly, watching Thorndike intently. She was aware that he spoke of the horse in present tense. Sensing her observation, he gave her an amused glance, then picked up his coffee cup.

"Yes, that would be wonderful. Now would you

like to go to the races, or would you prefer the beach?"

He directed his question to Edward, but his eyes remained on Mary Lou.

Edward clapped his hands in delight. "The beach this morning, and the races later!"

"Spoken like a true politician," Thorndike grinned, then turned to Mary Lou. "Is that acceptable? Or will it interfere with Edward's studies?"

"I think Edward is entitled to a little vacation, too," Mary Lou smiled fondly at the boy. "Besides, the study of the ocean and sea life is fascinating in itself. I'm sure we can manage a little bit of work and have fun, too."

"Mrs. Doisneau?" Thorndike looked at her questioningly.

"I have plans to visit with friends," she said. "I have no desire to watch a bunch of sweaty horses running down a track in the hot sun. Ridiculous sport."

"Yes, it is." Thorndike's eyes met Mary Lou's, and she had to stifle a giggle. "I have to meet with some business associates, but perhaps I can join you for lunch. Would you like one of Feltman's Coney Island hot dogs?"

Edward nodded enthusiastically, while his grandmother shuddered. "Wasn't it rumored that those dreadful sausages were made of dog meat?"

"I believe it was. Care to join us?"

The twinkle was back in his eye, and this time, Mary Lou couldn't resist laughing as Mrs. Doisneau shook her head in horror.

*   *   *

The ocean was beautiful, glittering beneath the morning sun and rushing to the shore like a thousand racehorses. A soft mist rose from the sea into the air, scenting the breeze with a salty tang and softening the sun's rays into a comfortable warmth. Women clad in scandalous bathing costumes consisting of Turkish-style pants and loose-fitting blouses tiptoed down to the water, then ran shrieking back to the sand. Men watched appreciatively, flexing their muscles for the benefit of the ladies.

Edward enjoyed himself thoroughly, alternating between wading in the cold surf, building sand castles, and collecting samples of shells and sea creatures for his schoolwork. Very quickly he was able to identify clams, oysters, scallop shells, and even some of the shore birds. Piling the shells and seaweed beside Mary Lou's chair, he proceeded to catalogue everything diligently in his workbook.

Mary Lou smiled, then went back to her casebook. She'd had an interesting communication from Emily that morning. The police had questioned Bill Cooke, and the man claimed to have an alibi the night Damien had been stolen. But the servant's story had fallen through. Worse, one of the villagers heard him speaking threateningly about Thorndike in the tavern after his dismissal.

Frowning, she reviewed her notes, wondering if she wasn't completely off-track herself. If the servant was the culprit, then where was Damien? Had he killed the magnificent horse out of spite, or to revenge himself against Thorndike? That seemed extreme, but Mary Lou reminded herself of the apple.

Whoever had put it in Damien's stall certainly meant to harm him.

But she remained deeply dissatisfied with the notion of Bill Cooke as the criminal. Was everything else then just a coincidence? She supposed that could be the case, but it seemed highly improbable and far too simplistic. But perhaps that's because I want it to be, Mary Lou realized. The thought startled her, but she was forced to admit the truth of her feelings. She didn't want Bill Cooke to be the culprit because she wanted to find the man herself. And she didn't want to leave Graystone.

Slamming the book shut, she squeezed her eyes closed. She had to stop all this daydreaming about Pierce Thorndike. She was, after all, simply his son's governess. No sooner had she steeled her internal resolve than a familiar voice broke into her thoughts.

"I daresay, whatever you're reading can't be that bad."

Glancing up, she shaded her eyes against the sun and saw Pierce's friend Peter Whitesell grinning at her. Forcing a smile, Mary Lou got to her feet, and after brushing away the sand, extended her hand.

"Mr. Whitesell, I recall meeting you at Graystone. How nice to see you again."

"The pleasure is absolutely mine," he said cordially, then bent to kiss her hand. "I saw Edward and thought you'd be nearby."

"Did you see my shells?" Edward reached into a bucket and withdrew a sample from his collection. "Crustaceans. There's a crab inside this one."

"How nice," Peter said politely, but withdrew a step in repugnance.

Mary Lou laughed at his squeamish expression. "Are your children here with you?"

"No, they're at the hotel. I didn't bring their governess, who isn't nearly as attractive as you," Peter said wistfully. "If she was, I, like Pierce, would be tempted to include her as well. Where is our Draconian friend, anyway?"

"Behind you."

Mary Lou held back another chuckle as Thorndike approached. Peter looked guilty as hell, then shrugged ruefully as he realized Thorndike had overheard him. Pierce put a hand on his friend's shoulder and spoke with feigned seriousness.

"I thought I told you not to go stealing my governess."

"You can't blame me for trying," Peter said cavalierly. "After all, she is bright, beautiful. Your son adores her—"

"I think we're all aware of Miss Finch's stellar qualities," Thorndike said wryly, giving Mary Lou a warm look. "Would you like to join us for lunch? We're having hot dogs."

"Good God, no," Peter shuddered. "But I hope to see you tonight. The Mitchells are hosting a party. You will come?"

His question was intended for Thorndike, but his eyes met Mary Lou's. Thorndike stepped deftly between them.

"We'll see. I have a meeting with my lawyer, then some business to conduct. Perhaps we can catch up for a drink."

"I'll make it a point." Bowing once again to Mary Lou, Peter walked away, appearing quite pleased with himself. Thorndike muttered a curse while Mary Lou finally expelled her laughter.

"I'll have to keep an eye on him," Thorndike said dryly. "He seems determined to coerce you into his employ."

"Perhaps I should seek him out," Mary Lou said, wanting to tease him. "After all, he may pay more."

Thorndike gave her a look betraying his lack of appreciation. "Miss Finch, if I didn't know better, I'd think you were trying to make me jealous."

Mary Lou grinned, delighted at his admission. She was about to annoy him further when she saw that Edward was paying close attention to everything she said, and appeared more than a little upset. Taking his hand, she indicated the boardwalk. "I believe you said something about lunch. Shall we?"

16

—🍃—

Feltman's was a pretty clapboard structure that rose up on Surf Avenue like a beacon. Delicious smells of hot dogs, clams, and beer permeated the air, while the open porch was filled with hungry customers. Patrons also crowded into the shaded beer garden out back, where a carousel whirled to the bawdy tunes of a calliope.

Edward immediately wanted to go for a ride on the carousel, so Pierce gave him some change and watched him run off. Mary Lou waited until he was seated on a noble white charger before taking a chair at a nearby table.

The waiter took their order, and Mary Lou surveyed the crowd. A group of men gathered at a special table beneath a maple tree, ordering noisily and enjoying pitchers of beer. One or two of them looked familiar, and Thorndike answered her thoughts.

"Those are the jockeys and trainers," he explained, waving to one of the men who immediately grinned and waved back. "That's one of our jockeys, Toby Nelson. And there is our new trainer, Mickey Conway. You might have seen him at Graystone."

Mary Lou nodded. "I may have. And isn't that the blacksmith from Graystone?" Her eyes narrowed as she recognized Old Willy. He appeared to see her at the same time, and his eyes narrowed, giving her an ugly glare.

"Yes, he probably came with the grooms. With so many horses in town, there is liable to be plenty of work. The black man is Curtis Jones. He was a runaway slave who has a hell of a reputation as a trainer. He works with Belmont's horses."

"Grand Master," Mary Lou said thoughtfully. At Thorndike's sharp look, she explained, "I heard some of the servants discussing his horses."

"That is one of the horses scheduled to run in the Saratoga race. He is a favorite, along with Golden Heels. You'll probably meet several of the owners tonight at the party. Most of the Coney Island Jockey Club will be there, including Travers, Lawrence, Vanderbilt, and Belmont."

Mary Lou's mouth went dry even as the waiter brought a tray of hot dogs and lemonade. "You want me to go to the party?"

"Of course." Thorndike looked at her as if the question never entered his mind.

"But . . . It sounds like a fancy affair . . . I don't think it would be appropriate for your governess to attend."

Her words hung in the air for a long moment, then Thorndike's eyes met hers. "Are you uncomfortable being with me?"

"No, that's not it, but—"

"Then is it because of what happened between us in the library?"

Mary Lou's mouth dropped, and she had to forcibly close it. Somehow she didn't think Thorndike was going to mention that night. Her cheeks burned as she recalled him taking her gown from her, and worshiping her naked body with his eyes. She stared at him and he smiled softly.

"I would like to say that I am sorry, but that wouldn't be entirely honest on my part. I could blame it on the brandy, but that wouldn't justify my actions. Nothing I could say would really make a difference; I behaved inexcusably. What I promise is that I won't force my attentions upon you in that manner ever again. Will you forgive me?"

Mary Lou felt the color rise in her cheeks. That night was one of the most beautiful in her life, and he was once again sorry. She adopted a cool tone. "There is nothing to forgive. I know that you weren't . . . entirely yourself."

"That doesn't excuse—"

"Please," Mary Lou said softly. She didn't think she could stand having him apologize again. "Let's not mention it anymore."

Thorndike nodded. "I understand. So if you think

we can get past that night, I would like you to accompany me."

"I don't think that's a good idea," Mary Lou said softly. When Thorndike continued to stare at her, she continued. "I . . . don't have anything to wear."

"We can remedy that." Thorndike glanced down at her skirt stained with beach sand and chemicals. "There are quite a few good shops here. I would be happy to advance you the money."

"No!" Mary Lou said, truly appalled. "A nice outfit would cost far too much. I simply couldn't accept that from you."

Thorndike rubbed the back of his neck in a way Mary Lou recognized betrayed his irritation. "Miss Finch, we must seek a remedy here. I have many plans for this summer, and they all involve you and my son. There will be many parties like this one. Also picnics, balls, and other social activities. We have been invited to dine with the Mitchells tomorrow, and to watch the races with the Whitesells. I understand your wardrobe as a governess may not be complete, so you must allow me to compensate for that. Consider it an order."

Mary Lou's mouth dropped, but before she could argue any further, she saw Pierce divvying out the hot dogs as if the conversation had ended. His attention was no longer on her, and instead he gazed thoughtfully at the carousel. Mary Lou followed his glance, and realized at the same moment he did that the music had stopped. All of the other children had left the ride and had joined their parents for lunch. The carousel was empty.

"Edward!" Thorndike rose, calling for his son. "Edward, where are you?"

A chill went up Mary Lou's spine as she gazed at the empty white horse. Surely Edward would appear at any moment, laughing at the joke. Instead, the minutes ticked by as if they were hours, and neither she nor Thorndike could see a hair of the child.

"I'm going to search the grounds," Pierce said, his voice thick with anxiety. "He must have run off to play. Wait here."

"No, I'll go for the police." At Thorndike's startled glance, Mary Lou indicated a patrolman circling the grounds. "He may have seen him."

Pierce nodded, appearing grateful for the help. They split up, Mary Lou heading for the street, while Thorndike bellowed out Edward's name. Glancing toward the jockey's table, she saw Willy following her with his eyes, but Edward was nowhere in the vicinity. Mary Lou turned away, still feeling the hostile glare behind her.

Other people began to realize that a child had disappeared and quickly joined in the search. Charles Feltman himself came out of the restaurant and began to assist in the effort to find the boy.

The policeman admitted he hadn't seen anything, but at Mary Lou's insistence, rounded up a few other patrolmen and began to scour the adjoining restaurants. Mary Lou returned to Pierce, and indicated the path to the ocean.

"I'm going to search the beach once more. Perhaps Edward went back for a shell, or to play in the water."

Thorndike nodded, but she could tell he barely

heard her. Her heart pounding, she ran toward the shore. A thousand ugly scenarios played out in her mind, and she forced them away, refusing to give in to panic. Yet the thought of Jimmy Dwyer's death and the missing stallion refused to leave her. Was it possible that Thorndike's enemy would stoop so low as to kidnap his child?

That thought made her stomach turn, and she ran faster, tripping over the dunes. It seemed that there were a hundred children on the sand, and dozens of them looked just like Edward. Peering under the umbrellas at one freckled face after another, she ignored the disapproving looks of their nannies and the curious grins of the children. Nothing mattered except that they find Edward. When she met with no success, she returned to the beer garden.

"Did you find him?" One look on Thorndike's face gave her the answer. Tears started in her eyes as she realized the truth. Edward was gone.

"Oh, Mr. Thorndike, I am so sorry! I should have been watching him . . . "

"It isn't your fault," Thorndike said abruptly, then gentled his tone. "I am equally guilty. He is my son, after all. But where in the hell could he have gone? I refuse to believe someone took him—"

He stopped short, as if unable to continue that thought. Mary Lou recalled her own idea, that Thorndike's enemies could be responsible for Edward's disappearance. It seemed the same notion had occurred to him, as unthinkable as it was.

"I'm going to the police station," Thorndike said. "There are Pinkertons all over the place due to the races. I'll hire a few of them immediately."

"No!" Mary Lou said as his meaning penetrated. "I refuse to believe that he's been kidnapped. Let me return to the hotel and talk to Bridget. Perhaps she's heard something."

Thorndike nodded, but not a single ray of hope penetrated his eyes. Distraught, Mary Lou made her way back to the hotel, allowing blind tears to fall. It was all her fault, if she hadn't been so busy arguing with Thorndike . . . the guilt made her physically ill.

Bridget was nowhere to be seen, and Mary Lou remembered that she'd intended to spend some time with friends. Dispiritedly, Mary Lou was about to return to the seaside to search again when her gaze fell on the row of doors down the hall.

Once when she was a little girl and frightened, she'd walked home from school and climbed into bed. She had awakened hours later, much to the consternation and panic of her father. It was odd how the memory surfaced at this exact moment, and Mary Lou couldn't help but wonder if Edward had done the same thing.

Fetching a second room-key from the desk, Mary Lou ran upstairs and turned the lock. There, bundled beneath the thin white blankets and sheets was Edward, fast asleep.

The relief that swept over her caused her legs to buckle and she nearly fell. Mary Lou eased herself into a chair to catch her breath, blinking to make sure she wasn't dreaming. Edward snored, then rolled over. His hand opened and a seashell tumbled to the floor. The sound didn't wake him and he continued to sleep, blissfully dreaming while his father and the police frantically searched the island.

One of the maids went by the door carrying an armload of sheets. Mary Lou stopped the woman and asked her to bring up the manager, refusing to leave Edward's side. It was almost a superstitious fear, that some unknown danger was still stalking him, and only her presence could prevent him from disappearing again. The manager arrived shortly, appearing disgruntled at having been interrupted in his work, but when Mary Lou explained the situation, he immediately sent a boy to the police station to fetch Thorndike.

Edward awoke a short time later, rubbing his eyes and yawning. When he saw Mary Lou, he appeared startled, then a guilty look came over his face.

"Edward," Mary Lou said softly. "What were you thinking of, coming back here? You were supposed to join us for lunch after the carousel ride."

She fought to keep the emotion from her voice, the outrage and fear and anger, but was only partially successful. Edward shrugged, looking sheepish.

"I . . . you were talking, and I . . . "

At that moment, Thorndike burst into the room. His gaze settled on his son, looking small and helpless in the bed. Crossing the floor quickly, he wrapped his arms around Edward, and gave him a fierce bear hug.

"Edward, is it really you? My God, you scared the life out of me. Where were you, what happened?"

The little boy put his arms around his father and started to cry. Tears wracked his slender body and Mary Lou felt a touch of compassion for him.

"I just thought I'd come back here."

"Why? Without telling anyone?" Thorndike held him a few inches away and gazed into his face. Anger replaced fear and he shook the lad. "Was this another one of your pranks? Do you realize what you put me through? Miss Finch? Even the police are still looking for you!"

Edward sobbed harder, and Mary Lou rose, putting her hand on his back in a comforting manner. "Edward, tell us why you did this. This is much more serious than snakes or worms. You could have gotten lost or hurt. You could have even been kidnapped. Your father and I were scared to death that something terrible had happened."

Edward glanced up, his face red and tear-streaked. "You wouldn't care if something happened to me!" He thrust his finger at Mary Lou.

She stared at him in bewilderment. "I certainly would. Why would you say such a thing?"

"I heard you talking to Mr. Whitesell. You might go to work for him and leave me. I heard what you said. I heard everything."

Mary Lou's eyes met Thorndike's, and suddenly it all made sense. Reaching for his hand, she forced him to look at her and she spoke very seriously.

"Edward, I told you before that I'm not going anywhere. You don't have to do this, not to me or your father. There is nothing bad enough you can do that would scare me off, nothing that will stop me from being your teacher and your friend."

He looked at her, blinking away tears, as if wanting to believe her but unable to. Taking a deep breath, Mary Lou continued.

"Edward, I lost my mother, too. I know how you feel. You think if she could disappear, anyone else can too. She didn't die because you were bad. Do you understand me?"

Something changed in Edward's face, and he broke down, sobbing hysterically. Pierce held him tightly, then looked at Mary Lou in wonder. Forcing a smile, she once more reached out to the boy and caressed him. To her surprise, Edward turned from his father and came into her arms, holding her as tightly as he had Thorndike.

"Promise you won't go away. Promise."

"I promise," Mary Lou said, her own eyes becoming moist. Looking into Edward's face, she spoke softly. "There will come a time when you won't need me as a teacher anymore, but I will always be your friend. You have my word on that."

The boy looked at her for a long moment, then nodded. Mary Lou gave him a smile, which he reluctantly returned. Thorndike patted his head, but spoke solemnly.

"Edward, I understand what you may have thought, but I will have to punish you for what you did today. I was going to let you come to the party tonight, but I'm afraid you'll have supper and an early bedtime instead. Do you understand?"

"Yes." Edward nodded. Instead of being defiant, he almost seemed relieved. "You don't have to worry anymore. I'll be good."

"I believe you." Thorndike and his son solemnly shook hands.

Father and son communicated without words, and it seemed that Edward grew a full inch before their eyes. Unbearably touched and feeling awkward at being present at what should have been a private moment, Mary Lou stood up decisively and gave Edward a frank look. "I don't know about you, but drama always makes me hungry. I think they serve a late lunch downstairs, if anyone is interested."

Edward leaped up eagerly and raced for the steps, everything forgotten with the promise of food. As Mary Lou started to leave, Thorndike stopped her, taking her hand. Their eyes met and she saw a soft sheen of moisture in his.

"Thank you," he said, his voice breaking. "For my son."

Mary Lou nodded, a dangerous welling of emotion inside her that she refused to name. Why, oh, why hadn't Emily been the one to take this case? Mary Lou could be home right now with an apple tart and a bubbling test tube, far from the devastating master of Graystone and the mystery that enshrouded them all. But even as she formed the thought, she realized it was far less appealing than it had once been.

"You look marvelous, Miss."

Bridget stood back in admiration as Mary Lou turned around, displaying her gown. She had purchased it secondhand a few years ago, when it became apparent she had to have one nice costume for parties and balls. Those invitations seldom arrived, however, so the dress, a soft blue satin with a pink sash, had remained in relatively good condition. Bridget had artfully masked the few worn spots with lace, and from a distance, she looked very presentable indeed.

"Thank you." Mary Lou beamed. A polite knock on the door announced Thorndike's arrival. Bridget flung open the portal, then waved her hand at Mary Lou as if she was personally responsible for her success.

"Doesn't she look grand, sir?"

Mary Lou blushed, but the look on Thorndike's face made it all worth it. Bridget had also helped her style her hair, weaving a few flowers into the curls. Thankfully, her hair had grown enough since the Bunsen burner incident that it no longer looked even remotely boyish, but actually flattered her face and drew attention to her eyes. Thorndike was speechless for a long moment, then his gaze met hers with stark approval.

"You look absolutely beautiful," he said sincerely. Then his eyes narrowed as he studied her dress. "I don't remember that gown, but it doesn't look quite new. You did do as I ordered, and had a wardrobe made up?"

"I did not," Mary Lou said firmly. "This is one of my own. I am not entirely without means, sir."

Something danced in Thorndike's eyes, and deciding not to argue with her, he extended his arm. "You, Miss Finch, have got to be the most stubborn woman I've ever known. Fortunately, you are stunning as well. Shall we go?"

Mary Lou laughed, then accepted his arm. She felt exactly like a princess, walking down the hall with her prince, going to the ball. For a woman with very little social experience, it was a heady feeling, and she enjoyed every moment.

When they reached the bottom of the stairs, Edward's grandmother stood waiting. Mrs. Doisneau startled upon seeing Mary Lou, then her eyes glittered coldly.

"I wasn't aware servants attended this event. And I am rather surprised that you've left Edward alone after what happened today." She turned to Thorndike. "Surely it would be better for the girl to remain behind?"

Mary Lou's hand tightened on Thorndike's arm, but he caressed it softly and spoke with cool authority.

"My son is with Bridget, Madam, and is already asleep. Miss Finch is here at my invitation. Do not concern yourself in my business, Mrs. Doisneau. I assure you, when I wish for your advice, I will ask for it."

The woman looked as if she'd been slapped, but she raised her head in a modicum of dignity. "I suppose my concerns for my grandson are of little matter, now that my daughter is no longer with us. Please excuse me if I seemed to overstep my bounds."

With that, she took herself off to the party, dabbing suspiciously at her eyes. Mary Lou sighed. "Thank you for defending me, but she is right. I really should stay behind with Edward. . . . "

"Edward is well taken care of, as you know," Thorndike said, his voice brooking no disagreement. "I think it troubles Mrs. Doisneau to see me in the company of another woman after her daughter's passing. I understand her feelings, but it would be the height of folly to indulge them. Clarissa is gone, and no amount of wishful thinking on her part will change that."

Mary Lou nodded, an uneasiness sweeping through her. She noticed he didn't say "on his part," and once more she wondered about their relationship. She didn't have time to give it much thought, however, for they walked into the ballroom, which nearly took her breath away.

A glittering chandelier sparkled from the ceiling, lending a festive air to the scene below. Women dressed in beautiful ball gowns glided effortlessly across the dance floor, while gallant men in dark formal-wear escorted them. A huge table was set up in the corner, groaning under the weight of shelled clams, shrimp, oysters, and crab legs, while waiters expertly picked their way through the guests with trays of golden champagne. An ice sculpture of a swan perspired on another table, where jellies and punch awaited those heated from dancing. The awnings were furled and the windows flung open, revealing the sea bathed in twilight.

It was magnificent, as was the company. Thorndike led her into the room, reeling off the names like a glamorous society directory. Bet-a-Million Gates. Diamond Jim Brady. William Vanderbilt. August Belmont, Jr. Jesse Lewisohns. Abe Hummel. They were a spectacular group, all horseracers who handed out hundred-dollar tips, made private wagers worth more than a working-man's yearly salary, and indulged lavishly in a lifestyle provided mainly by the previous generation. Once again, Mary Lou was struck by the unlikelihood that any of these men had stolen Damien. They had more money than they could spend in a lifetime.

Thorndike moved easily among the crowd, and Mary Lou was once more aware of his striking good looks. The dark suit he wore, coupled with a crisp white shirt and black tie, only enhanced his brooding appearance and made his eyes seem the color of the sea. Mary Lou could see the female company send him furtive glances before their regard would return to her with curious speculation.

"Would you like to dance?" Thorndike asked.

"Why yes, I would," Mary Lou said, surprised. "But I have to admit, I haven't had much practice."

"Neither have I," Thorndike said, but he belied his words a moment later when he swept her onto the floor and waltzed magnificently. Mary Lou found it ridiculously easy to follow him, and more pleasurable than she had ever dreamed. When the dance ended, he gazed regretfully into her eyes and spoke softly.

"I'm sorry, but I see someone I have to speak to. Please wait for me. You don't mind?"

"Not at all," Mary Lou spoke truthfully. Dancing with Pierce was heady indeed, and she needed a moment to regain her composure. Watching him walk away from her, she sighed. A prince from a fairy tale. It didn't seem so far-fetched after all.

17

But he wasn't hers.

Her fantasy faded as she saw Thorndike walk past the ice sculpture to the Widow Norcross. A pang of jealousy swept through her, and she wondered if he'd known all along that she would be here. Of course the widow would have come for the race, Mary Lou reminded herself. Still, she couldn't help but speculate that Thorndike had planned to meet her.

The thought made her drop her glass. Blushing furiously, Mary Lou tried to clean up the spilled champagne with her handkerchief, but a waiter rushed forward and insisted upon taking care of the mess himself. Voices echoed around her, and she could hear some of the women speaking in hushed tones.

"Governess, I think. He does have a son."

"Odd little creature, isn't she?"

"Kind of him to include her."

Glancing up, she saw a group of wealthy-looking women peering over their fans in her direction. One of them had on a dress that appeared to be trimmed in real gold, another wore a diamond pendant that was as large as a walnut around her neck, while the third had a tiara nestled in her dark curls. Heat stung her cheeks, and Mary Lou realized she was the subject of their conversation.

This was his class of people, not hers. These were the kind of women he could court, and perhaps someday wed, not a penniless teacher like herself who no longer even had a dowry.

"Hello, Miss Finch." Peter Whitesell approached, appearing dashingly handsome in a midnight-blue jacket. "You looked lonely standing there by yourself. Would you care to dance?"

"Yes, I'd love to," Mary Lou said fervently. Anything to get away from those women and her own heartbreaking thoughts. Peter set his glass aside and led her onto the floor. Feeling a dozen eyes on her, Mary Lou followed Peter's lead and whirled to the sound of the music, pretending none of it mattered at all.

"Are you having fun?" Peter asked.

"No," she said honestly.

He laughed, the sound charming in the wake of the ladies' whispered barbs. "It will get better. I understand they have Henry Pain doing fireworks tonight. It is supposed to be spectacular. They say he demonstrates celebrated war scenes with Roman candles and fire rockets."

"That sounds wonderful," Mary Lou sighed.

"It should be. I just hope it doesn't spook the horses overmuch."

"Do you mean for the race tomorrow?"

Peter nodded. "It doesn't take much to throw a horse off. A case of the jitters. A loose stirrup. A jockey out of sorts. Almost everyone has his horses stabled here, close to the hotel. The noise is sure to upset the thoroughbreds."

Mary Lou's pulse quickened at the mention of the stables, and she recalled the blacksmith glaring at her at Feltman's. While it seemed unlikely that he or anyone else would dare bring Damien here, it was worth taking a look around. Perhaps someone would know something, or she could pick up some kind of lead. The case had grown very cold at this point and any information would be welcome.

She became aware that Peter was looking at her strangely, so she smiled politely and continued the conversation. "Are you racing tomorrow?"

Peter nodded. "Blue Danube. I don't expect much from him, but I'm holding Rajah back for Saratoga. I don't want to tire him."

"Is he your favorite?"

"At present. He's good, but not nearly as good as Damien. Has Pierce heard anything about him yet?"

"No." The music stopped, and Mary Lou allowed Peter to lead her off the floor. "We're all hoping the police find him before Saratoga. He means a lot to Mr. Thorndike."

"Yes, I know. Pierce always manages to focus on the wrong things. It nearly drove Clarissa to distraction."

"What an odd thing to say," Mary Lou commented.

Peter gave her a startled glance, then smiled in a self-deprecating manner. "I apologize. It just concerns me that Pierce seems to have acquired a powerful enemy. As his friend, I can't help but worry."

"I know." Mary Lou put her hand on his shoulder. "You are a good friend to him. I'm sure he appreciates that."

Peter gazed at her hand for a long moment, then took it in his own with a sigh. "Would you care for another dance? I think our mutual friend is occupied for the time."

Mary Lou glanced over his shoulder and froze. Thorndike was waltzing with the widow. "I think I'll go for a walk instead," she said, withdrawing from Peter's arms. "The cool air will do me good."

A strange smile curved Peter's mouth and he glanced once more in Thorndike's direction. "You are an intelligent woman," he said softly. "And very beautiful. I wonder if Pierce truly appreciates you."

"I'm sure he doesn't," Mary Lou said bitterly. "After all, most men of means don't appreciate their help, do they?"

With that, she walked swiftly off the floor, hoping that no one would notice her leave. It was time she stopped all this foolish daydreaming and remembered her place. She was, after all, simply a servant.

*   *   *

Thorndike watched Mary Lou in Peter's arms, then saw her dash quickly out of the ballroom. He danced the widow to the edge of the floor and gave her an apologetic shrug.

"I must go. My attorney will escort you. I'm afraid I've neglected Miss Finch for far too long."

"So I see." The widow smiled indulgently as Mary Lou disappeared through the verandah. "I daresay she'll be fine. Poor thing, she probably isn't used to affairs like this, with all this wealth and so many glamorous people. But we do need to talk, Pierce. I have concerns I need to share with you."

"Meet me at the stables in half an hour," Pierce said impatiently. "I want to check on my horses."

"How very romantic," the widow replied.

Pierce left her side, feeling a rush of irritation at her words. Surely Mary Lou didn't leave because she felt out of place . . . yet as he glanced at the assortment of jewelry, costly Worth gowns, and sumptuous food, he understood that it could all appear overwhelming to someone like his lovely scientist.

He berated himself for having neglected her for so long, yet it couldn't be helped. Vivian could be a demanding woman at times, and tonight was apparently one of them.

A movement near the stables caught his attention, and Thorndike saw a flash of powder-blue disappear around the back. Mary Lou. He changed his direction, frowning as he realized that once more he'd caught her sleuthing, after his express orders to the contrary. Outrage rose within him as he recalled his previous warnings to her. Evidently, she had failed to take him seriously. It was time he changed that.

Snatching up a lantern, he rounded the corner of the building and saw her crouched at the doorway. One eye was shut, while the other peered into the lock with steady concentration. Her nose wrinkled charmingly, and her mouth was screwed up, betraying her intense concentration. A wire stuck out of the keyhole, and she jiggled it carefully.

"Perhaps these would help." Thorndike dangled the keys to the stable in front of her face.

He experienced a moment of intense satisfaction when she leaped to her feet and stammered in reaction. "I . . . I . . . "

"Lost an ear bob?" Thorndike said sarcastically. "Miss Finch, for a woman who seldom rides, you seem inordinately interested in horses. Obsessed, one might even say."

Mary Lou crossed her arms and tapped her foot impatiently, eyeing the keys. Finally she threw up her hands in resignation.

"All right, you've caught me. Would you mind opening the door before someone else comes out? This sort of thing is best done unobserved."

"Yes, I imagine it is," Pierce said, obliging her and unlocking the door. Before she could step inside, he held out his arm and stopped her. "You and I will discuss this later."

Mary Lou sighed, well aware of the consequences of her actions. Thorndike opened the door, and she entered, gazing about in the darkness at the dozens of stalls. Retrieving the lantern, Thorndike joined her and placed the light on the floor. Ignoring Mary Lou's curious glance, he approached one of the stalls, then brought a dark bay into the aisleway. Inspecting the horse thoroughly, he ran his hand down the animal's legs, testing for soundness. Next, he carefully examined the beautiful gelding from mane to tail, feeling for injuries and talking to the horse in a reassuring manner. When he finished, he led the thoroughbred back into his stall, secured it, then opened the next gate.

"Mr. Thorndike." Mary Lou apparently couldn't stand it anymore. "Would you mind telling me what you're doing?"

Thorndike barely looked up from his work. "I'm checking my horses." At her quizzical expression, he shrugged. "I've already lost one. I have no plans to lose another. This is the first time these horses have been off my property, and I am understandably cautious."

"I see," Mary Lou said. It seemed as if she wanted to say something more, but stopped herself.

When he finished with the third horse, Thorndike secured the stall. Brushing his hands, he stood before her. "And you Miss Finch? Have you accomplished whatever you have set out to do?"

He stood directly before her, blocking her escape, making it quite clear that she was not going anywhere without an explanation. Mary Lou sighed. He could see the play of ideas racing about her head in her change of expression: trepidation, suspicion, doubt. Finally, she gazed directly at him. "I decided I'd look for Damien."

Her words hung sharply between them, Mary Lou's face daring him to show his own hand.

Thorndike silently acknowledged he was surprised—this was as close to the truth as she had ever come. Could she finally be starting to trust him?

Lifting her chin, he gazed into her green eyes. "Why on earth would you be so concerned about my horse? While I appreciate your interest, I assure you it is not necessary."

"Why?" Mary Lou demanded, intelligence sparkling in that fierce gaze. "Why is it I'm the only one who seems concerned? Why aren't you looking for the horse? You don't seem to care at all! Please, tell me what's going on here?"

Pierce struggled to keep a tight rein on his temper. "I understand that for a bright and curious woman like yourself, this mystery must be seductive. But I will once again remind you that I will not tolerate you sleuthing. Trained professionals are investigating this case, and I have no desire to find you in Jimmy Dwyer's condition. Whoever took my horse will stop at nothing, not even murder. Am I making myself clear?"

"Who?" Mary Lou demanded. "Who are the trained professionals?"

"Miss Finch." Raw anger filled him and his fingers tightened on her shoulders. "My refusal to discuss this case with you has nothing to do with your intelligence, nor my trust in you. The less you know, the safer you are. Do you understand that?"

He was shaking her, and had some satisfaction in seeing her eyes widen as his words finally penetrated. "Yes, but—"

"There is no 'but.' I will not have this conversation with you again. As much as I appreciate the work you've done with my son, I will not hesitate to take action if you continue snooping. You mean that much to me."

Her lips parted in surprise, and Pierce realized that he'd finally gotten through to her.

"Do you . . . mean that?" Mary Lou asked softly.

"Yes," he said. "I'm afraid I do."

"I see." To his surprise, the defiance he expected didn't come. Instead, a suspicious moisture glistened in her eyes and she turned away from him as if embarrassed.

"Miss Finch . . . "

"I . . . think perhaps we should go back inside," she said weakly, looking down at the ground.

At that moment, the sound of fireworks exploding rent the night. He stared at her, measuring her words. She was right. They should return to the ballroom before they were missed. But then Mary Lou raised her face and what he saw in her eyes took his breath away. Pain and passion, as intense as the fireworks exploding outside. An overwhelming urge to comfort her possessed him, as it did the time she burned her hair. All notions of propriety fell aside, and he took her in his arms.

"Mr. Thorndike . . . " Mary Lou protested breathlessly.

"Pierce," he demanded. "Call me Pierce."

"Pierce, I . . . "

He smiled, then his mouth took hers, startling her in its swiftness. Mary Lou pressed herself fully against him, stretched on tiptoes, her hand sliding behind his neck as a moan came from somewhere deep within her. It was all the encouragement he needed. Roman candles boomed outside, while his heart was alight with the same lusty explosion. Pierce turned her in his arms to kiss her more thoroughly, recklessly abandoning what little reason he still had. . . .

"Pierce!" a voice came from the darkness. Mary Lou sprang from Pierce's arms and whirled in astonishment as the Widow Norcross stepped into the lamplight. "Oh! I wasn't aware you were occupied. Please forgive me."

The widow turned delicately away. Mary Lou glanced down in embarrassment at her disheveled appearance, then her face flushed red. "I have to go." Picking up her skirts, she started for the hotel.

"Miss Finch." Pierce put a hand on her shoulder to stop her. "Wait."

"I must see to Edward," Mary Lou said, refusing to meet his eyes. "The noise may have awakened him."

"I will speak to you later," he said, his voice firm, reluctantly releasing her. "Please wait up for me."

Mary Lou did not answer, but fled across the lawn. Thorndike could have sworn he heard a choked sob. Turning angrily toward the widow, he swore beneath his breath.

"I'm sorry," Vivian said softly. "We had an appointment. I suppose I should have been more discreet, but I was so surprised . . . perhaps it is for the best, however."

Thorndike looked at her incredulously. "Whatever do you mean?"

For once, the widow appeared disconcerted. "Why, I should think it obvious. I know you are attracted to Miss Finch, but you certainly couldn't mean anything serious. I would think it best if she sees that now."

"Mrs. Norcross," Pierce struggled to keep his tone even. "My relationship with Miss Finch isn't anyone's concern but mine, and I certainly have no intention of disgracing her. I trust you will relay that information to anyone else impertinent enough to speculate about it."

"I see," Vivian said, her brows arching so high it seemed they'd fly off her face. She placed a gloved hand over her lips to suppress a gasp. "Goodness, I had no idea."

"Idea about what?" Pierce said furiously.

"That you cared for the girl."

The words struck him like a bolt of lightning. Could Vivian be right? Although he admitted he had feelings for Mary Lou, he hadn't examined the depth of his emotions.

There was no bitterness in the widow's voice, but Thorndike felt her pain. "I'm so sorry. You know I never meant to hurt you or lead you on."

"You didn't." Vivian forced a brightness into her voice that she obviously didn't feel. "You were always honest with me. If I chose to hope otherwise, then that was my decision, and I certainly can't blame you. Let's change the subject—I didn't come out here to catch you and your pretty Miss Finch in a dangerous liaison. I came to tell you that there was an attempt made last night to break into my stables."

Pierce's face grew hard. "What! Are you saying—"

"No. No one got in. I've hired quite a few grooms this year, as you know, and all of them live on the property. Whoever it was certainly didn't expect the place to be so well guarded. They left almost as soon as the alarm was given."

"My God." Pierce shook his head. "The police—"

"Have already been there. They advised me to move my best horses, given what has happened at Graystone. I have already made the arrangements. Half of the horses have been moved to Nina Benninghoff's stables, just outside the city. Do you know her?"

Thorndike shook his head.

"She has a wonderful trainer and has just leased a new place. Not too many people know of its location yet, so the horses should be safe for the time being."

"When I think of the danger to you—"

The widow rose, a firm smile planted stiffly on her face. "Do not even speak of it," she said sharply. "You know as well as I do that whoever would threaten the horses is an enemy to us all. Fortunately, we were given the alert and can take the appropriate steps. I will be in no personal danger, especially with the racing season upon us. I am staying here until all three races are finished, then will move on to Saratoga. But I think you should take care, Pierce. We both know what this means."

Pierce nodded. "Vivian, how can I—"

"Please don't thank me." She turned smartly, then glanced back. "A woman's pride can only take so much. Now go see your little governess. I think she has entirely the wrong idea about us."

18

❦

She'd been a fool.

Mary Lou couldn't help the sobs that emitted from her throat when she finally returned to her room. Putting on a clean nightgown, she gave into her tears and threw herself across the bed.

She had no one else to blame for her present dilemma. Why should she have been surprised to find out that Thorndike had been planning a rendezvous with the widow? It was obvious there was a depth of feeling between them. The widow was a beautiful and accomplished woman, certainly in Thorndike's class, and much more appropriate for him than a lowly governess. . . .

The sobs wracked her body. Why then, had Thorndike acted as if he had feelings for her? And why had he kissed her, knowing the widow was due at any moment? Was he playing some cruel game with them both? Or was he like every other male of the species, simply looking for the most receptive mate?

That thought was not only scientifically plausible, but logical as well. Mary Lou turned her head into her pillow, cursing the science of biology, the male gender, and her own weakness. Reaching beneath the pillow, she pulled out a handkerchief and immediately recognized it as Thorndike's. He'd given it to her the day he'd consoled her over her burned hair, and she'd kept it beneath her pillow ever since, dreaming on it, even bringing it with her to the hotel . . . Good God, she'd been such a fool.

A knock sounded lightly on her door, and Mary Lou froze. A thrill of apprehension crept up inside her as she recalled Thorndike's words, and the danger that seemed to follow them. A sigh of relief escaped her a moment later when she heard his familiar voice:

"Mary Lou? It's Pierce. Open the door."

It was a command rather than a request. Indignation replaced her fear. She might be nothing more than a governess, but she had some rights, and those included a peaceful night's rest and the privacy of her room. She also didn't want him to see that she'd been crying over him, while he was no doubt blissfully engaged with the widow.

"Go away!" Mary Lou hissed back.

She was startled to see her doorknob turn back and forth, as if he was testing the lock. Thankfully, she had bolted the door. The knob finally stopped moving, and the knocking resumed.

"Miss Finch, stop this foolishness and open the damned door!" he snarled.

Mary Lou stood up, her arms crossed, her own anger welling inside her. "I told you to go away!"

"If I have to break this down—"

Startled, she slid open the bolt, but kept the chain fastened. Surely he wouldn't create a scene in the hotel, but then, one never knew with Thorndike. Opening the door a scant inch, she peered through the crack.

"What do you want?"

"We need to talk." She could hear the frustrated fury in his voice. "Will you *please* open the door?"

"No."

"Miss Finch," Thorndike thundered. "This is ridiculous. I will not stand outside in the hall like some chambermaid and try to reason with you. Open the door!"

As an answer, Mary Lou slammed it firmly in his face. She had a moment's satisfaction when she heard him curse, then to her surprise, heard a second voice in the hall. Curiosity overcame her and she peeked through the crack just in time to see one of the other guests, an elderly man wearing a red and white striped robe and nightcap, stick his head out of his doorway.

"What in blazes is going on here! I thought this a respectable hotel . . . Are you drunk?" He tugged on the belt to his robe, glaring suspiciously at Thorndike.

Pierce appeared anything but pleased, and Mary Lou tried to swallow the laughter welling up inside her. "No, I'm not drunk. Please go back to your room. I'm sorry to have awakened you."

"What is it then? Marital troubles?" The man persisted, turning to Mary Lou. "Come on, girlie, and let him in. I need to get some shut eye!"

"I am not his wife!" Mary Lou said indignantly.

The little man's eyes seemed to bulge out of his head and he glared at Thorndike. "Then what are you doing . . ."

"My . . . niece is just being stubborn," Pierce said, fuming at Mary Lou, who choked back laughter.

"Niece?" The man's brows narrowed at Mary Lou, then he turned back at Thorndike. "You uncles certainly have enough of them running about here. Now be quiet, I'm trying to sleep!"

He slammed his door indignantly. Mary Lou stifled a grin just in time as Thorndike turned around. His face was livid and he spoke through gritted teeth.

"Open the door."

"No."

"I can't talk to you out here."

"You're going to have to."

"Miss Finch, you are the most stubborn, determined, bull-headed woman—" She started to close the door again when he slipped his boot between the portal and the jamb. His blue eyes glittered in outrage. "I'm not leaving until you hear me out."

"There is nothing you can say that will make a difference," Mary Lou said blithely, trying to hide the hurt in her voice. "I know you have an . . . understanding with the widow, and it was my own foolishness to think otherwise. I should have recalled the biological differences between men and women, particularly during the mating season . . ."

"Miss Finch!" Thorndike looked appalled.

"But what I cannot accept is your staging a kiss just in time for Mrs. Norcross's entrance. Was that simply a means to satisfy your ego, or was it a message?"

"How can you possibly think such a thing!" Thorndike thundered. Mary Lou had never seen him so angry, and she wondered at the wisdom of pushing him so far.

The little man peered out of his door again and they both shouted, "Go away!" Indignant, he slammed the portal shut, muttering all the while about the lack of respect for decent guests.

As soon as the man's door closed, Thorndike pushed hers open, snapping the chain in the process. Mary Lou gasped, then stepped hastily backward. "Sir! How dare you!"

In answer, he kicked her door closed. An implacable light gleamed in his eyes and he took a step closer to her.

"Mr. Thorndike, this is highly improper . . . if anyone should discover your presence here, it would endanger my reputation beyond repair."

"No one will know a thing, particularly if you had listened to reason to begin with," he said determinedly. "Miss Finch, I am keenly disappointed that you think so little of me."

"What else am I to think?" Mary Lou said, trying desperately to stop the pounding in her chest as Thorndike approached her. Surely he wouldn't . . . not here, like this. A thrill of excitement swept through her, but she sternly squashed it and put a chair between them. He reached out and easily tossed it aside, continuing toward her like a predator closing in on its prey.

"You'd better stop right there," Mary Lou said, realizing she had backed up to the wall. A table stood beside her and she picked up the first thing she laid her hands on, a thick bible, and brandished it before him like a weapon.

Thorndike saw the book, and grabbed it easily out of her hand. Sliding his arm roughly around her waist, he pressed her to his chest. When he spoke, his voice was steely. "I have come to several conclusions this night, some of which you may not agree with, but you will hear me out."

"You have no right—" Mary Lou gasped, struggling, feeling every inch of him against her sensitive skin. The thin nightgown she wore was no protection at all, and she suddenly wished she hadn't changed out of her dress.

"Ah, but I do. You see, not only are you under my employ, but the depth of our relationship has gone far beyond that, as you well know."

Mary Lou's head flew up and she glared at him. "Let me go—"

"Not on your life. We need to get a few things straight. The Widow Norcross and I are simply friends, and have been so for years. There is nothing more between us."

Mary Lou gazed at him, the outrage draining from her as if someone had stuck a balloon with a pin. "Then why . . . ?"

"Do I see her?" Thorndike's eyes glittered strangely, and he gave her a rueful smile. "I admit, after my wife died, I took solace in her company. It wasn't in a physical way—it is indeed, a close friendship. The widow admitted she had feelings for me, but I made it clear I couldn't reciprocate those emotions. Friendship, she said, would suffice."

"And you believed her?" Mary Lou asked incredulously, knowing it would never be enough for her.

He nodded. "The widow has been married, and understands these things a little better than you might. I needed a friend; she needed an escort and protector. We thought it was a reasonable exchange, and I felt things were under control. Until recently."

Mary Lou's eyes widened. "Not because of me—"

"Exactly because of you. The widow realized that there was something between us before I did. I think as long as I wasn't seriously involved with another woman, she could accept my friendship. Now, I have doubts."

"Then why are you still involved with her?"

Thorndike sighed. "There are other reasons, besides our long-standing friendship. I am partly responsible for any pain she feels, for even though I was honest, she was hurt. I cannot just desert her now."

"I know," Mary Lou nodded. Pierce was far too noble to just forget someone he considered a friend. "But that doesn't explain why she was there—"

"I had forgotten I was supposed to meet her. She wanted to tell me in private that someone had attempted to break into her stables."

He smiled self-deprecatingly, and softly touched her face in a gentle caress. Mary Lou felt her defenses crumble, although she desperately tried to cling to reason. "But . . . if someone broke into her stables . . . wouldn't that mean . . . ?"

"We don't know what it means yet," he said thoughtfully. "The police are investigating."

"But—"

Thorndike smiled, extending the caress to her throat. "Didn't I tell you no more sleuthing? Besides, I think the time for logic has long passed."

"I'm so sorry I doubted you," Mary Lou said softly. "It's just when I saw her standing there—"

"I know," Thorndike said, pulling her closer into his arms. "You have to understand, Mary Lou, I never meant for any of this to happen. It's wrong, and I know it, but I can't seem to help myself. My God, I've tried so hard to hold what I felt inside me, but I want you so badly I can hardly think. Please, Mary Lou. Let me love you."

"Yes," she answered breathlessly. "Yes."

His mouth covered hers in a kiss that was achingly sweet. Mary Lou sighed, surrendering completely. She wanted this man, needed him, and she'd known it from the first time she'd met him. It was indefensible, irrational, and totally illogical, but it was the truth, and she didn't have the strength to resist him.

Reaching up on her toes, she slid her fingers through the silky black hair at the nape of his neck. Her heart felt as if it would burst inside her. The empty ache inside her disappeared, and was replaced by a strange sense of completion. She held him tightly, bringing him even closer, wanting everything his hard-muscled body promised.

And he gave. Pierce groaned at her enthusiastic reaction, then deepened the kiss, his tongue meeting

hers in an exciting rhythm that mimicked the sexual
act itself. Heat pulsed through her veins, and her skin
became shockingly sensitive as Thorndike eased his
lips from hers and began feathering kisses along her
throat. She gave him no resistance when his warm,
callused hand covered her breast, searing her
through the thin cotton of her nightgown. Instead,
she arched her back, giving him even greater access,
gasping at the hardening of her nipple and the tortur-
ous ache his caresses generated.

His lips replaced his hand, his tongue hot and wet
against her sensitive skin. Mary Lou sighed as he
knelt before her, tasting her through her clothes.
Then his hands slipped beneath them and raised the
gown over her head, rendering her naked in one swift
motion. Cool air struck her skin, replaced by his
warmth a moment later when he carried her to the
bed and placed her gently on top of the sheets. To
her amazement, he moved the gaslamp closer, revealing every inch of her pale skin in the soft light.
Instinctively she tried to cover herself, but just as before, when she looked into his eyes, she saw adora-
tion there.

"You are so beautiful," he murmured, scorching
her with his gaze. "Do you know how often I've
wanted this, dreamed of you this way? You are so
soft, so sweet, your skin is like honey and cream . . . I
can't get enough of you."

All self-consciousness left her. The shy, plump little girl vanished, as did the wallflower who was never
asked to dance at fashionable parties. Instead, she
was beautiful, and she gloried in it.

His mouth caressed her everywhere his eyes had

just adored her. Mary Lou moaned, clutching handfuls of the sheets as he cleverly aroused her. He seemed to know exactly where to apply pressure, where a gentle flick of his tongue would be most pleasurable, and when to stop being gentle at all and roughly nip her.

"Please," Mary Lou begged. She never realized the sensitivity of the skin on the back of her knee, her inner thigh, or even her fingers when Pierce put them one by one into his mouth. Straining against the covers, she felt like she had a fever, but one that gave her intense pleasure. Her body was alive, pulsing and hot, tense as a violin string about to break. "I need . . . "

She didn't know what she needed, but thankfully, he did. To her shocked amazement, he moved lower, down past her round belly, to the golden triangle between her legs.

"Is this what you want?" he asked teasingly, drawing a finger seductively between her innermost folds. "Or this?" The same finger entered her, while his thumb caressed the most sensitive part of her, making her gasp with stunned amazement. "Or perhaps this . . . "

His lips replaced his hand and she thought she'd die from the pure bliss of it. His tongue was merciless, flicking deeper and higher, rendering all conscious thought impossible. Arching against him, she heard herself cry out as wave after wave of shocking pleasure ripped through her, reverberating throughout her body from her blonde curls to her toes.

She'd barely caught her breath when he was inside her. A slight stinging pain brought her quickly back to reality, but that was soon obliterated as he rocked gently against her. Mary Lou squirmed, then his hands gentled her as if calming a nervous horse, running them along her flanks and beneath her, guiding her movements to his rhythm. She caught it and moved with him, rewarded by the growing sense of urgency that was becoming familiar.

"Once more, sweetheart. Relax. You feel so good, so hot and wet . . ."

Mary Lou gasped as the passion soared within her. Unwittingly, her teeth sunk into his shoulder, the frenzy coming upon her. She welcomed his thrusts as he drove hot and hard within her, demanding a response, and he got it. Mary Lou cried out as her body shook with release, each throbbing spasm more incredibly pleasurable than the last. A guttural sound came from his lips and he pulled out from her at the last minute, breathing heavily, then collapsed in her arms. His heart joined hers in a rapid beating.

He held her tenderly for a long time, gently stroking her hair as if she was something too precious for words. Mary Lou sighed blissfully. Never had she felt so womanly, so full of joy. It was as if the ache inside of her, the years of disappointment and pain, was completely gone.

Pierce lifted himself on an elbow and peered down into her face. "What are you thinking? I can hear your mind turning from here."

"Just that I understand now why fruit flies and honeybees and polar bears are so enraptured with each other," Mary Lou said honestly. "I had no idea this could be so pleasurable. It certainly explains a lot. What are you laughing at?"

"Nothing," he said, though his voice choked suspiciously. He picked up her hand, pressing a kiss to the back of her wrist, gratified to feel her pulse jump in response. "It will never be boring, will it Miss Finch? Not in a hundred years."

19

❧

The Widow Norcross returned to the ballroom and quickly snatched a glass of champagne from a tray. Dashing the sparkling liquid down her throat as if it was water, she put the flute aside and took another. As she lifted the drink, Robert Cornwall stepped beside her.

"I wouldn't drink too much of that if I were you," he said softly. "You'll have a hell of a headache tomorrow."

"Well, that's tomorrow, and this is tonight." Vivian drank the second as quickly as she had the first, hoping it would numb the raw ache inside her. She gestured for a refill when the lawyer's frown stopped her. "Oh, pooh, Robert, don't be so stodgy. The fun is just beginning."

"So it went that badly, did it?" The lawyer waylaid the waiter before he could give the widow any more liquor. Instead, he took the glass himself and quietly sipped the champagne.

"I don't know what you mean," Vivian said sharply. "I went out for some air and to see the fireworks. Quite exhilarating, I assure you."

"I'm sure," Robert said, not bothering to hide the sarcasm in his voice.

The widow gave him an outraged glare. "You know, Robert, at times you can be a good friend, but at others you are truly annoying. Why don't you do everyone a favor and mind your own business?"

"Because I wanted to see how long it would take you to stop chasing moonbeams," Robert said, sipping his own drink. "You are far too beautiful a woman to waste your life pining away for something that will never be yours."

The widow looked at him in astonishment. "Why . . . how dare you!" She trembled in fury. "You don't know anything about it!"

Instead of getting angry, Robert laughed. "I suppose I don't. Perhaps I granted you too much intelligence to know when the game is up. Too bad. But I've waited this long for you—I suppose I can wait a little while longer for you to come to your senses."

Vivian's mouth dropped. "You, sir, are no gentleman!" she spat, but the words generated something within her. A spark of awareness. A hint of some long-forgotten emotion. A male–female challenge.

Again, Robert laughed, as if her reaction was entirely expected. "Come, Vivian. Let's dance. The night is still young and we've wasted so much of it already."

Without waiting for a response, he whirled her onto the dance floor. Vivian forgot her anger as the music swept over them, and she gazed at Robert as if seeing a stranger.

How had she been so blind? This man apparently cared for her, and had for some time. Had she been so wrapped up in wanting Pierce that she hadn't seen Robert clearly at all? In truth, she had never noticed how handsome he was, how intelligent and charming . . . and he was an excellent dancer.

When the music stopped, she put her hand to her head to stop it from spinning. It must have been the champagne. She'd drunk too much of it, and it always went to her head. Nothing made sense—it couldn't. She loved Pierce, and Robert was simply his lawyer . . . And yet . . . she could feel that something had shifted in her, like the sand beneath the onslaught of the ocean.

"Vivian?" When the widow looked up, Robert was gazing at her with concern. "Are you all right? Perhaps a cup of coffee and some fresh air will help."

Vivian smiled. "I think that sounds wonderful."

Thorndike was gone when Mary Lou awoke. A note lay upon the indented pillow beside her and she picked it up, feeling her heart overflow at his simple message.

> I thought it best if I left before everyone woke. Thank you for last night. You have brought joy and beauty into my life once more. T

There were no words of love or commitment, but Mary Lou hadn't expected that. She knew that Pierce had broken his vow not to become intimately involved with her, just as she had broken her own. Her emotions were in turmoil, but even under those circumstances, she had no regrets. Last night she had felt beautiful, cherished, and cared for. To wish it never happened would have truly been a loss indeed.

She dressed slowly, her hands tracing the lines of her body as if they had become foreign to her. Now that Thorndike had made love to her, she would never be the same. The thought of a possible pregnancy entered her mind, and a shiver of anxiety swept through her. Although Thorndike had attempted to protect her from that by withdrawing, she knew enough about biology to know that no method of contraception was foolproof. How would he greet the news if such a thing occurred? And what would happen to her? Pregnancy fears aside, her heart was another matter. It belonged to him now. How could she go back to being just his governess? Yet how could she do anything else?

"Miss Finch, you look stunning." Peter Whitesell gave her an appreciative glance as Mary Lou joined them, Edward at her side. The little boy glared at his father's friend, and Mary Lou gave his hand a reassuring squeeze.

Thorndike's eyes met hers and in silent communication, conveyed his own compliment. Mary Lou felt a flush of color climb into her cheeks. Whereas

Peter's gallant words didn't affect her at all, a mere glance from Pierce had her blushing like a schoolgirl. The erotic night they'd spent together came swiftly to mind and she found her face getting even hotter.

"I'm . . . sorry I'm late," Mary Lou stammered. "Bridget told me to meet you here. Are we going to a race?"

"Yes, the Suburban. We have a horse running in the third, and Peter's is in the fourth. Everyone will be there. Unfortunately, we cannot leave until all the races are over, around five o'clock. Edward, do you think you want to stay that long?"

Edward nodded eagerly. "Yes, some of the other boys will be there and I can play with them."

"Why can't we leave?" Mary Lou asked, puzzled.

It was Peter who answered her. "The Pinkertons are trying to crack down on illegal activities. For a while telegraph men were sitting on top of those poles and giving signals to their men below as to who was winning. Now they get locked up if they even so much as wave to each other, and they prevent the guests from leaving before all the races have been run."

"There were other things going on as well," Thorndike said smoothly, seeing Mary Lou's attention perk up. "Men were sneaking into the stables and racing a horse during the night into exhaustion, so it couldn't perform the next day. That sort of thing."

"Oh," Mary Lou answered casually.

Thorndike gave her a knowing smile. "None of that, of course, need concern you. The stands will be well guarded. We have plans to lunch with the

Mitchells, as you may recall, and Mrs. Doisneau will join us then. By the way, is that a new gown? It is charming."

His gaze took in the new yellow flowered gown she wore. Mary Lou smiled, and when Peter bent down to talk to Edward, she feigned a sharp look. "You know perfectly well it is. I thank you for the advance, but I intend to pay it all back."

"Can I choose the method of payment?" To her amazement, Thorndike teased her, delighted when the color rose again in her face. Mary Lou was about to scold him when he bent down as if to kiss her hand, then spoke softly. "I hope you understand why I left when I did last night."

"Yes." Mary Lou shivered. This man had merely to touch her and she melted.

"We need to talk," he continued, pretending to search the crowds for someone while he spoke under his breath.

Something caught at Mary Lou's heart. Did he have regrets? He didn't appear so, and thankfully, he wasn't apologizing. Instead, he seemed charmingly happy, his eyes sparkling, and there was a light-heartedness about him that she'd never seen before. He was also devastatingly handsome. She admired the lightweight summer suit he wore, the immaculate shirt and tie. Her eyes lifted to his and he moved closer, whispering to her alone.

"Stop looking at me like that. I swear, it is taking every ounce of control I have not to pull you into my arms."

Mary Lou smiled, though her breath caught. She was feeling much the same way. If it was possible for the color to rise even more in her face, she was certain it did. Thankfully, another woman joined them, taking the attention from her. Two children were holding her hands, and the woman looked completely flustered and out of patience.

"Would you please take them? I've had them all morning."

Peter looked embarrassed, then turned to Mary Lou. "This is my wife, Carolina, and my children, Grace and Jonathan. You know Pierce, but this is Miss Finch, his governess."

"Hello." Peter's wife nodded briefly in her direction. Mary Lou had a glimpse of a fashionably dressed woman who appeared older than her years, and far from happy. Her hair was pulled back into a severe chignon beneath a charming straw hat, and her face seemed unnaturally tight. She thrust the children at her husband as if wanting to get rid of them as quickly as possible.

"I am meeting Mrs. Williams for tea," Carolina said. "And these two are driving me insane." Another thought occurred to her and she glanced quickly at Mary Lou. "Perhaps you wouldn't mind watching them along with Edward."

Pierce started to say something, but Mary Lou smiled quickly. "Of course not, they can all play together. I don't mind, really."

Thorndike didn't appear happy, but the woman, rid of her baggage, had already gone. Peter stared after her for a moment, his expression annoyed, but then shrugged and engaged Pierce in conversation about business.

The children ran ahead, and Mary Lou raced after

them to the promenade where the jockeys were walking the horses. The children were delighted with Peter's offer of taffy, and chased each other gleefully around the stands. Pierce tried to help her keep the children in line, but he and Mary Lou were clearly outnumbered, and the taffy created a sticky mess.

"That's the one I want! With the blue colors!" Grace called out, pointing to one of the jockeys dressed in a brilliant sapphire.

"There's ours!" Edward cried as he spotted a beautiful bay. The jockey was wearing Graystone's gold, and he waved to the children as he passed, causing more shrieks.

"That's Toby," Thorndike said. "You may recall seeing him at Feltman's. He's riding Pippin."

Mary Lou nodded, remembering the jovial little man who'd called to them over his hot dogs. A few more horses walked by and Thorndike identified them.

"That's Belmont's Silverado. There's Domino, Mitchell's new colt. Looks like he's got Greenwood riding him—he's a hell of a good jockey. And that's Pinsticker and Cashbox."

Mary Lou glanced down at the program that Thorndike had produced and could see the horses listed exactly as he described them. The children shouted and waved to the horses, thrilled when a jockey waved back.

The stands began to fill as people took their seats, and Thorndike and Mary Lou herded the children toward their box. Others soon joined them, and he introduced Mary Lou to more than a dozen guests, including the Mitchells. Within a few minutes, the trumpets sounded to signal the start of the race. Only then were her charges persuaded to take their seats and succumb to her ministrations with a damp handkerchief.

All at once, the horses burst from the gate. Mary Lou saw a few horses surge to the front of the pack, while the others began to fall behind. She could hear a megaphone somewhere above, and the names of the horses called.

"And there is Pinsticker out in front, followed closely by Silverado. Pippin is coming up fast on the inside, as are Cashbox and Domino. It's Silverado taking the lead, Pippin coming up right beside them—"

"Go!" Edward and the other children screamed, each rooting for their chosen horse. As the horses rounded the bend, everyone got to their feet. The air was charged with electricity, and suddenly Mary Lou could understand why this became an uncontrollable passion. Even she and Thorndike were shouting as Pippin took the lead.

"And it's Pippin out front, Pippin by a nose. Cashbox inching up. Silverado's taking the lead . . . Pippin's fighting for ground—this one's close . . . "

Through a blur of color Mary Lou saw Thorndike's horse suddenly fall back, and a wash of gold tumble to the ground. Her breath halted as the unthinkable became apparent, reinforced by the announcer a moment later.

"And Silverado wins the race! Wait a minute folks, there's been an accident . . . Toby Nelson, Pippin's rider has taken a bad fall. He's not moving. There's no need for panic, please stay off the field. The doctor is arriving already."

Mary Lou felt a sickness begin inside her . . . the jockey had fallen. He could easily have been killed beneath those churning hooves, and there was no guarantee yet that he was alive. Turning to Thorndike, she saw the same stricken expression on his face as he gazed onto the field. A man appeared to capture Pippin, but the horse had already stopped and seemed to stare at the fallen jockey as if somehow responsible. The doctor arrived and knelt beside Toby, shaking his head as if the news were bad. The crowd began to file onto the field in spite of the warnings, and Thorndike got quickly to his feet.

"Wait here," he said to Mary Lou. "Keep Edward with you. I checked the horses last night, but never thought about the jockey."

He disappeared into the crowd. Mary Lou watched in horror as two men carrying a stretcher placed Toby's battered body on the makeshift bed. She could see blood staining the gold of his jacket. Edward and the other children pressed against her in silent horror, and they saw Thorndike join the doctor at the scene. His words came back to her and Mary Lou suddenly realized what he'd meant.

Toby's fall hadn't been an accident.

20

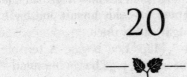

Thorndike returned a short while later. From his grim expression, Mary Lou knew the news wasn't good. Picking up Edward, he turned to her and Peter, indicating the tables below.

"We'd best join the Mitchells. It appears they're waiting for us."

"How is Toby?" Peter asked quietly.

Thorndike appeared as if he didn't want to discuss it. "He's had convulsions. The doctor thinks he's had a seizure of some kind. He's also got broken ribs, a fractured skull, internal bleeding, and contusions. His breathing sounds bad and he may have punctured a lung. They don't know if he'll make it."

Peter whistled softly, shaking his head in

sympathy. "Did he appear to be ill? It isn't like Toby to take a fall."

Mary Lou watched Thorndike closely. Pierce shook his head, his eyes narrow with anger. "That jockey never fell off a horse in his life. If he had one fault, it was that he was intensely honest and loyal. Toby couldn't be bought, at any price."

"Do you mean—" Mary Lou began. A terrible suspicion began to piece itself together in her mind.

"Yes, I think it very likely someone deliberately caused his fall. I don't know any particulars yet, but call it a gut feeling."

Peter grimaced, while Mary Lou felt her heart grow heavy. It seemed that an invisible hand was capable of reaching out at any time and striking at will. She'd once thought the danger was at Graystone, but apparently nowhere was safe.

Thorndike must have had the same thought, for he held Edward closer, then looked at her with an intense expression. "I think it might be a good idea to cut our holiday short. I would like to meet with the police and give them this information. Would it be too difficult to pack up quickly after lunch?"

"Not at all," Mary Lou responded. "I'll get to it right away."

"Don't you think you're overreacting a bit, old man?" Peter said. "I understand your concern, but nothing has been proven. The jockey could have just had a bad stomach. He'll be fine."

"Yes, I'm sure you're right," Thorndike said politely, but Mary Lou could tell he wasn't convinced.

Lunch was a subdued affair in light of the jockey's

fall. Margaret Mitchell, an older woman dressed in a dark suit cut in a severe masculine style, greeted Pierce fondly, then extended a hand to Mary Lou. Her husband, a rotund man with the agreeable look of wealth, gave them a greeting that was equally jovial. Their bluff welcome turned somber as they mentioned the accident.

"Tut, tut, my boy. It's a rare shame, that. I hear the boy, Toby Nelson, was a true genius with a horse."

"He is exceptionally talented," Thorndike said with keen regret. "I can only hope he'll pull through."

Mary Lou saw the pained effort it took for him to make polite conversation. She was almost relieved when Peter's wife rushed up, breathless, waving an enormous lacquered fan at her heated face.

"I'm terribly sorry I'm late. The accident and everything, you know. Why, all these people in the way . . . everyone's talking. Oh, there are my little ones."

Scooping up her children, she barely gave Mary Lou a glance or a word of thanks. Instead she gushed up to Margaret Mitchell, admiring everything from her sophisticated dress to her upswept hairstyle.

Margaret accepted her compliments and called for a waiter. The Mitchells and the Whitesells all took their chairs, and Mary Lou reluctantly joined Pierce, while the children sat at a nearby table. Much as Mary Lou wanted to get to know the Mitchells, dining with them at an elegant lunch seemed presumptuous on her part. At any minute she expected someone to yank her out of her seat for the grossest impertinence, and direct her to the children's table.

Thorndike, sensing her thoughts, put her napkin on her knee and his hand on the back of her chair, as if to prevent her from fleeing.

The waiter brought oysters and wine, and lemonade for the children. A bewildering array of silver serving pieces were on the table, as well as several different-sized dishes and glasses. Although Mary Lou was no stranger to formal dinners, having joined her father in a few at the University, she wasn't prepared for an elaborate feast of this kind. By watching Pierce covertly, she was able to discern what fork to use, and which glass was hers.

"So I went shopping at the Elephant Hotel . . . it really is shaped just like an elephant. You can view the ocean from inside his eyes . . . "

Carolina Whitesell talked incessantly, through the crab salad, the baked bluefish, the roast lamb with vegetables, and the apple tart. When the waiter cleared places for dessert, Carolina finally took a breath. It was as if everyone was waiting for that moment, for Peter firmly steered the conversation away from sightseeing and shopping.

Glancing at Joseph Mitchell, he indicated the track. "So you have a horse running today?"

"Yes. My son Charles has Caesar in the ninth, and we have Western Light running tomorrow. Charles has high hopes for Caesar, though he seemed a little footsore today. Altogether he's been making a good showing as of late. I certainly hope he does well. My boy has invested a fortune in that horse."

"Joseph!" His wife said, appalled. "I'm sure no one is interested in Charles's finances."

"Well, I am," Joseph replied, none too happily. "That boy seems to think money grows on trees. I'm not bailing him out this time. He's on his own."

A stilted silence followed the man's words, and everyone picked at their meal awkwardly. Mary Lou listened intently even as she pretended to eat.

Carolina shrugged, as if bored with the conversation. "I think that all of these horses cost far too much money, anyway. Some of them are worth more than our house, for goodness' sake! Even all this," she waved to the track. "It seems as if some people don't know what to do with their money."

Mary Lou flinched, concentrating on her coffee. It was well known that the Mitchells spent quite a lot on their horses. The silence was deafening, and when she did look up, she saw Peter giving his wife a look of disgust.

"Darling," he gritted slowly. "Would you mind if we took our coffee and cigars over there? I know how much the smoke bothers you."

"Not at all," Carolina seemed very happy with the prospect. "Then we can talk of more interesting things. Margaret, have you been to Lundy's yet? I hear the food is spectacular!"

The men retreated, and the children began racing around the table. Mary Lou found herself once more in the role of chaperone for all of them as Carolina blithely ignored her offspring to continue her chat with Margaret Mitchell.

The races started again, but no one made a move to return to the box, nor did the men appear overly eager to rejoin them. As Carolina Whitesell chattered on, it was apparent why. Mary Lou pulled one of her children out from beneath the table, wondering how handsome, debonair Peter had acquired such a wife.

It was late when Thorndike returned, apologetic but distant. Apparently, Peter had wanted to discuss a business venture with Joseph Mitchell, and had deftly utilized the luncheon as an opportunity to make his proposal.

"Unfortunately," Pierce said once they were out of earshot. "We won't be able to leave now until Friday. I have to make the arrangements for the horses and the ship's crew. That is, unless perhaps you'd prefer the train?"

Mary Lou's eyes brightened so much that Thorndike smiled. "The train it is. And when we return home, there is something I need to discuss with you."

His voice sounded serious and Mary Lou felt a tightening in her stomach. Something was wrong— she could tell by his tone and the way he was acting. She gazed at him, but he refused to meet her eyes. She was about to question him when Edward joined them, excitedly showing them a lollipop that Peter had purchased for him. The carriages arrived, and she watched the Whitesells pile into one, then she and Edward joined Pierce in the other. They rode back to the hotel in silence.

Early in the evening, Mary Lou heard a tap on her door. When she answered it, to her surprise, Curtis

Jones, one of the jockeys, stood outside with a bundle in his hands.

"Excuse me, Miss," he spoke softly, shifting uncomfortably from one foot to the other. "But I was looking for Mr. Thorndike. I need to give him these."

"Mr. Thorndike's room is next door," Mary Lou said. "Isn't he there?" The jockey shook his head in the negative, and Mary Lou gave him a reassuring smile. "He may have gone out. He sometimes likes to take a walk on the beach before dinner."

"Oh." Curtis looked awkwardly at the bundle, then beseechingly at her. It was obvious that he had walked a considerable distance and didn't relish the idea of having to come back.

"If you want to leave that for Mr. Thorndike, I will be happy to give it to him when he returns."

"Thank you, Miss." Curtis handed her the armload, which appeared to be a curious collection of clothing and personal grooming implements. At Mary Lou's questioning look, he quickly explained. "It's Toby's things, his clothes and pipe. There is also his flask of gin. He wasn't a drinker, just took a taste for luck. I thought Mr. Thorndike . . . that is, he might be able to send them home in case . . . "

Curtis lowered his face, but not before she saw the sheen of tears welling in his dark eyes. Putting a hand on his shoulder, she gently squeezed it. "That was very kind of you, and I'm sure Mr. Thorndike will take good care of his belongings. I'm hoping Toby will be all right."

"We all are, Miss." The little jockey wiped his face in embarrassment, then flashed her a look of anger. "Whoever did this to him, I hope they get him!"

"Curtis," Mary Lou put the bundle on her bed then turned back to the door. "Are you saying you think his fall wasn't an accident?"

"Yes, Miss, I do. The police came and questioned me, and I told them the same thing. I watched Toby ride the worst of them, even Stormy. Remember him?"

Mary Lou shook her head. "No, but go on."

"He was a hell horse, all fire in his eyes and rearing straight up. Toby had that horse going as smooth as silk. There ain't a horse been born what could have thrown him."

Mary Lou nodded, then handed the jockey a coin for his trouble. Curtis seemed reluctant to accept it, but then stuck it in his pocket and gave her a wan smile. "Thank you, Miss. But that ain't why I'm helping. Toby was a good'un, know what I mean?"

"Yes, I do," Mary Lou said softly. "And I'm sure his family will be grateful for your thoughtfulness." As the jockey started to leave, Mary Lou stopped him once more. "Curtis, you didn't happen to see Willy Starkey around last night or this morning, did you?"

The jockey paused, his brow squinting thoughtfully. "Now that you mention it, Miss, yes. Why, did you need a horse shoed?"

"No, nothing like that. Thanks again, Curtis."

Mary Lou closed the door, then sank down onto her bed thoughtfully. The blacksmith appears, and the next day, an experienced jockey takes a fall. The connection seemed far-fetched, but something in Mary Lou's gut believed, as Curtis and Thorndike did, that Toby's injury wasn't accidental. What, then, could have happened? Could someone have tampered with his breakfast or dinner, possibly slipped him something in his drink?

After undoing the bundle, she rolled it out on the bed. There was nothing remarkable: some shirts and trousers, all unbelievably small, a razor and a shaving cup, comb, a jackknife and block of wood Toby had been whittling, a pipe and a pouch of tobacco and . . . the flask.

Mary Lou opened the tin and smelled the pungent scent of liquor. Half the flask was empty, so Toby must have indulged frequently, perhaps even that morning, yet he didn't have a reputation for being a drunkard.

Mary Lou rolled up the articles except for the flask, and neatly retied them with the piece of twine Curtis had used. A vague hypothesis formed in her mind. Anyone could have crept inside Toby's room and put something in the flask. While not all poisons were flavorless, the gin was peculiarly strong, perhaps strong enough to hide the bitter taste of an alkaloid. It would take but a few simple tests to know for sure.

She was about to put the flask away when a light knock sounded on her door. Before she could respond, it opened, and she saw Pierce standing on the threshold.

"We're dining early this evening and I thought . . . " his eyes fell to the odd assortment on her bed. "What is all that?"

"Toby's things," Mary Lou said, clutching the tin in her hands. A red flush crept up on her cheeks, but she continued as if he hadn't just caught her sleuthing once more. "Curtis brought them. He thought you could send them home."

"I see," Thorndike said, his voice telling her he saw a lot more. His gaze lowered to the flask that she attempted to hide behind her back, and one black brow lifted sarcastically. "And what were you doing with that?"

Mary Lou held her head high. "I was merely rewrapping the package. Curtis carried it so far that the twine had come loose."

"So you decided to keep his flask in case you wanted a nip of gin?"

"Well, I . . . " Mary Lou stammered in reply.

Thorndike gave her a steady stare. "Come now, Miss Finch. I don't think you would be tempted to filch liquor from a man who may not live until morning."

Sighing, Mary Lou put the flask down on her bed and faced him squarely. She knew enough about Thorndike to know when the game was up. "I was going to run some tests on the liquor when we returned. It occurred to me that perhaps someone may have tampered with Toby's gin. It would at least prove your theory about his fall."

"Mary Lou," Thorndike said, steel in his eyes. His voice was barely a whisper. "Haven't we had this conversation before?"

It dawned on Mary Lou that he was furious. She suddenly wished she had never laid eyes on Toby's things. He advanced a step closer and she took one back, feeling completely vulnerable and at his mercy.

"Well, yes, but this isn't exactly the same thing—"

"Miss Finch, I was going to wait until a more opportune time to have this conversation, but it appears you've forced my hand. I cannot put anyone else at risk any longer. Your services are no longer required at Graystone."

Mary Lou stared at him, stunned. "You aren't suggesting . . . "

"That you're dismissed? That's exactly what I'm saying."

He meant it. He didn't want her. Not even as his employee. Pain shot through her, and only her pride kept her from weeping and begging him to reconsider. When she looked up at him, determinedly blinking her eyes to keep the tears from falling, she saw nothing in his face to engender any hope of changing his mind.

"I am sorry it had to come to this," he said. "You have to know how grateful I am, and how much our relationship meant . . . "

It was too painful to hear him say the words. Mary Lou stopped him before he could go on. "What about Edward?"

"Edward has progressed so well that he is ready for school," Thorndike said firmly, although she could hear a catch in his voice. "You are, of course, welcome to stay in touch with him."

"I see," Mary Lou said softly, the words seeming to stick in her throat. She noticed he hadn't included himself in his offer. "When, sir?"

"As soon as we return. I will telegraph Beecham to gather your belongings, and I will be happy to arrange compensation for the rest of the month." Reaching into his pocket, he pulled out a wad of bills and handed them to her.

"Please accept this."

She felt like a prostitute, being paid for services

rendered. Bile, bitter and acidic, rose in her throat and she pushed his hand away from her. Outrage replaced the pain, and she faced him directly.

"Keep your money, Mr. Thorndike. I may be poor, but never that poverty-stricken. Or is this how you usually dispose of your mistresses? What did the Widow Norcross cost you? Or didn't you have to make that payment?"

She was rewarded with a flash of anger in his eyes, followed by a cold shuttering of his emotions. It seemed to take every bit of his effort not to reply back in turn, but instead he put the money by her bedside and turned toward the door.

"If you leave the money there, the hotel will return it and I will simply have it deposited into your account. I'm sorry, Miss Finch." Then he was gone.

Mary Lou stared at the closed door, unable to believe what had just happened. Thorndike had discharged her. A sick feeling overcame her and she sank down onto the bed, the reality of the situation finally hitting her.

Why? Why had he done this? She thought he was happy with her. He'd made love to her with a desperation that was heartbreaking. And he seemed to appreciate how she had helped his son. Then why? Was it regret that he'd seduced her, that he'd violated his own moral code? Maybe he wanted to get rid of her, and this was the easiest way?

Frantically, her mind went over the last few minutes and she winced at his expression when he saw her going through Toby's things. Surely that wasn't the reason. Even though he'd threatened before, she never truly believed he'd carry out his threats.

Her mind went back to Toby's fall. Never had she seen Thorndike look so ominous. She suddenly understood. He was afraid for her, and in his mind, the logical way to protect her was to send her away. Toby's injury had proven to him that no one in his circle was safe. What were his words: *I cannot put anyone at risk any longer.* Thorndike's solution was obvious: Edward in school. Herself back in Boston.

The tears she'd concealed from him spilled forth now. She didn't want to leave Thorndike, or Edward, or even Graystone. She just couldn't envision going back to her old life in the little cottage with only her father, the servants, and her science to keep her company. Her time with Pierce had irrevocably changed her. Graystone had become her home, Edward was like her own son, and Thorndike . . . well, he had become the world to her. Yet what else could she do?

21

—🌿—

"I won't be returning with you to Graystone," Mrs. Doisneau announced that night at dinner, as the waiter placed a roll on her bread plate.

Thorndike sipped from his wineglass. "Indeed, Madam? Have you had a change of plans?"

The elderly woman nodded. "I've been invited to the Mitchells', and would prefer to remain there for the summer. I would like to visit with Edward during the Saratoga season, that is, if you still intend to bring him to the races?"

"That was, and is my intention."

"Good. I shall join you there. I doubt that my presence will be missed in the meanwhile. You all seem to have become quite comfortable together."

Mary Lou choked on her wine, understanding the

woman completely. Obviously Thorndike hadn't told her she'd been fired.

"Whatever you wish, of course," Thorndike said smoothly. "Given what has happened to my jockey, I personally don't believe Graystone is safe right now for anyone."

Mary Lou knew the last was meant for her. Putting down her fork, she found she couldn't eat another bite. Mrs. Doisneau gazed at Thorndike curiously, but said nothing, and the awkward silence continued.

Thankfully, dinner ended quickly, and Edward's grandmothe the table as soon as she reasonably could be excused and took Edward to his room. Thorndike rose as if dismissing her, but before he could leave, Mary Lou placed her hand on his arm.

"Sir, I would like to speak to you a moment."

"I don't think there is any need—"

"Please," Mary Lou said. She looked up at him, letting him see the urgency in her eyes. He glanced down at the hand on his arm, and she could sense his reaction to her closeness. An involuntary shudder went through him and he nodded reluctantly, taking his seat once more.

"Thank you," Mary Lou breathed gratefully. At least he would hear her out. "I have given a great deal of thought to what you said earlier, and I believe I understand why you have come to this decision."

"Miss Finch—"

"And while I appreciate your concern, I cannot let you do this. I will not leave your employ."

Thorndike gazed at her, incredulous. "It is not up to you to decide—"

"Nor is it entirely up to you," Mary Lou continued in the same reasonable tone. "Your enemies do not have geographical limitations. You don't know that Edward would be safer in school, nor can you be sure Toby's fall wasn't an accident, at least until I do a chemical analysis. You are overreacting, which is understandable given the circumstances, but I cannot let you make a rash decision that you may later regret."

"Miss Finch!" Thorndike thundered. He seemed to be contemplating strangling her. "You can be assured that I have come to this decision only after much thought, and certainly not on an impulse. I must do what I feel is right, and take whatever steps I deem necessary to protect the people around me. I cannot let this situation continue."

He slammed his fist upon the table, attracting the notice of the diners around him. Yet Mary Lou felt a wave of relief sweep over her. She had been right. Thorndike was acting out of concern and a desire to protect her. She had taken a terrible risk, but it had paid off.

"If you really mean that, then you will listen to me. We are going to be with you until returning from Saratoga, if I am correct." At his nod, she continued. "So does it make sense to disrupt Edward's education now, when you will be with us anyway?"

"Mary Lou," he said softly, his voice much less sure than a minute ago. "While I appreciate what you're trying to do, I cannot help but feel you would be safer away from here. My God, if anything were to happen to you—"

The passion in his voice made her breath stop.

Mary Lou felt an answering passion inside her threaten to spill forth. Could his concern possibly be because he truly cared for her? Overcome, Mary Lou reached out and touched his hand, squeezing it between her own. Somehow, she found the strength to speak softly.

"Nothing will harm me, not as long as I'm in your care. I truly believe that. I plan to continue my investigation, Mr. Thorndike, with or without your protection or consent. I have my own reasons for delving into this case, and they haven't changed. But I would prefer to stay. And that is my final offer."

He stared at her a moment, then a wry smile curved his mouth. "You drive a hard bargain, Miss Finch. I give you a reprieve, a way out of this mess, and you throw it back in my face. Whatever am I going to do with you?"

"I imagine you'll think of something." Mary Lou smiled in return, but Pierce's expression grew serious once more and he withdrew his hand.

"All right, I will let you stay, but under these circumstances. You must trust me and tell me whatever you have learned. There are still things I cannot completely confide in you. I know I can't expect you to understand, but you will soon. Everything will work out for the best, and everyone will get his due. I know that dozens of people have invested their life's savings in Damien, and I have no intention of letting any of them down. But until we know what is really going on, and who is behind all this, I must keep you safe."

Mary Lou looked at him in surprise. What did he mean he had no intention of letting the investors down? It was almost as if Thorndike knew. But how could he? And if he truly understood her purpose in coming to Graystone, why had he let her remain?

The return trip was mercifully uneventful. Mary Lou was surprisingly happy to arrive at Graystone once more, with the sun fading on the porch and Beecham waiting for them in the hall. It was an odd feeling, as if she'd . . . come home.

Even her room seemed welcoming. Bridget had placed fresh flowers in a vase and had turned down her bed that morning, little niceties, but they made her feel cherished and appreciated. As she realized she was becoming attached not only to the inhabitants of Graystone, but even the place itself, she felt a moment's concern. The day would come when her case was solved, and then what? Would she return home to her quiet, lonely laboratory? Would Thorndike return to the widow's side?

She couldn't think of that now. To dwell on the future would surely drive her mad.

A note waited for her beside the bed. Picking it up, Mary Lou saw it was from Officer Merrimack. She tore it open quickly, and a thrill went through her as she read the contents.

Starkey owed over five thousand.

The enormity of the brief note struck her fully. She had been right. The blacksmith had gotten himself into considerable debt.

Coincidence? Was it also coincidence that Willy was present the night of Damien's disappearance?

That he had motive and opportunity? That he was also at Coney Island when Toby took his fall? As a scientist, Mary Lou didn't believe in such things. Putting the letter aside, she turned to her trunk. After unpacking her clothes, she came to the bottom of her trunk and found the flask. Weighing the tin in her hand, she realized that this innocuous container could possess a deadly poison. Thorndike, she knew, wouldn't be happy to discover her testing it, but he hadn't argued when she insisted it was the only way to know for sure if Toby's injuries were deliberate.

Slipping out to the cottage, she tried to quell her mounting curiosity. Once inside, she lit a lamp and placed it on the table. Opening the tin, she sniffed the gin, detecting an acrid scent along with the juniper berries. Mary Lou dipped her finger inside and placed a drop of gin on her tongue. At once she detected a bitter taste, reminiscent of an alkaloid substance. She set up a test tube and poured a sufficient quantity of gin inside it. Dropping several ounces of alcohol in the tube, she allowed it to stand, then filtered it and added acid, reducing the alcohol. As expected, the alcohol evaporated. Next she diluted the substance with water and shook it with ether, leaving the resulting mixture to stand while she scribbled furiously in her notebook.

Next, she drew off the ether, placed the remaining material on a white dish, and added sulfuric acid. At once, a spectrum of colors emerged before her eyes: blue, violet, red, and yellow.

Mary Lou gazed at the rainbow results. There was but one poison that reacted in such a way: strychnine.

No wonder the jockey had fallen from his horse! It was clear that Toby's fall was no accident.

Putting the test tubes away, Mary Lou made copious notes. She had to tell Pierce about the poison and about Willy, but she wasn't at all sure how he'd take the news. Yet her results were important. A man's life had been threatened, and he needed to know.

"Miss Finch, can we work down at the pond today?" Edward jumped up and down in excitement the next morning as Mary Lou attempted to finish breakfast. Bridget put another scone before her and hushed the boy, who raced outside to chase Max. The dog barked, delighted that everyone had come home, and Thorndike grumbled behind his paper.

Yes, everything was back to normal, as normal as it could be. Mary Lou sipped from her cup of coffee, amazed at how right it all felt. Even Thorndike was resigned to her presence. After their confrontation in Coney Island, he seemed easier around her, freer, as if her firm refusal to leave reassured something within himself. Mary Lou didn't dare to hope or read too much meaning into it, but she felt the subtle shift in their relationship.

Edward ran back into the kitchen, where Mary Lou blocked him from running around the table. "We can work down at the pond as long as you finish your multiplication tables. Do you have them?"

Edward nodded eagerly. "Yes, upstairs."

"Why don't you fetch them? When you're done, perhaps we'll study the lives of freshwater fish, and see if we can figure out how to outwit old Sam."

"Yes!" Edward shouted gleefully, then ran upstairs. Thorndike lowered his paper enough to meet her eyes.

"So, taking on old Sam, are you? I wouldn't have too much confidence in that. We've tried for years and only ever hooked him once."

"That's because you didn't study his living habits, and understand things from his point of view," Mary Lou said. "I think I can increase our odds."

"Perhaps I'll join you later," Thorndike said. Even Bridget stopped drinking her tea and gazed at him in astonishment. "I can't remember the last time I went fishing."

"Why, I'll be thinking it's been more than a year, sir," Bridget said happily. "It was before . . . "

Her voice trailed off and Mary Lou realized what she meant. It was before Clarissa died, before Damien's disappearance, before Mary Lou ever set foot on Graystone. Both she and Bridget understood the significance of Thorndike's offer, and her heart lifted.

"You are certainly welcome to join us," Mary Lou said softly. "I think Edward would enjoy that."

Thorndike's glance met hers once more, and this time, she could have sworn she saw a merry twinkle. "Yes, I think *Edward* just might at that."

Mary Lou blushed. Was she really so transparent? Thankfully Bridget only seemed pleased that Thorndike was relaxing his usual stern routine. She joined Edward outside, only then allowing a smile to cross her face. Thorndike could be exasperating, but he was also full of surprises.

The pond glimmered softly in the morning light.

A dragonfly hovered just above the water, then was gone in a silver flash, while waterbugs inched their way across the pond's surface. Ivory flowers peeped between the leaves of floating lily pads. It was a peaceful place, surrounded by cattails and pine trees, and Mary Lou could see why Thorndike and Edward enjoyed it so much.

Edward skimmed a few stones across the water, then settled obediently down to his books, while Max took the opportunity for a morning nap and curled up beside him. Mary Lou encouraged Edward to read out loud, helping him over the difficult parts as he explored pond life. His attention span had increased appreciatively, and Mary Lou changed the lessons frequently to keep his active mind interested. Even more significant, Edward's pranks had ceased since his disappearance at Feltman's, and she felt optimistic that she could make significant progress with him now that some of his own demons were put to rest.

That thought led to other, equally troubling ones. She'd told Thorndike last night about the poison, and he was very upset, but hadn't scolded her for investigating. She'd also told him her suspicions about Willy. While Thorndike admitted her theory made sense, he couldn't believe the blacksmith was behind such a terrible deed.

". . . feed primarily on organisms, insects, and smaller fish. They are egg layers, and spawn deep within the water plants, providing a safe nursery for their young. Can we put our feet in the water?"

Mary Lou laughed, her eyes opening. Edward's

segue, while not the most graceful, was nevertheless appealing. "Yes, I think that sounds like a fine idea."

Joining him at the water's edge, she took off her shoes, then rolled down her stockings, tucking them neatly inside her boots. Max sprang to life and dove into the pond, only his small nose poking above the surface. Edward removed his shoes and socks, then he and Mary Lou dipped their feet into the pleasantly cool water. Edward shrieked, withdrawing, then put his toe just along the edge of the pond. Mary Lou splashed his foot with her own, earning another shriek, then Edward returned the favor. Max jumped out of the pond and shook himself dry, drenching them all over in the process. The two of them giggled and played like children until a voice interrupted.

"Well, well. I wasn't aware that bass could be caught using toes as bait."

Edward laughed, and Mary Lou gave him a haughty look. "We haven't started fishing yet, so you have no room to criticize."

"I see." Pierce's eyes settled on her pale thighs, fully exposed as she'd tucked her dress up around her to keep it from getting wet. Edward missed the exchange as he rolled up his pant legs, determined to wade deeper into the pond. When Pierce's gaze met hers, Mary Lou's breath caught.

Passion burned there so intensely that a physical rush seemed to spread through her. In that moment she never wanted anything so desperately as she wanted him to make love to her. Swallowing hard, she had to look away to regain her composure.

Thorndike picked up the rod and his son came to

stand close beside him, while Mary Lou's dog sat at his feet. A rush of emotion filled her as he smiled at Edward, then allowed the boy to hook his own worm and toss the line into the pond. Edward seemed so happy in his presence, and thoroughly enjoyed his father's attention.

"I would say he's living beneath those lilies," Thorndike said, shading his eyes against the sun. "Wouldn't you agree, Miss Finch?"

Mary Lou shrugged thoughtfully. "This time of year he's probably looking to eat all he can, so he may be hiding in those rushes over there, where the insects are. What do you think, Edward?"

The boy tossed the line toward the lily pads. "I think I'll try both."

"A born diplomat," Thorndike said warmly, giving Edward an approving nod before bending over the boy as if to impart a secret. "Stick with the lilies," he whispered audibly, with a wink for Mary Lou.

Edward laughed, then solemnly threw his line once more and allowed it to fall between two large flowers. Sinking to the ground, he patiently loosened his line, allowing the string to fall gently upon the water's surface. Occasionally, he jerked the pole so that the bait would move enticingly, hoping to lure the big bass from his hiding spot. Thorndike came to sit beside Mary Lou, his eyes wandering appreciatively over her bare legs. Embarrassed, Mary Lou rose and allowed her dress to fall to her ankles.

"I think I'll go for a walk," she said, hoping to regain her composure. Thorndike's effect on her was unsettling, particularly before lunch.

"I'll come with you. Edward, we'll be right back."
The boy barely looked up and only nodded, so intent
was he in his quest. Pierce joined Mary Lou in the
grove of pine trees. Silently they enjoyed each other's
company, and Mary Lou felt a deep sense of peace in
his presence, along with a compelling sense of sexual
awareness.

"Miss Finch, I gave your information to the police," Thorndike began. "They were very impressed
with your study."

Mary Lou nodded. "I just hope it helps."

"The good news is that Toby is going to be fine.
He is recovering nicely. Apparently, he hadn't im-
bibed much of the gin. Like most jockeys, he spends
much of his time flipping, so he hadn't eaten or drunk
much before the race."

Mary Lou looked at him, puzzled. "Flipping?"

"They gain weight, then have to lose it to com-
pete," Pierce explained. "It is not only unhealthy, but
dangerous, for it leaves many jockeys in weakened
condition. Fortunately, Toby is naturally slender, so
he wasn't as affected as another rider might have
been. The police said had he been in worse shape, he
wouldn't be here now."

Mary Lou shuddered to think of how close they'd
come to another killing. "Why would anyone want to
hurt him? What is the point of all this?"

"I don't know," Pierce said darkly, his voice angry.
"But I intend to find out. Until then, I want everyone
in my household to exercise extreme caution.
Especially you."

Mary Lou's eyes raised to his and what she saw in

his face made her heart stop. A thousand emotions seemed to war for control, but before he could say anything else, a shriek interrupted them.

"I've got him! I've got him!"

Pierce stepped away from her, then called to his son. "We'll be right there!"

Together they returned to the pond to see Edward's pole nearly bent in half. Max barked as if understanding what was going on and demanding their help. The boy struggled, his heels dug deep into the mud, his face tight and determined.

"I've got him! I know it's him!"

"My God," Pierce said, astonished. "I think it is!"

22

Pierce rushed to Edward's side, helping him to brace against the tension of the rod. "That's it son, you're doing fine. Let out a little line, then pull back. Don't worry, I've got you."

Mary Lou smiled as Edward, excited beyond words, did as instructed. The wily old bass darted among the rushes, then dove into the deeper water beneath the lily pads. Max rushed down to the water, then ran back, barking in excitement. Edward reeled in slowly, trying to land the huge fish, while Thorndike held him tightly around the waist. It was a good thing his father was there, Mary Lou realized a moment later when Old Sam, tired of the game, made a run for it and dragged them both into the water.

"It's him, I just know it!" Edward cried, knee-deep in the pond. "Did you see him?"

"Yes," Pierce replied hoarsely. Max joined them, racing up and down the edge of the pond, barking at the fish. Old Sam, as if hearing them, leaped into the air, breaking water. The sun flashed on his silver body, and rainbow scales gleamed in the glittering light. Edward gasped and even Thorndike stood transfixed as his old nemesis seemed to laugh at their efforts before diving back into the pond.

"My God, he must be fifteen pounds! Did you see it, Miss Finch?"

Mary Lou nodded, sharing in the excitement. In truth, the fish was a monster, having lived a good many years in the pond. She almost felt sorry that his life was about to come to an end when he suddenly broke free and disappeared into the rushes. Edward stared at the empty line dangling in the water with a look of disbelief.

"He's gone!"

"Yes, he managed to get away." Pierce ruffled his hair comfortingly. "But you got closer to landing him than anyone ever did. A fine job!"

Edward beamed, then gazed out to the water once more. Mary Lou saw his expression soften as he, too, seemed to realize that Sam's escape meant another day of excitement. "Did you see him jump? He's beautiful!"

"I saw him." Pierce smiled, his eyes meeting Mary Lou's as he climbed out of the water. "So did Miss Finch. He is incredible."

Edward grinned at his teacher. "You were right, he does live in the rushes. Maybe if we study more, we can think of other ways to catch him."

"I'm sure you will," Mary Lou said confidently. "He is a beauty."

Edward joined her and his father on the bank, wringing out his trouser legs. Thorndike did the same thing, and Max once more shook himself, earning a shout of laughter as the boy and his father got wet all over again. Mary Lou watched them, her heart melting like warm butter. It felt good to be here, engaged in this simple activity with Pierce and his son. It felt . . . like a family.

That notion induced a deep sense of guilt. She'd barely given her own father much thought since coming to Graystone, and she realized she'd been so angry at his investment decisions that she hadn't wanted to think about him. A thousand memories came back to her as she recalled her father holding her on his lap while showing her how to use the microscope, of him rescuing her from school on a hot day to take her swimming, and bringing her candy, of all things, when she was sick. Watching Pierce and his son now, she understood that her father had only been trying to help her. He'd honestly thought that by investing in Damien, he could increase her dowry, thus ensuring that some man, some day, would want her.

"Is something wrong?" Pierce asked a moment later.

Mary Lou glanced up, startled, then shook her head. "I was just thinking that I haven't written to my father in some time. I should do so soon."

"Why don't you invite him to Saratoga?" Thorndike said quietly. "I would like to meet him."

"You would?"

"Yes, I would. He must be a remarkable man after all. I think I would enjoy his company."

"I'll be happy to invite him," Mary Lou couldn't stop the grin from spreading across her face. "I'll write to him tonight."

They returned to the manor house, all of them giggling and laughing like children. Bridget beamed when they told her about the huge fish, and she bustled to set out the tea, clearly delighted to see her master so happy. Even Beecham went so far as to smile when Edward related the tale to him, and seemed considerably impressed with the boy's skill.

After supper, Edward and the servants went to bed. Mary Lou was about to do the same when Thorndike stopped her.

"Miss Finch, would you mind staying in the library for a while? I find I have a need for company tonight."

His manner was so boyishly charming that Mary Lou could only smile in agreement. Taking her seat across from the fire, she yawned drowsily as Pierce did his work. The sense of silent companionship made her feel wonderful, and she could easily envision all her evenings like this one, basking in the warmth of Thorndike's appreciative gaze. Mary Lou fell instantly asleep, and this time in her dreams, the prince arrived on a beautiful white horse and carried her off into the clouds.

Mary Lou opened her eyes the following morning, aware that the gray light of dawn was just beginning to creep into her room. Lazily, she remembered sitting downstairs with Pierce, falling asleep before the fire . . . that thought made her eyes fly open. How did she get into her room? And how had she gotten undressed?

She was clad only in a shift. Her dress lay carefully across a chair, her boots waiting neatly below. Had Thorndike carried her, undressed her like a child, and put her to bed? She blushed at the thought, yet she was also unbearably touched by his gesture.

Yawning, she rolled back onto her stomach, wanting nothing more than to continue the delightful dream she'd been having, but a tap on the door interrupted her reverie. It became even more insistent a moment later, and she heard Beecham's stiff voice.

"Miss Finch, are you awake? Mr. Thorndike would like to see you at the stables."

"All right." Mary Lou forced herself upright and stretched her hands high above her head as she yawned. Glancing at the clock, she shivered.

"It's only five! What does he want at this hour?"

"I would suggest you go see, Miss. He's been waiting for quite some time now."

Mary Lou crept reluctantly out of bed and dressed quickly in the early morning chill. Running a brush through her hair, she tried to assemble the riot of curls into something presentable, but failed miserably. Waving her hand at her reflection in disgust, she tiptoed down the stairs.

The sun glowed softly in the dawn sky, bathing the fields in soft light and making her path easier to see. The chill was even more pronounced outside, and she shivered again, goose bumps springing out all over her skin. The grass was wet with dew, and she could feel the dampness soaking her stockings just above her boots.

She saw the horses first, two of them saddled and waiting by the barn. Mary Lou couldn't suppress another yawn as she approached Thorndike, noticing to her annoyance that he looked as perfectly polished and pressed as he would at ten o'clock in the morning. Dressed in dark riding clothes, he was even more handsome than ever, and she had to ignore the sexual awareness that his presence effortlessly generated in her.

"Did you wake me to go riding?" Mary Lou asked incredulously.

Thorndike smiled. "That wasn't my only objective. I wanted to talk to you alone, and had no desire to compromise your reputation. Do you mind?" He gestured to the gray mare.

Mary Lou gazed at the horse uncertainly. "I'm not much of a rider," she confessed. "The last time I rode I fell and broke my arm. What are you doing?"

He'd lifted her in spite of her reservations and placed her gently on the mare. The animal took a few steps, but then quieted at the gentle sound of his voice.

"Kahlua will take good care of you, won't you, girl?"

The mare, who'd pinned her ears back threateningly, perked up and gazed at Thorndike with a soft, liquid eye. "See? It's all in how you talk to them."

Mary Lou rolled her eyes. It seemed he could charm any female. Pierce walked around the mare, checking the stirrups, his hands lingering on Mary Lou's ankles far longer than seemed necessary.

Swallowing hard, she ignored the hunger that leapt up inside her at his slightest touch, and forced herself to look straight ahead as if completely unaffected by his nearness.

"Ready?" He gave her a knowing smile, then mounted Blackwatch in a graceful, fluid motion. Mary Lou nudged her horse forward to follow his.

Kahlua laid her ears back again at the touch of Mary Lou's leg, but went into a brisk trot, more interested in Pierce's horse than her inept rider. Fortunately, Mary Lou didn't have to do much more than hang on as they cleared the paddocks and started for the fields shining in the rosy light. At once Thorndike went into a canter, and Kahlua followed, changing gait far too quickly for Mary Lou's liking. Panic filled her as the horse seemed to race across the wet grass, and any attempt she made to slow her was ignored.

Thorndike glanced back and saw her expression, then slowed his mount's gait. When Mary Lou drew up alongside him, he gave her a reassuring smile.

"You're doing fine, don't worry."

Mary Lou laughed nervously, gritting her teeth with anxiety. There was nothing to do but surrender, she realized, for the horse was genuinely enjoying the race in the fresh morning air. Forcing herself to relax, Mary Lou choked down a shriek as the mare bucked playfully, then cantered across the fields.

It was like flying, becoming a part of the horse and losing the clumsy human ability to run at such slow speeds. Once she relaxed, the horse responded, and Mary Lou experienced a thrill she never dreamed existed. The crisp air blew through her hair, with scents of flowers and dank moss, while the horse's graceful three-beat gait covered ground effortlessly. When Thorndike saw that she was all right, he increased Blackwatch's speed, allowing Kahlua to catch them, then they raced together into a beautiful world of flashing light, sound, and fragrance.

She was giggling when they finally slowed. Thorndike brought his mount back to a trot, and Kahlua obediently followed the lead horse. Mary Lou caught her breath, exhilaration pounding through every inch of her body. They approached a silver stream and Thorndike halted the horses, then helped Mary Lou down.

His hands firmly grasped her waist, and when she slid into his arms, it was the most natural thing in the world for him to kiss her. Sighing, she reached up and embraced him fully, her body pressed tightly against his, her heart pounding in wild rhythm with his own. The warmth of his heat contrasted pleasantly with the chill air, and she never wanted to leave his arms.

"My God," he whispered, holding her close. "I just can't get enough of you. I don't understand it. I never felt this way about any woman in my life."

Mary Lou looked up at him, thinking of his wife. "What about Clarissa?" she asked gently. "Surely you were in love with your wife."

Thorndike gently disengaged from her, then ran his hand through his hair, looking off toward the brightening sky. "I suppose there was a time I was. Or thought I was," he amended. "I didn't realize there was such a difference between infatuation and real love. Do you understand?"

"Yes," Mary Lou said, wanting to know and yet afraid at the same time.

"Once I married her, I discovered she was nothing like I thought, that her loving words were all a facade designed to get what she wanted. I could have lived with that, for I believe in keeping vows, but when Edward was born—"

"Yes?" Mary Lou gently encouraged him.

"It was then I learned she was cruel. She had never wanted children, and thought she was barren. Apparently there had been many men before me, and none of them resulted in pregnancy. When she discovered she was expecting, she tried to rid herself of my child by throwing herself down the stairs."

"No!" Mary Lou couldn't repress the exclamation of distress.

Thorndike looked at her, his face filled with pain at the memory. "It turns out she had a long history of emotional difficulties. Her mother thought that a strong man and marriage would cure her, but Clarissa's torments were much of her own making. When Edward was born, I tried to protect him. She would fly into rages, and terrify the boy. When she died, like most children, he blamed himself."

"I'm so sorry," Mary Lou said haltingly, remembering Edward's reaction the day he broke the microscope slides. "Such painful memories are best forgotten."

"I know, and I've tried. The servants, God bless them, hid all this from the police, for they were suspicious of me already. You see, Clarissa kept up her liaisons with other men once she was out of childbed."

"Didn't you mind?" Mary Lou asked, appalled.

Thorndike smiled bitterly, then came to stand beside her. His hand caressed the cool flesh of her upper arm, and she shivered with warmth and desire.

"Of course I did. But by then, I knew I had never loved her. I almost felt sorry for the men she entangled. She had this way of making you believe you were the only one, all the while she laughed behind your back."

His hand rose and caressed her throat, then slid into her hair. Mary Lou closed her eyes, feeling the delicious sensations race over her. She felt him cup her face, then gently trace her profile as if it was something precious he wanted to memorize. Yet she had to know the rest if she was ever able to trust him. When she opened her eyes once more, she gazed deeply into his.

"Pierce, how did she die? I need to know the truth."

23

His silence, following her question, was deafening. The only sounds were night music: the crickets and katydids, and the rustle of a raccoon near the stream. Thorndike sighed, then pulled her closer into his arms.

"I suppose you deserve to know, especially now. Clarissa told me she loved someone else and wanted a divorce. I couldn't do that—the scandal would affect Edward for the rest of his life. Instead, I made her a proposition, and I shudder to think of it even now. I said she could leave, go to Europe, live with her lover if she so desired, but Edward would stay with me and we would remain married."

"Did she agree?" Mary Lou asked, unable to

believe this proud man would offer his wife such an arrangement.

Thorndike shook his head. "She nearly went insane. All she heard was that I was telling her 'No.' She ran out the door, into the rain. It was pouring that night, lightning and thunder everywhere. No one else was awake. The servants, used to her rages, had long since gone to bed, and Edward, bless him, was also asleep. I stood in the library, watching the storm, knowing I should go after her."

Mary Lou felt the tears coming to her eyes, and she quickly wiped them away. "And did you?"

"No," Thorndike said after a long moment. "I couldn't make myself follow her. We'd gone through scenes like this so many times before that I just couldn't do it again. I was certain she was in the barn or the cottage laughing at my fears, waiting for me to come for her so she could triumphantly throw my weakness in my face. She was the type who knew how to destroy the best in people."

Pierce looked off into the distance as if seeing the scene once more in his mind. Mary Lou reached out and gently touched him, running her fingers through his hair in a reassuring caress. He smiled, kissed her hand, then continued.

"My groom found her the next morning. Apparently, she'd fallen and broken her ankle in the rain. She developed pneumonia as a result, and never recovered. Clarissa died a few days later in her own bed, cursing the day she ever laid eyes on me."

Mary Lou shuddered, picturing the woman raving at him. She remembered having a discussion with one of her professors about evil, and whether or not it truly existed. Mary Lou in her innocence thought not, that it was madness that prompted wickedness, but now . . . nothing seemed that simple any more.

When she looked into Thorndike's face, her heart tightened. This man had endured so much pain, yet he continued to do right by his son and everyone else. A rush of pure emotion swept through her, and she smiled gently, kissing his hand this time.

"Pierce, you can't blame yourself. She wasn't a child—she was a grown woman, and she made her own decision to run out that night. That isn't your fault."

"I know," he said softly. "I've told myself the same thing a hundred times, but it's no use. I can't help but think that had I gone after her, she would be alive today. But there's more."

"What?" Mary Lou encouraged him.

Thorndike looked deeply into her eyes. "I'm not sorry now that she's dead, and that is the worst part of all."

Mary Lou saw how much that admission cost him and she wrapped her arms around him in a gentle embrace. "It is natural for you to feel that way. This woman abused your son, was unfaithful to you, let you know in every possible way that she didn't love you . . . how could you feel otherwise?"

He looked at her with tender appreciation and whispered reverently, "How did I ever find you?"

Brushing a stray lock of hair from his forehead, she offered her mouth to him in response, and he eagerly accepted the invitation.

His kiss was tender, filled with emotion. Mary Lou could feel his arousal, the beating of his heart, the change in him as he began to react to her nearness, but it was much more than that. For the first time in years, he was opening up to a woman.

"Do you have any idea what you mean to me? I shudder to think of what I would do without you."

Mary Lou smiled, her heart tightening painfully. One day, they would both have to find out, for theirs was an impossible situation. He was a gentleman, while she was . . . his son's governess. One day Edward would grow up and no longer need her, and then . . .

But she wouldn't think of that now. Instead, she tenderly brushed a lock of hair from Pierce's forehead, and gazed into his eyes. Something in her expression affected him deeply, for his kiss turned ravenous, an urgent need demanding to be filled. Mary Lou cried out, pressing against him, wanting nothing more than to feel his naked body against her own. Tossing his jacket and trousers into the field of flowers, he stripped her of her clothes, then lowered her onto the makeshift bed. There was none of the artful seduction he'd used before, no sense of him holding back. It was as if he couldn't control himself, as if some raw, overwhelming need drove him to possess her. Mary Lou gasped as he impaled her with one quick thrust, holding her body prisoner with his own. A sexual rush pounded in her veins as he raised himself on his arms, and she saw him, godlike and naked in the moonlight, his muscular body a play of pure beauty in the waking dawn.

It was as if they were creating life all over again. Mary Lou cried out as he plunged into her, hard and urgent, adding to her primitive sense of excitement.

She tried to caress him, to add to his pleasure, but he grasped her hands impatiently and pinned them at her sides. Instead he seemed determined just to give to her, rocking her body beneath him in a tumultuous rhythm, taking her to a level of pleasure she never knew existed. The unbearable sensations sent shock waves through her, and she lifted herself to him, blindly encouraging him, wanting everything he could give.

And he gave. Mary Lou felt him release her hands to grasp her waist, holding her tightly even as he drove deeply into her. A hoarse moan rent the night and she was astonished to realize it had come from her. Her body arched bow-like and he slid his hand beneath her, murmuring to her, hot words of sex and love and passion. Suddenly she felt an explosion of pure eroticism. Poignant spasms racked through her, and her body strained against him, her heels digging into the earth, her hands clutching wildly at his back. It was as if he understood what she was feeling, for at that moment he withdrew, then plunged even deeper inside her, giving her more, taking her into a white-hot world where nothing but pleasure could possibly matter. It was the most sensual, incredibly satisfying experience, and when he withdrew, joining her in ecstasy, she felt completely a woman.

Their hearts beat frantically and they lay side by side in the field of daisies. Dawn edged out the moon, and the warmth of a newborn sun warmed their limbs. Black-eyed susans stared questioningly down at them, bobbing in the gentle breeze. Mary Lou closed her eyes and reveled in the sheer pleasure of it all, her body aching blissfully from Thorndike's sexual onslaught. Never had she felt so alive, so beautiful, so sexy.

When he kissed her, she opened her eyes and saw an apologetic smile on his face. "I'm sorry, I didn't mean for it to happen that way. I should have been more gentle, considerate . . . "

"Please don't apologize," Mary Lou said softly. "I thought it was wonderful."

He reached out and gently touched her stomach. "Unfortunately, I didn't withdraw this time. I couldn't bring myself to—" he gave her a rueful look. "Forgive me. And if anything goes wrong, tell me."

Her face reddened furiously. He was talking about pregnancy. As a woman of science, she should have taken this into consideration, yet she, too, had been caught up in the moment. There were female contraceptives, articles which were purchased discreetly through magazines. Why hadn't she prepared for this? Good God, what if he was right? She could be pregnant within a few days . . .

Rising abruptly, she indicated the horses. "We should be getting back before everyone wakens."

Thorndike nodded, watching her closely. "Is everything all right?"

"Yes," she choked, the words sticking in her throat. "I just think we should hurry."

They dressed and returned to the horses a moment later. Before they mounted, Thorndike turned to her with a serious expression.

"You must be even more careful the next few days. I spoke to the police. Willy is back. The police caught him prowling around Whittaker's property. That cantankerous old man chased him with his gun,

then called for help. The police think he may have
been using Whittaker's place to survey this property.
They also think—"

"Yes?" Mary Lou asked.

"That there is something to your theory, that he
may have been involved in Damien's disappearance
and Toby's fall. Apparently, one of the jockeys overheard Toby arguing with him about his treatment of a
horse the day before the race. They almost came to
blows."

"My God," Mary Lou shuddered.

"There's more. When Toby left to mount the
horse, Willy was seen hanging around his room. So he
had access to the gin."

"Was anyone else nearby?" Mary Lou asked softly.

"I don't know. Certainly others were around as
well. All the same, I wanted to tell you what has transpired. I don't want you going anywhere alone until I
know it's safe. Understood?"

"Yes," Mary Lou said thoughtfully. So Willy
Starkey was back. Mary Lou thought of Toby and
shuddered. If the blacksmith had been responsible
for poisoning the jockey, the question that remained
was why? Was it really just because they had argued?
Injuring Toby wouldn't help Willy's financial condition; it would only hurt Thorndike. Perhaps . . . a
thrill of excitement went through Mary Lou. Perhaps
there was more to all this than any of them realized.

Riding back to the house, Mary Lou was deep in
thought. Suddenly, Thorndike's horse reared at the
approach of a wooden footbridge. Pierce tried to

reassure him, but Blackwatch refused to put even one hoof on the planks. Dismounting, Pierce handed Mary Lou the reins, then squatted down to survey the structure.

"It's been completely destroyed," he muttered, touching the underside of the wood. "Someone hacked away the underpinnings."

Mary Lou drew in a deep breath as Thorndike's words sunk in. "Do you mean—"

"Yes. If we had crossed, the bridge would have collapsed, taking us and the horses with it." His gaze lifted and met Mary Lou's. "Chances are, one or both of us would have been seriously hurt."

She couldn't repress a shudder. "Are you certain that it was deliberate, that the bridge wasn't just in need of repair?"

Thorndike straightened, and gazed at the footbridge with an ominous expression. "No, the supporting beams have been neatly cut. Whoever did this did it intentionally."

"But no one could have known we would ride here this morning," Mary Lou protested. "After all, we didn't even come this way the first time out."

"No, but I usually ride this way every night," Pierce said softly. "If it wasn't for Blackwatch—"

Mary Lou put a fist to her mouth, stifling a sob. Thorndike patted his horse gratefully, and the black stallion nuzzled him as if responding to his thanks. Mounting, he indicated the path of the stream. "We'll have to follow it down to a place where we can cross. Unfortunately, it will mean getting home a little later than I intended."

Mary Lou nodded, reflecting that this was the

least of her concerns. A thrill of fear crept over her as she glanced back and saw the water rushing beneath the bridge. The stream was deep and treacherous at this point, which is probably why the bridge was erected here to begin with. Yet now, the beauty of the land and the soft welcome of the morning appeared threatening, and even the woods beyond seemed filled with danger.

If Pierce felt the same apprehension, he didn't show it, but instead guided the horses until they reached a shallow part of the stream. Gently, he urged Blackwatch across, then glanced back to ensure the mare followed. Kahlua seemed much more hesitant, but as the stallion leaped across the stream, she had no choice but to follow. Mary Lou felt her heart in her throat as the mare jumped clear across the stream bed, then settled down on the opposite bank, giving her a look as if to say, "What's your problem?"

They made it safely back to the barn, but Mary Lou couldn't dismiss her feeling of apprehension. She remained convinced that somehow everything was related: the missing horse, the murder, the jockey's fall, and now the broken bridge. Yet nothing had been proven, and according to Pierce, the police didn't even have a murder weapon. If, as they surmised, someone had hit Jimmy with a barn tool, wouldn't it have been lying near the scene of the crime?

Thorndike was also moody and thoughtful. More than once Mary Lou started to say something, but his manner was so forbidding she didn't dare. Yet as they started down the path, Mary Lou suddenly stopped, her gaze fixed on the pond as if this was the first time she had seen it. "Pierce," she said, her voice rich with excitement. "Have you dredged that pond since the killing?"

Thorndike looked at her as if she'd truly lost her mind. "No. Why would I do that?"

"Because I would say with some certainty that the murder weapon is resting on the bottom."

24

Thorndike gazed at Mary Lou, bewildered by her statement. "Why would you say that?" he asked.

"Think about it," Mary Lou said, the puzzle finally coming together. "A man broke into these stables to poison your horse. He was surprised during the theft by your trainer, who had no intention of letting an interloper escape with Damien. They struggle, then the criminal hits the trainer with a blunt object. In the meantime, the horse breaks free."

"What would the killer do then? He would run outside, most likely still holding the weapon. He sees the horse galloping toward the neighboring property. He isn't about to give chase dragging a heavy object with him, one that might even implicate him with fingerprints. So he tosses it into the pond, chases down the horse, and makes off with him."

Thorndike nodded, staring at the pond. The glassy surface seemed placid and calm, hardly the place to conceal a murder weapon. And yet . . .

"I'll have it searched," Thorndike said abruptly. "Now do you think you can confine yourself for the afternoon to nothing more dangerous than tea?"

Mary Lou smiled. "I think I can manage that."

Thorndike's inscrutable gaze met hers, then he turned to the barn and began shouting for the groom. She returned to the house as the grooms and the stableboys, armed with an assortment of rakes and shovels, began combing the bottom of the pond. Max and Edward joined in, the little dog barking orders while Pierce's son observed the happenings with keen interest. It was barely noon when a triumphant shout interrupted the tea, and Mary Lou raced down to the pond. One of the grooms held a dark metal object aloft.

"It's a blacksmith's hammer!" He cried, wiping the object clean with a piece of burlap. "Wasn't but ten feet from the edge."

Pierce turned and gave Mary Lou a look of sincere admiration. "The police never thought of that and they were here twice. Well done."

Mary Lou smiled, pleased with his praise. "It was nothing." Her clear green eyes raised to Thorndike. "But you do know what this means?"

Thorndike nodded. "I'll have the police arrest Willy Starkey at once."

*   *   *

When Thorndike returned, Mary Lou and Edward were just sitting down to supper. Edward couldn't contain his excitement when his father walked through the door. Mary Lou watched the small boy and realized that Edward had been harboring a good deal of fear regarding the murder.

"Tell us what happened!" he cried. "Did they get him?"

"Yes." Pierce handed Beecham his coat and hat, then turned to the assemblage. "As soon as I handed them the blacksmith's hammer, they put out a warrant for Willy and he was brought in even before I left. They also notified the Boston police to release Bill Cooke, since he couldn't have committed the crime."

Mary Lou sighed with relief. "Thank God. There is just one thing that concerns me," she said when Pierce joined them at the table. "I can understand Mr. Starkey's desire for the horse. Damien is worth a good deal of money, and Willy had easy access to him. He saw the horse every week, knew the layout of the stables, and the habits of your staff. I can also see him tampering with the jockey's food, particularly if he had argued with him. However, I am wondering why he would have cut the bridge in an attempt to hurt you." Her gaze raised to Thorndike's.

"I was wondering the same thing," he said slowly. "The man must have a personal vendetta against me. I've had very little contact with him. However, now that we've got the culprit, I should think we can find brighter things to discuss."

He seemed purposefully evasive, and Mary Lou wondered if he really believed what he was saying. It seemed impossible that Willy would go to such lengths just to satisfy a grudge, and Thorndike, she was certain, was too intelligent to accept such a simple answer.

After dinner, they retired to the library, where Edward played until it was time for bed. Thorndike took him upstairs, and Mary Lou stared into the fire, a feeling of utter relief washing over her. The killer had been caught. And as for the horse, Mary Lou thought it would be only a matter of days before Willy confessed where he'd hidden the thoroughbred. She would telegraph Emily and tell her the case was closed. Her cousin, she knew, would be genuinely thrilled for her.

It was all coming together, yet a new fear stirred inside her. What would happen now? Once the horse was found, there really wasn't a reason for her to stay . . . except that she had fallen in love with the master of Graystone.

Mary Lou curled into a chair, blinking back the moisture stinging her eyes. What if Thorndike made no declaration to her now that the murder had been solved? Could she just stay on indefinitely, hoping? Her pride burned at that, yet what was her alternative? Even if he did want her, he couldn't marry her. She was his governess, little more than a servant in the eyes of society.

Pierce returned, and sensing her melancholy mood, reached for her hand. Pulling her to her feet, he put his arms around her in a comforting manner.

"What is wrong, Mary Lou? Is it the shock of everything? My brave girl, you've been through so much because of me."

He smoothed a tear from her eyes and Mary Lou nodded, unwilling to confess the truth. "That must be it. I was experiencing a reaction, I suppose."

"That's understandable. Why don't you leave for Saratoga a few days early? I think you will like it there. It's a beautiful place, with a lot to do. Perhaps it will serve as a distraction."

"Wouldn't that inconvenience your business?"

"Not at all. I can wrap up a few things here, and join you on Friday. Would you like that?"

"Yes, I would," Mary Lou said softly.

"Good. And remember to invite your father. I would like very much to meet him. I also think it may comfort you to visit with him."

Mary Lou nodded, but his words made her stomach tighten. Was he intending to get rid of her now? Perhaps that was why he wanted her father to come to Saratoga. "I'll pack tonight," she managed. "Can Edward come with me?"

Thorndike smiled. "Yes, my son can go with you. I trust him in no one else's care the way I do yours."

It was a long train ride to Saratoga Springs, but Mary Lou didn't mind. She felt strangely glad to be gone, to have a chance to sort out the welter of feelings that possessed her.

Settling back into her seat, Mary Lou could only hope the horse appeared in time for the race, but even if that happened, there was no guarantee that Damien would still be in prime condition. Living at Graystone, she saw the endless training of the horses, the care taken with their feed, the constant inspections by the grooms and the veterinarian to ensure they were in top form. While it would be foolish of Willy to let him deteriorate, until Damien was back at Graystone, no one could be certain of his fate.

Edward played quietly with a toy horse, pretending to gallop along the edges of his seat. The horse obediently skirted Mary Lou's shoulder, then leaped behind her as Edward came easily into her lap to finish the game.

Putting her arms around him, Mary Lou held him tightly. Edward had come so far, so fast. She was extraordinarily proud of him, and felt his joys and sorrows almost as keenly as he did. A startling thought came to her and she forced down the tightness in her throat. She was not only in love with Pierce, but she was also in love with his son.

The train pulled into the station, and Mary Lou's eyes widened at the sight of the United States Hotel. The famous piazza was already crowded with guests, while others strolled the lawns and surrounding streets. Carriages lined the block, waiting for patrons, while families assembled at the station for loved ones. She had heard that the resort sometimes swelled to forty thousand guests during the season, and from the amount of people she saw just within a few blocks, it seemed entirely possible.

"Edward," she directed as the passengers moved toward the doors. "Give me your hand. It's terribly crowded."

Edward immediately pocketed his horse and slipped his hand into hers. As they descended, Mary Lou was glad she had taken this precaution, for the crowd was even thicker on the ground. A porter rushed up and took down her bags, then turned to her with a smart salute.

"Miss Finch?" When Mary Lou nodded, he smiled. "I'm Dan, and I'm here to show you to your cottage. Are these all the bags?"

"Why, yes," Mary Lou said, holding onto Edward firmly. "We're staying in one of the cottages?" she asked in surprise.

"Yes, right around back. They are very elegant and perfect for families. Mr. Thorndike has stayed with us here for years. Just follow me."

Mary Lou watched in amazement as the boy easily piled the luggage upon his shoulders, then grabbed the remaining bags with his hands. He refused all offers of help, but dashed in a zigzag pattern through the crowd, and expertly made his way to the cottages, which were situated among the gardens. Opening the door of the largest and most grand, he placed the bags inside and gestured to the room.

"It has a marble fireplace, parlor, bathroom and water closet, along with five bedrooms. I will show you the rooms."

Gazing in appreciation at the stunning cottage, she saw that it was furnished much more luxuriously than any hotel room she'd ever seen. Every detail was expertly appointed, from the Brussels carpets to the carved rosewood sofa and the elegant dining table. Running a hand over the glassy smooth wood, Mary Lou wondered aloud, "But where does the food come from? Is there storage?"

"Why, no, Miss," the porter answered briskly.

"There is room service. Just place your orders with the front desk, and anything you desire will be brought here."

Bowing, he exited, closing the door behind him. Edward raced through the rooms, choosing a sunny one for himself, then proceeded to settle into his unpacking. Mary Lou surveyed the remaining bedrooms, all of them gorgeous. When she reached the master bedroom, her breath caught as she surveyed the enormous canopy bed, the huge armoire, the dressing table, and mirrors. It was a room meant for lovers, a place where the wealthy yet unhappily married could find privacy and pleasure. A second fireplace graced this room, and Mary Lou saw a silver champagne bucket waiting beside the bed. Her face grew hot as she pictured herself and Pierce here, and wondered if he'd had the same thought when he'd ordered this cottage.

As she gazed at the sumptuous surroundings, the restlessness she'd been feeling crystallized. She couldn't continue this affair as simply a mistress. While another woman, the widow perhaps, would be content with finding pleasure in his arms, she couldn't settle for that, particularly with his son involved. Yet she understood Thorndike's dilemma; there was no way he could marry a governess.

Her heart squeezed tightly, but she knew what she had to do. She'd stay with him until her father came to Saratoga. And then she'd go home.

25

—❧—

Thorndike arrived a day before he was expected. Mary Lou was just returning from the springs with Edward when she saw him enter the cottage, a bouquet of roses in hand.

Edward broke free from her grasp and ran into his arms. "Papa! You came early! We weren't expecting you until tomorrow."

Pierce gave his son a fierce bear hug, then his eyes lifted to Mary Lou's. "Yes, I found I couldn't stay away. I hope I'm not interfering with your plans?"

The look on his face made her shiver, and Mary Lou had to remind herself of the conversation at hand. "No, we just went to the springs. I didn't know they were saltwater. The feeling is incredible."

"Yes, they've been there for hundreds of years, I

suppose." Pierce smiled. "People used to come from miles away just to bathe in them, in the hopes of curing an illness or fighting off a plague. The waters are supposed to be tremendously beneficial."

"They bubbled out of this great big rock. You should have seen it!" Edward declared.

Thorndike smiled. "I've brought you something. It's in my coat on my bed."

Edward disappeared immediately, and Pierce turned to Mary Lou. "I've also brought you something. I hope you don't mind." He handed her the flowers.

Mary Lou touched a petal of the beautiful pink blossoms. "They are lovely, but you shouldn't have."

"Why not? You certainly deserve them. They are almost as beautiful as you."

Mary Lou felt her face become the same shade as the flowers, but she ignored her embarrassment and buried her face in the blooms. "They smell wonderful."

"Why don't we put them in some water? I've made arrangements for us to dine tonight at the hotel. Peter is here with his children, and he's invited Edward to have supper with them. I think that will be much more entertaining for him than the dining room."

"Has his wife agreed to those plans?" Mary Lou asked, concerned. She recalled the woman's lack of interest in all the children, even her own.

As if reading her mind, Thorndike smiled. "They've hired a servant to watch over the children this evening, so it is perfectly fine. Edward has visited with them before."

Edward came racing out of the bedroom, a beautiful white toy horse in his hand. "He looks just like Damien!" he shouted, displaying the toy for Mary Lou to see.

"He is gorgeous," Mary Lou said sincerely. "Maybe he'll bring luck and Damien will return in time for the race."

"Do you think he will, Papa?" Edward asked hopefully.

Thorndike smiled. "Perhaps. Now why don't you get cleaned up? You're having supper with the Whitesells tonight."

"Hooray!" Edward shouted exuberantly. "Can I go now?"

"Tub first. You look like you've been rolling in the mud. I've ordered a bath drawn for you—it should be waiting in your room."

Although Edward didn't appear too happy with the notion of a bath, he obligingly went to his room, more than pleased with the prospect of supper with the other children. Mary Lou thoughtfully picked up the toy horse, which Edward in his haste had left behind, then turned to Thorndike.

"He really does fit the description of Damien. Do you think he will magically reappear in time for the race?"

Thorndike shrugged, but she could sense an excitement about him. "The police are questioning Willy even as we speak. There is a very good chance that, given the kind of sentence he will receive without cooperating, he will decide that it is in his best interest to tell all."

"But you seem so . . . optimistic."

"I suppose it is just my sunny nature," he said with a grin. "I have reservations in the restaurant for eight. Is that agreeable?"

"But—" Mary Lou thought of the formal dining room in the hotel, where it was rumored that men gave hundred-dollar tips and women dressed so extravagantly that they had to turn down the gaslights to avoid being blinded by glittering jewelry. "Are you certain you want me to go with you?"

"Quite certain. Oh, and Miss Finch?" He paused before leaving the room. "I promise you I have a late night planned, so please rest up. You will definitely need it."

With a wicked grin, he walked out of the room.

The dining room was even more splendid than Mary Lou had anticipated. She'd barely approached her seat when a waiter rushed over, held her chair for her, then put her napkin on her lap. Before she could thank the man, he disappeared and another seemed magically to take his place. This one poured water and lit the candle gracing the center of the table, giving her a polite smile, but remaining properly distant. Another man appeared with the wine list, then still another to take their order.

Mary Lou giggled when the last man left. "How many waiters do we have?"

"There are over fifty employed here," Pierce said, smiling at her astonishment. "Canfield took over the restaurant and gaming hall a few years ago. He insisted that everything be the best, for he rightly saw that a precedent would be set by the way he conducted the dining experience. I understand he has the best wine cellar in the state, and instantly tosses out any china that shows the slightest chip or tablecloth that isn't immaculate."

"I can see that," Mary Lou traced the cloth with her finger in wonder. It was perfect Irish linen, creamy-white and gorgeous.

"Do you remember that little pond outside?" Pierce asked. When Mary Lou nodded, he grinned. "If you wanted fish for dinner, you could select one fresh from the water. The kitchen boy would catch it in a net and bring it into the kitchen to be cooked according to your desire."

"You're joking!" Mary Lou grimaced. "I don't think I'd be too happy sending a live fish to his demise."

"You needn't worry." Pierce leaned closer as if to impart a great secret. "I learned that they actually have a large pipe in the kitchen connecting to the pond. When no one is looking, they slip the fish back into the water and cook one that is already prepared. The customers never notice the difference."

Mary Lou laughed, tears coming to her eyes. "That is unbelievable. Perception is everything."

"Not always," Pierce said softly, giving her a warm look. "Appearances, as you know, can be deceiving. Remember Willy? Part of the reason the police didn't pursue him is that he seemed so unlikely a suspect."

The waiter brought a serving of shrimp cocktail, and Mary Lou had to admit it was absolutely the best seafood she'd ever sampled. A light Italian wine was served with it, followed by sorbet. Everything was impeccable, from the crystal glasses to the glowing china.

Dressed cucumbers came next, and as she ate the crisp greens, Mary Lou spotted a familiar figure across the room. "Isn't that . . ."

"Diamond Jim Brady and Josie Mansfield," Pierce replied, anticipating her question. "They attend every season. The waiters love to have that table. Brady gives out enormous tips when he's feeling extravagant. And do you see the man over there?" He inclined his head toward a well-dressed gentleman with a huge, blue-black beard who dined with a beautiful woman.

"Yes. He's very distinguished." Mary Lou nodded, tearing her eyes away from the gorgeous Josie Mansfield.

"That's George Kessler. He's a wine merchant. He sent the champagne." He indicated the bottle cooling beside him.

"Did he do that for all the tables?" Mary Lou asked, incredulous.

"No, just the people he knows like wine. It's business as well as a nice gesture, for he assumes you will then order from him in the future. And there is Miss Lillian Russell. I understand she loves crepes, and the chef prepares them especially for her every night."

Mary Lou saw the celebrated Miss Russell take her seat, giving the waiter a gracious smile. Up close, she was extraordinarily beautiful, if a little plump. A woman after my own heart, Mary Lou thought mischievously as Miss Russell dove into the crepes and sampled them, closing her eyes in ecstasy. A vacant chair stood on the other side of her table, and Mary Lou frowned. "Is she alone?"

"She's with Jesse Lewishon, the banker, but his health has been failing. He'll probably join her at the gambling tables later. His physician warned him he'd have to choose between his health and Miss Russell. You can see his choice."

Sampling a slice of steak perfectly prepared, she smiled. "Well I guess that's true love."

"You might call it that," Pierce said. "Miss Russell is actually having a rough time of it today. She wished to go to the track this afternoon, and asked Mr. Tom Williams for a ride in his carriage. Unfortunately, he only allows one blonde and one brunette in his carriage at the same time, and he already had a blonde."

"So he refused?" Mary Lou asked in astonishment.

"Left her standing on the piazza. I hear she was more than a little perturbed."

Mary Lou giggled at the thought of the beautiful star pouting on the porch. The whole place was incredible, the people beautiful, the food spectacular. Pierce's company was wonderful as well, for he continued to point out the various guests, sharing funny stories about their lives or his business dealings with them. Mary Lou discovered that instead of seeming distant and unreachable, they appeared just as human as herself. Many of them had made their own fortunes, coming from the same simple beginnings as her own family.

She didn't know if it was intentional on Pierce's part, but his jovial manner helped her considerably to relax. Between that and the champagne, by the time

Jim Brady approached their table to say hello, she found herself chatting with him and his stunning companion as if she'd moved in such circles for years.

When they'd finished dinner, they went for a walk in the gardens. Strains of beautiful music filled the air, and Mary Lou glanced at Pierce appreciatively. "Do you hear that? It sounds wonderful."

"The hotel holds morning and evening concerts during the season," he explained. "Victor Herbet, the composer, leads them. I understand he is engaged at a fabulous salary. You can meet him later, if you want to. He is always in the dining room drinking pilsner until very late."

"It is like a fairyland here." Mary Lou sighed. "I've never seen so many famous, wealthy people in one place."

"It's part of the allure," Pierce said. "Wealth attracts wealth. Aside from the money, which, granted, can do peculiar things to people, most of them are quite interesting."

Mary Lou leaned against the rough bark of a tree, watching the moon rise. "Miss Finch," Pierce said softly. "Did I ever tell you how beautiful you look in the moonlight?"

Mary Lou felt her lips part in surprise. "No . . . "

"Well let me tell you now. I feel incredibly lucky to have a woman like you in my life." He came to stand beside her, picking up a golden curl and touching it with his fingers. "I was just wondering if I could persuade my lovely scientist into a new kind of experiment."

"Such as?" Mary Lou asked breathlessly.

"It starts like this." He lowered his head to kiss

her. Mary Lou's body reacted immediately with anticipation, flaming the spark of desire his words had
generated into a roaring heat. She knew she should
stop him, but somehow couldn't bring herself to object. Just as his mouth touched hers, a voice interrupted them.

"Good evening, Mr. Thorndike, Miss Finch. Are
you enjoying the fine weather?"

Pierce groaned, regaining his composure immediately. Turning and shielding Mary Lou with his body,
he forced a smile.

"Mrs. Doisneau. I wasn't aware you had arrived."

"Apparently not." She nodded stiffly, then her
gaze fell on Mary Lou. "Miss Finch, I believe that is
you, is it not?"

"Hello Mrs. Doisneau," Mary Lou said miserably.
She could feel the disapproval radiating from the
woman.

"Are you enjoying the night air?" she continued
mercilessly. "Very romantic this evening, isn't it? The
full moon, the music . . . "

"Mrs. Doisneau, did you want something?" Pierce
asked impatiently.

The woman smiled coldly. "I'll be on my way; I
can see you two would prefer to be alone. Is my
grandson with you?"

"He is supping with the Whitesells tonight,"
Pierce said through gritted teeth.

"How very convenient," she continued, her voice
rich with meaning. "Good evening, Mr. Thorndike.
Miss Finch."

With an icy nod of her enormous hat, the woman
stalked away. Thorndike looked furious. He extended

a hand, and Mary Lou took it, but his mood had changed entirely. They walked in silence back to the cottage, Thorndike brooding, Mary Lou lost in her own thoughts. She understood now why his mother-in-law had this effect on him. Pierce felt a tremendous guilt where his late wife's death was concerned, and her mother exploited that fully.

There was a chill in the air and when they stepped inside the cottage. Mary Lou shivered, drawing her arms around her.

"Are you cold?" Pierce asked.

"A little." Her teeth chattered.

"Let me start a fire before I fetch Edward." He reached out and massaged her shoulders, warming them with his hands. His eyes fell admiringly on her summer gown, a lighthearted affair of muslin sprigged with violets that she had proudly purchased for half-price since it was the end of the season. Pierce tore himself away from her, then bent down to prepare the fire.

Mary Lou sat on the sofa, her heart aching for him. Thorndike was a good man. He cared for his son, treated his servants well, and was respected and liked by everyone who knew him. Yet his past seemed determined to haunt him. A tenderness grew inside of her, and she knew she was lost. She could resist his artful seduction, but not his pain. If they only had a short time left together, she couldn't refuse him.

"How is that?" Pierce straightened, a soothing fire roaring behind him.

Mary Lou smiled, then didn't repress another shiver. Lifting her eyes to him, she confessed softly, "May I ask one more thing of you?"

"Certainly. What is it?"

"Would you kiss me the way you were going to before Mrs. Doisneau interrupted?"

Pierce looked surprised, but he took her in his arms. His lips gently nuzzled her throat before he kissed her, softly at first, gently exploring her soft mouth until she moaned with anticipation. Seizing the opportunity, he deepened the kiss, taking her into his arms and cupping her head in his hands. Then he slipped his tongue between her lips to taste her fully.

Mary Lou sighed as the blood began pounding in her veins. It was like an electrical charge, lighting her up more indecently than one of Edison's lamps. Her body hummed, pressing against him, wanting even more contact with his, while her blood seemed to sing in her veins. There was only one explanation for the effect this man had on her, Mary Lou realized, and it wasn't science. The refrain echoed through her mind: *So this is love.*

She felt it in every inch of her skin as he feathered kisses along her throat, spreading fire wherever he went. She knew it in her heart when it seemed about to burst with emotion. She experienced it in every one of her senses: from the scent of his lime water filling her head to the feel of his hard, muscled body beneath her curious fingertips, to the taste of him, incredibly sweet when she heatedly kissed his shoulder in a ragged demand for more.

Thorndike smiled, seeming pleased by her response. Turning her in his arms, he undid the buttons to her dress, impatiently fumbling with them. Mary Lou giggled when he swore under his breath. "I think dressmakers hate men," he said, finally freeing her from the confines of her clothes. "No man would ever invent anything this damned difficult to get out of."

"Perhaps it is part of our mating ritual," Mary Lou said teasingly, breathless as his eyes swept her with erotic appreciation.

"Really?" Thorndike's eyes deepened to a hot, glowing sapphire. "Well perhaps we can elicit a few mating cries from you then . . . "

He bent his head, nipping at the tender skin beneath her breasts, then took one hard nipple into his mouth. Mary Lou gasped, unashamedly pressing herself closer to him, responding to the delightful urgings of her young body. Thorndike knelt before her, adoring her, sliding his hands against her satiny flesh, glorying in the creamy roundness of her belly, the firm flesh of her legs, the smooth silk of her inner thighs.

"Oh my," Mary Lou bit out breathlessly as his mouth and tongue moved lower, teasing her, making her crave him more intensely than chocolate. "I . . . don't think I can stand," she whispered raggedly.

"You're going to have to a little bit longer," Thorndike said, abruptly separating her legs and kneeling between them.

"Why . . . I . . . oh, Pierce, what are you doing?"

Mary Lou's response was lost as he rose to ravish her with his lips and tongue. Pure liquid heat flashed through her and Mary Lou arched in pleasure, a thousand nerve endings exploding within her at once. Within seconds, she was crying out, feeling the spasms shuddering through her, taking her to a place where nothing else could possibly matter except the erotic sensations that were filling her. This time her knees buckled, and Pierce lowered her to the Brussels rug, where she lay panting in the firelight.

"Don't worry," he whispered in her ear. "This time I came prepared. You don't have to worry about pregnancy, unless . . . "

Unless it had already occurred. Mary Lou understood what he was saying. Yet she was touched that he had gone out of his way to protect her. Gazing at him with eyes filled with desire, she begged.

"Please, Pierce. I want you so badly."

Her words affected him immediately. Pierce quickly thrust inside her, and Mary Lou gasped, startled as he rolled her on top of him. Holding her firmly, his hands on her waist, he slowly withdrew, then entered her again, each time deeper, making her cry out and bringing her to a new level of fulfillment until she arched once more in ecstasy. Only then, when she finally could no longer bear it, he joined her, reaching the ultimate fulfillment. Tenderly, he brought her down into his embrace, holding her as if she were something incredibly precious.

Mary Lou sighed, feeling utterly content and safe in his arms. An overwhelming feeling of love filled her and she closed her eyes, trying to hold back a tear. Her feelings for him seemed to grow with each moment. How could she continue to hold back what she felt?

Pierce saw the moisture lining her eyelashes and he tipped her head up toward his. "Mary Lou," he whispered. "What is the matter? Did I hurt you?"

She shook her head, quickly wiping at her eyes in embarrassment. "No, nothing like that. It's just . . .

everything that's happened the past few weeks. I think it has been building up inside me."

"I understand." Thorndike smoothed the curls away from her face. "You've been through a lot living at Graystone. You are brave as well as beautiful. Somehow I have to make it up to you."

Mary Lou looked at him and he smiled teasingly. "Maybe I can see my way clear to giving you a raise."

Her heart dropped. She was just a governess to him, but the thought didn't even make her angry. How could it? That's what she was. Mrs. Doisneau saw that clearly; so did everyone else.

"I think you'd better get Edward," she said softly, trying to keep the hurt from her voice. "Peter will be wondering where you are."

"You're right." Thorndike rose and extended a hand to her. Helping her to her feet, he gently kissed her forehead. "I'll be right back."

He dressed quickly, then giving her a warm smile, left the cottage. Mary Lou stood at the fireplace, watching the flames.

So she was in love. Yet Thorndike never admitted any such feelings of his own. He seemed perfectly content with the idea of her as his mistress. Even this cottage was a place where married men could entertain other women. And why wouldn't he think this was enough? It really was the most practical arrangement.

Yet in the fairy tales, it wasn't supposed to end this way. The handsome prince was supposed to fall in love, take her away to his castle and marry her.

But Cinderella wasn't the governess, either.

26

— 🍃 —

Mary Lou awoke a short while later. The moon shone through her bedroom window, bathing the quilts in silver. Thorndike had gone to get Edward, but it seemed hours had passed and she hadn't heard them return. Rising reluctantly from bed, she tiptoed out into the hall and peered into the master bedroom.

It was empty. Puzzled, Mary Lou returned to bed, wondering where on earth he could be. A sudden fear swept over her. Perhaps Pierce had gotten hurt, someone could have attacked him . . . she remembered the bridge at Graystone. He could be lying out there, helpless and hurt even now . . .

Forcing the terrible thoughts from her mind, she lay awake for a long time, then finally heard the key turn in the lock. Listening intently, she heard Pierce murmur something to Edward, and the boy replied sleepily. She closed her eyes quickly when Pierce looked in on her. It seemed he stood there a long time, gazing at her, and it was all Mary Lou could do not to open her eyes and demand to know what was going on. Instead, he closed the door softly, and she could have sworn she heard him chuckle.

Scowling, she pulled the covers higher, wondering where he had been. The widow flashed through her mind, but Mary Lou dismissed the thought, assuming that even Thorndike didn't have that kind of stamina. Where then, did he go at night?

It was a mystery, one she wasn't sure she would ever solve. Maybe he just spent some time walking in the warm night air. That seemed the most likely explanation, and yet . . .

It was a long time before Mary Lou fell asleep and even then, her dreams were haunted by visions of a beautiful white horse.

"Can we go down to the stables and see all the horses now?" Edward asked the next morning, his mouth full of eggs.

"I suppose," Pierce said, his eyes meeting Mary Lou's over his coffee cup. "Do you mind?" he asked softly.

"Not at all," she managed. "I was planning to go for a walk anyway."

"Don't forget we have the Astor's Ball tonight," Pierce said to her, taking Edward's hand as he rose from the table.

"The Astor's Ball?" Mary Lou asked in astonishment. "You didn't tell me anything about that! Isn't that the party that is written up in every society newspaper?"

"Just about," Thorndike said easily. "It starts at eight."

"But I don't have anything to wear—" Mary Lou protested.

Edward ran outside and Thorndike paused at the door, his brow knotted seriously. "Then I suppose I'll have to take you naked. Either way, you're going, Miss Finch. In fact, now that I think about it, I hope you don't find anything appropriate to wear."

He dodged a biscuit that just missed his face and gave her a lecherous smile. "Until then," he said, closing the door quickly before the jam followed.

Mary Lou put the jar back down on the table and sighed. The Astor's Ball! It was only the most talked-about event of the season. Caroline Astor was stringent with her guest list, and usually only invited New York's upper-crust. How on earth was Mary Lou Finch supposed to fit in there?

With renewed determination, she ventured to her room, but not before finishing the last buttermilk biscuit. Diving into her trunk, she fished out the few gowns she had, wondering desperately if she could make one of them over in time. Perhaps her taffeta wouldn't be too bad if she pinned some fresh flowers on it, or her tarlatan, if she could get the chemical stains out. . . .

It would never do. Mary Lou sat down on the bed, gazing at the dresses, aware that none of them possessed the kind of sophistication needed for an event like this. Thorndike, she knew, wouldn't understand.

A dark coat and white shirt was the uniform for men, and suited almost any occasion, while women's gowns were ruthlessly scrutinized. And if she wasn't dressed appropriately, she would not only embarrass herself, but him.

A gold gown glittered in the bottom of the trunk. Mary Lou withdrew the dress and laid it thoughtfully across the bed. Frowning, she realized this dress wasn't hers.

It was a beautiful brocade satin ball gown, crafted in the Parisian style with a keyhole neckline trimmed in black lace. It was a much more daring dress than Mary Lou had ever worn, and she held it up against her body, surprised to see that the size was close to her own. The garment was clearly worth a small fortune, and the sumptuous material felt wonderful against her skin. A black lace reticule tucked inside the folds matched it perfectly, and would look wonderful dangling from her arm. It was a ball gown fit for a queen, but how on earth did it get in her trunk?

Pierce, Mary Lou surmised. He must have purchased the gown for her. Annoyance warred with pride inside her. Was this his way of telling her that her own clothes were not suitable? Or maybe he sought to delicately impose his dictates by inviting her to such a grand party, giving her the dress and no time to object?

She wasn't sure what his motivations were. Yet the dress glimmered invitingly, and she could imagine wearing it into the ballroom, the gold satin shimmering around her legs, her bodice practically bare ... Determined, Mary Lou took off her dress and slipped on the sumptuous gown. Turning, she faced herself in the mirror and gasped in surprise.

She had been transformed. Like a moth changed into a butterfly, the metamorphosis couldn't have been more astonishing. The gold of the gown complemented her skin tone perfectly, while the black lace framed her face and drew attention to her ample bosom. Pulling up her hair, she smiled at the effect, pleased to see she was at least the equal of Miss Russell. A slight giggle escaped her as she visualized Thorndike's reaction, particularly after his threat to escort her unclothed.

That thought decided her. Although her pride still burned, she would be foolish not to accept his gift and wear the gown. She couldn't wait to see the look on his face, for not even Thorndike could have envisioned how different the dress made her look. She wouldn't appear the dowdy scientist or schoolmarm, Mary Lou thought in amusement. At least not tonight.

When Thorndike returned, she put the gown away, determined to surprise him. Joining him in the parlor, she found him reading the newspaper while Edward played on the rug.

He glanced up from the racing pages, and gave her a warm smile. "Did you have a nice walk?"

Mary Lou nodded, then feigned a yawn. "Yes, but I think I'll lie down for a while. I want to be ready for tonight."

Thorndike's eyes narrowed. "Why do I get a feeling that you have something up your sleeve, Miss Finch?"

"I don't know," Mary Lou said innocently, giving him a wide-eyed look. "Perhaps you're just the suspicious type."

He lifted one brow, giving her a penetrating glance before Mary Lou left the room, giggling. It felt good, she thought, to hold the cards for once.

If Mary Lou had thought the party at Coney Island extravagant, the Astor's Ball at Saratoga made it seem like an afternoon tea. With a black velvet cloak over her lovely dress, she walked into the grand ballroom at the United States Hotel with her arm looped through Pierce's. Standing at the entranceway, she blinked in wonder at the fairyland before her. In addition to the brilliance of chandeliers, the sumptuous quantities of oysters, sweetbreads, champagne and Roman punch, the glittering diamonds, rubies, and emeralds, the hall was festooned in each family's racing colors. Bouquets of flowers shaped like horseshoes graced the ballroom, some in gold, some in red, white and blue, one in orange and white, and even a few in violets and pinks. Some bore the romantic names of racehorses, including Iron Mask, Buster, Irish Lad, and Beldame, while others celebrated their jockeys. Even the waiters' ties coordinated with the racing colors, lending a jaunty air to the party.

Mary Lou scanned the flowers, looking for Graystone's colors, but she didn't see them, nor did she see Damien's name among the lauded horses. Could he possibly be found in time for the race?

"Mr. Thorndike and Miss Finch."

Mary Lou's head snapped up as the footman announced their names to the crowd. From the corner of the room she saw the celebrated Mrs. Astor glance her way. Reporters scribbled furiously, particularly when she handed her cloak to a servant. Turning, she eagerly anticipated Pierce's expression when he saw the beautiful gown.

To her surprise, his hand tightened on her arm and his eyes darkened furiously. "Mary Lou . . . where the hell did you get that dress?"

His voice cracked with disapproval, and he stared at her as if he'd seen a ghost. Mary Lou forced a smile, smoothing the folds of the beautiful gown. "I found this in my trunk. I thought you'd given it to me."

"I would have never done such a thing," Thorndike said, outraged. Several faces turned to look their way, and he lowered his voice. "Someone is playing some kind of evil game, and I won't have it!"

His face was a mask of fury, and his blue eyes blazed. Mary Lou felt an eerie thrill as she dimly began to realize what had happened. "It was hers, wasn't it?" Mary Lou asked softly. "This dress . . . it belonged to Clarissa."

Thorndike didn't reply for a long moment, then sighed deeply. "Yes, you are correct." When his gaze returned to her face, he smiled thinly. "I'm terribly sorry for losing my temper like that. It was just such a surprise."

"I didn't know," Mary Lou said softly. "I can easily return and change . . . "

Some of the tension left him and he shook his

head. "No, it is too late for that. Let's go inside. I just can't imagine why someone would have done this, or what they thought to gain."

Mary Lou didn't reply, but allowed him to lead her onto the ballroom floor. Guests looked at them curiously, and Mary Lou felt the eyes of the men settle on her and linger. A half hour ago, the attention would have been immensely appealing, but knowing this was Clarissa's dress, Mary Lou felt ashamed.

Thorndike swore beneath his breath. "I'll have to fight off a dozen lovesick swains tonight, I see." Then he began to laugh at his own dilemma. "I thought I had it bad with Clarissa, but it seems you fill out that dress exceedingly well. I shall have to be twice as vigilant." His gaze rested on the low cut of her neckline, naughtily lined with black lace.

Mary Lou forced a smile. The last thing she wanted to do was remind him of his dead wife. Why had someone played such a cruel trick on her?

Thankfully, a waiter approached. Pierce accepted two flagons of champagne from his tray and handed her a glass. Mary Lou sipped the bubbling wine, tightly clutching Clarissa's reticule, wishing she had never been tempted by the dress. Even one of her lab smocks would have been preferable.

"Good evening, Mr. Thorndike. Miss Finch." Mrs. Doisneau approached, her greeting as icy as the look in her eyes. Her gaze lingered on Mary Lou. "You are looking lovely tonight. Quite unlike yourself."

Pierce stiffened. "Miss Finch always looks lovely, as I'm sure you agree. This party promises to be the grandest yet, in honor of the big race tomorrow."

"I remember last year, when you brought Clarissa.

She was dressed so beautifully, in a gold gown trimmed in black lace, just like your dress, my dear. I had never seen her look so pretty."

A sudden silence followed her words. Mary Lou felt Pierce's hand tighten on her shoulder, then he put his glass aside. "Will you both excuse me? I see someone I must speak to."

With that he walked off, leaving Mary Lou in the company of Mrs. Doisneau. The older woman appeared very satisfied with herself and gazed at Mary Lou smugly. "Mr. Thorndike doesn't quite seem himself tonight, does he? I think it's time the man gave some thought to his actions, don't you?"

A terrible suspicion began to build in Mary Lou's mind. "Whatever do you mean?" she asked softly.

Edward's grandmother gave her a sharp look. "Come now, Miss Finch, we are all aware of your celebrated intellect. Surely you can figure it out. Why, is that Mrs. Ruscastle? I simply must make her acquaintance."

With that, the elderly woman vanished into the crowd, leaving Mary Lou alone. The waiter refilled her glass, and Mary Lou gazed at the crowd without seeing them. *She couldn't have,* the refrain played over and over in her mind. Surely Mrs. Doisneau couldn't have hated her that much, to have hidden Clarissa's gown in her trunk, knowing she would find it and wear it. Why would she do such a thing? It just didn't make sense.

And yet . . . The woman clearly resented her growing relationship with Pierce. Could this be her way of putting a stop to it, of coldly reminding him that he had just lost a wife?

Mary Lou drank the champagne as if it was water.

"Good evening, Miss Finch. Why, you look . . . ravishing."

Forced out of her reverie, Mary Lou smiled as Peter approached. "Thank you. It has been an interesting evening already."

"I'll bet. Where is the dragon?"

"He saw someone he knew and went to say hello."

"Well, a woman as beautiful as you shouldn't be standing here with a waltz playing. Come, let's dance."

Dancing, at least, was preferable to thinking. Mary Lou allowed Peter to take her into his arms and lead her onto the floor. The music filled the air, and the guests, dazzling in diamonds, twirled like spinning tops. It was a few minutes before Mary Lou realized that Peter held her more tightly than was proper. When she looked up at him, there was something strange in his expression.

"Mr. Whitesell, are you all right?" Mary Lou questioned softly. Following his gaze, she saw that he was staring at her gown.

"No. I mean . . . " His eyes returned to hers, and confusion reigned there. "When I saw you in that dress, it reminded me of . . . "

"Clarissa?" Mary Lou asked softly.

Peter nodded. "Yes. There is something about the way you look tonight . . . even your reticule reminds me of her."

"I know she had a dress very similar to this one," Mary Lou said. When Peter remained silent, she tried to converse easily once more. "She must have been very pretty."

"Yes, she is. I mean, was." Peter shook his head, then glanced down at her. "Please, forgive me. It was just so odd for a moment there . . . I almost felt as if she'd come back."

Mary Lou felt his hands tighten around her waist even more, and she withdrew a step, aware that Pierce was watching them from across the room. A strange sense of awareness came to her, as if something important was developing, a vision from a previous time enacting itself once again. But try as she might, Mary Lou couldn't seem to sort it out.

The music stopped and the guests applauded the orchestra. Mary Lou felt relieved when Peter released her, and quickly excused herself. Thoughtfully, she returned to Pierce's side, and he gazed after his friend with puzzled annoyance.

"What was that all about?"

"I don't know." Mary Lou was equally confused. Seeking to lighten Thorndike's mood, she gave him a teasing smile. "Perhaps he was trying to coerce me into accepting employment with him again."

"Doing what?" Pierce said hotly. "The way he was looking at you, I don't think he had schooling in mind."

"Whatever do you mean?" Mary Lou said, trying to keep the mood light. She smiled. "I think he's very charming, witty, handsome . . . don't you?"

Pierce looked furious for a moment, then, understanding, broke into laughter. He gave her a look of frank admiration. "Miss Finch, for a woman of limited experience in mating rituals, you appear to have caught on very quickly."

"Indeed?" Mary Lou asked innocently.

"Yes. I suggest we dance before I embarrass us both here and now, and show you just how effective your little game is."

Mary Lou smiled, and accompanied him onto the floor. The orchestra played "Blue Danube," one of the most beautiful waltzes ever, and Mary Lou felt her world spin as Pierce took her in his arms. While dancing with Peter had been pleasant, dancing with Thorndike was miraculous. Mary Lou put her head on his shoulder. The muscular strength of him made her feel warm and protected, while the closeness of his body made her long for far more attention than he could show her on the dance floor. When she finally lifted her head and looked into his eyes, what she saw took her breath away.

"Stop that," he said, his voice hoarse.

"Stop what?"

"Looking at me as if you want me to make love to you."

Those words, coming from him, made a shiver go up her spine. She smiled softly, and couldn't resist teasing him. "But what if I do?"

Pierce shuddered, then held her even closer. "I'm going to make you pay for that tonight," he whispered seductively into her ear. "Edward is sleeping over with the Whitesells, so I will have you all to myself."

"And?" Mary Lou asked innocently, smiling up into his eyes.

In response, he held her even more closely, and she could feel how much he wanted her through their clothes. "Enjoy yourself at my expense now," he said, his eyes smoldering. "But I promise retribution.

And this time I will have no mercy, no matter how much you plead or beg."

Mary Lou laughed, but couldn't repress the tremor of excitement his words engendered. He was a dangerous man to tease, and she was playing with fire. Pierce slipped his arm lower, then to her surprise, dipped her, bringing her back up with one smooth, liquid motion. In that moment she forgot everything except that she was in the arms of the man she loved. Gazing at him with unconcealed rapture, she let him sweep her gracefully around the floor, the swirls of music filling her head with beauty.

Gradually, the dance floor cleared, and Mary Lou didn't realize they were alone. It wasn't until the music ended, and the fabulously wealthy crowd applauded, that Mary Lou realized they had been honored. A blush came to her cheeks as she saw Mrs. Doisneau looking furious, Peter scowling, and Mrs. Astor inclining her head to her neighbor, obviously inquiring as to who they were. Her heart beat frantically as Pierce simply bowed to acknowledge the applause.

"Excuse me," Mary Lou whispered, then dropped his hand and picked up her skirts, disappearing into the crowd. She didn't look back to see the perplexity of his gaze, but she felt a sense of panic coming on. Entering the water closet, she secured the door behind her and nearly collapsed from emotion.

Everyone who witnessed their dance would know they were intimately involved. Although Pierce didn't seem concerned, Mary Lou couldn't help but wonder at the repercussions. While the Saratoga elite might look the other way at their own kind cavorting with glamorous nieces, a man having an affair with his governess was something else entirely. Even Peter had seemed appalled, and he was their friend.

Her breath finally returned to something resembling normal. Maybe she was overreacting. After all, Pierce didn't seem concerned. Maybe there was no need to be. Yet her cheeks were still flushed, and her face unnaturally red. Reaching inside her reticule for a handkerchief, she frowned as she saw a piece of paper tucked inside the linen square. Someone must have placed it there. She withdrew the note and unfolded it, holding it up to the light.

> *My dearest Clarissa, I cannot wait until this evening's end to hold you once more! Every time I look at him with you, his hand resting on your arm, I feel as if I want to kill him. You are my life, my love, my world. I cannot wait for the day when he releases you into my care. Only then will I find real happiness. . . . Peter.*

A sickness began inside her as the import of the note became clear. Pierce's wife had been having an affair with his best friend. Did Pierce suspect? Her thoughts went back to his confession about Clarissa's death. She had wanted a divorce . . . to marry Peter? Was Peter planning to leave his own wife for Thorndike's?

Crumbling the paper and stuffing it back inside her reticule, Mary Lou wished she had never read the hateful thing. Yet her heart went out to Pierce, trying desperately to make a marriage work that didn't have a chance. And how could Peter act as if he was Pierce's friend, when all the while he must have been laughing behind his back? *I feel as if I want to kill him . . .*

A dreadful suspicion came to her. Surely Peter didn't still harbor animosity toward Pierce. Clarissa was gone. He would have no reason to continue to hate him unless . . . he blamed Pierce for her death.

Mary Lou pushed the ugly thoughts from her mind and ventured outside to look for Pierce. She wouldn't tell him about the letter, nor her suspicions. What she would do was watch Peter closely, particularly where the children were concerned. Even now it troubled her greatly to think of Edward sleeping there.

As Mary Lou passed the library, the door was slightly ajar and she heard heated voices within. Immediately she recognized Pierce's deep tones, and the emotional ones of Mrs. Doisneau. Mary Lou was about to join him when Clarissa's mother's words froze her completely.

"Did you think a person in that room didn't know what was going on between you two? Must you flaunt your tawdry affair before everyone?"

"Madam, I am growing tired of this conversation. I have tried to assure you in the past, but this time you have overstepped your bounds."

"I think not," Mrs. Doisneau said indignantly. "As Edward's grandmother, I am well aware that gossip about you will affect him. Would you have other children refuse to befriend him because his father is rumored to be sleeping with the governess? Your only recourse is to get rid of her, now, before it's too late."

"Mrs. Doisneau, I understand your concern, and I promise to rectify the situation. Now if you'll excuse me—"

"I'm afraid I can't. Not until I know exactly when you will dismiss this creature."

Mary Lou withdrew, her heart in her throat. She didn't hear what Pierce's response was, but she could tell he was shouting. Making her way numbly down the hall, she couldn't stop the tears that clogged her throat.

She had to get away. There was no way she could face the crowd again. Mary Lou slipped out the side door, then made a run for the cottage.

27

"Madam," Thorndike said furiously to Mrs. Doisneau, his teeth clenched. "I understand your concerns and your feelings. In fact, I share them. That is why I plan to make Miss Finch my wife."

"Your—" Mrs. Doisneau stared at him in stunned disbelief. Fanning herself with a handkerchief, she appeared about to faint. "You can't possibly mean—"

Thorndike led her to a chair and helped her to sit, firmly closing her fingers around a glass of water. "Please compose yourself. Yes, I do mean to marry her. Miss Finch is truly the best thing that has ever happened to me. She is bright, witty, intelligent, wonderful with Edward, and most of all . . . I love her."

The woman gazed at him in surprise. "You . . . why I thought . . . "

"I know what you thought, and I know what you did. You put that dress into Miss Finch's trunk, hoping to remind me of Clarissa. Mrs. Doisneau, I understand that you loved your daughter, and you miss her terribly. I know how much you still grieve for her, but no amount of sorrow will bring her back. It is time for me to go on with my life, and through the grace of God I have found the woman whom I want by my side through eternity. I would truly like you to remain part of our lives, to visit with Edward and see him grow up. But I will no longer tolerate your disapproval of Miss Finch, your outrageous behavior, nor your disparaging remarks. Do I make myself clear?"

Mrs. Doisneau rose, her eyes glittering. "You, sir, will regret this."

"I am certain I will not," Thorndike replied with cold confidence. "Now if you'll excuse me, I plan to find Miss Finch and tell her exactly what I've told you."

Thorndike strode out of the room, leaving the woman to gape after him. A cold fury burned inside him, particularly knowing she had put that gown in Mary Lou's trunk. Still, he was amazed at how good it felt to declare his feelings for Mary Lou, and how right it seemed. Every time he envisioned his future, he could picture his little scientist, blowing up the cottage or running into the hallway to tell him of her latest discovery. A thousand images flashed through his mind: Mary Lou rapturously enjoying a chocolate cake, her eyes closed, her face a vision of bliss . . . Mary Lou in another kind of ecstasy, her body pressed close to his, her heart beating frantically while he showed her the results of his own experiments . . . yes, what he'd told his former mother-in-law was absolutely true. Mary Lou would fill his days with interest, and his nights with rapture. And he wouldn't have it any other way.

The crowd had thinned somewhat, but he didn't see her anywhere. Searching the room, he looked for Peter, thinking to ask him if he'd seen her, but Peter was gone also. Carolina, Peter's wife, was helping herself to a glass of champagne, and he ignored her smile of greeting.

"Mrs. Whitesell, have you seen Miss Finch?"

The woman shrugged in annoyance. "You mean your governess? Yes, I believe I saw her leave a few minutes ago. She went out toward the stables. Why, Mr. Thorndike, I don't believe we've had the opportunity to dance—" She winked flirtatiously at him.

"Maybe next time." Thorndike brushed quickly past her, ignoring her little huff of displeasure. Out to the stables . . . his footsteps quickened, as a nagging thought entered his mind. Mary Lou was extremely bright and curious. Surely she wouldn't discover the truth . . .

Thorndike was nearly running by the time he reached the barn.

Mary Lou had no destination in mind. The moon shone brightly, bathing the gardens in silver, but even the plants at night seemed foreign and vaguely threatening. The humiliation she felt made her want to disappear, to be swallowed up into the earth and never seen again. Yet if she had to do it all over again, she would have chosen the same path. Now she knew what it was to love. Thorndike had taught her that. And she also knew how much it could hurt.

The path forked. One side led to the barn, the other to the cottages. A dusky waiter brushed past, expertly balancing a tray on his shoulder. He rushed toward the cottages, bringing a romantic late-night supper to a couple who were no doubt entwined in each other's arms, just as she and Pierce had been last night. . . .

Forcing the vision from her mind, she was about to head for their cottage when she saw a man walking a horse behind the storage shed. There was something familiar about him and the bag slung over his shoulder. Curiosity overcame her and Mary Lou drew closer, recognizing him immediately. It was Thorndike's veterinarian. He was leading a dark horse into the stables, taking great pains to avoid being seen.

Why was he here and whose horse was that? Mary Lou had to find out, so she slipped silently into the barn. Dan Forester put down his bag, then led the animal into one of Thorndike's stalls. Quieting the horse with a sugar lump, he closed the gate softly. Casting a furtive glance around the stables, he left the barn, careful not to make a sound. He never noticed he'd left his bag behind him.

As soon as he'd gone, Mary Lou withdrew from her hiding spot behind the hay and went to the stall. The horse lifted his head in greeting, watching her with a strange kind of intelligence as she pet his nose. He was a magnificent animal, Mary Lou thought, every bit as beautiful as Damien must have been. But he was dark, and Damien, to all reports, had been a snowy-white. Was Thorndike intending to surprise them all with a secret entry tomorrow? It didn't make sense, but perhaps . . .

An oily substance clung to Mary Lou's hand and even in the darkness, she could see the dirt on her palm. Wrinkling her nose in repugnance, she realized that the horse was filthy. Surprised that the veterinarian would return a horse in such condition, she reached for a rag hanging beside the stall and gently rubbed at the animal's nose. More of the material came off.

A thrill began inside Mary Lou and she wished she had her magnifying glass with her. The veterinarian's bag lay at her feet and she reached inside, finding a bottle of rubbing alcohol. Shaking a bit of the vile-smelling liquid onto her cloth, she rubbed the horse's nose vigorously and managed to remove all of the substance within a quarter-inch square. This time when she looked she couldn't stop a squeak of excitement. Even in the dim light, she could see a patch of white hair beneath the stain. . . .

"Good evening, Miss Finch." A voice came from behind her. "I see you've saved me quite a bit of trouble, finding Damien like that. Did you ever hear the saying 'curiosity killed the cat'? This time I fear it is terribly close to the truth."

Mary Lou whirled around and found herself looking down the barrel of a gun. Peter Whitesell stood directly behind her.

*   *   *

Thorndike heard voices coming from the barn. A blacksmith's hammer and anvil stood beside the stables. Pierce picked up the hammer, a sense of dread coming over him as he crept closer and recognized the voices.

"Mr. Whitesell," Mary Lou said softly. "I am surprised to see you here."

"Are you?" Peter's voice was cold. "Come now, Miss Finch. We are all aware of your brilliance. Surely by now you must have realized a blacksmith could never have masterminded this."

"Yes, I did wonder about that," Mary Lou said. "As I see it, you were in love with Clarissa. You wanted her to leave Pierce and run off with you. But he refused to let her go. You blamed him for her death."

"He was guilty!" Peter shouted, then struggled to lower his voice. "He was guilty," he repeated. "He had no right to her. She didn't love him, she loved me."

Pierce felt blind fury shoot through him at his friend's betrayal, but none of that mattered now. Peter had Mary Lou, and he had a gun. Silently he crept closer, mentally applauding Mary Lou for distracting the man and keeping him talking.

"He had no right?" Mary Lou laughed harshly. "Mr. Whitesell, she was his wife and the mother to his child."

"Do you think that matters?" Peter said, waving the gun as he spoke. "I had to watch them together at social functions, parties just like this one. When he put his arm around her shoulders, or held her hand, I wanted to kill him. Don't you understand? She made love to me, but had to live with him! The situation was enough to drive me mad! Do you know what it is to truly love someone like that?"

Pierce could hear the anguish in his words, and apparently, Mary Lou did also. "Yes, I believe I do," she said softly. "But there is a vast difference between love and revenge."

"I was going to ruin him. The horse was only part of my plan. Unfortunately, now I will have to kill you. It's rather a shame when you think about it, but you've left me no choice. I have no intention of spending the rest of my life behind bars. Now if you will walk to the door, I have one thing left to do—" he shoved her roughly away from the stall, then turned to Damien and pointed the gun at the horse.

"No!" Mary Lou cried, throwing herself toward him. The gun exploded, and at the same time Thorndike's hammer came down onto Peter's head. Damien reared, his hooves pawing the air, his shrill whinny echoing in the barn. Mary Lou fell with Peter, his body hitting the ground with a thud, cushioning her fall. Yet the impact knocked the breath out of her and she struggled for consciousness.

Pierce put his arms around her and pulled her to his chest. "Mary Lou, tell me you are all right!"

A desperate fear seized him when she didn't open her eyes. This couldn't be happening, not now when he knew how much he loved her. He tapped her cheeks, trying to awaken her, and prayed to a God he hadn't called upon in years. Utter gratitude filled him as her lashes fluttered, and a moment later he was staring into her eyes.

"Pierce," she said softly. "I guess I got the wind knocked out of me."

"Thank God." Pierce held her tightly and to Mary Lou's surprise, she saw tears brighten his eyes. "When I saw you lying there I thought—"

"Shh." Mary Lou put a finger to his lips. "I'm all right." She turned toward the stall. "Damien—"

"Damien is fine." Thorndike breathed thankfully. "The gun was raised upward when it went off. Look!" He indicated the roof of the barn. Moonlight gleamed through a round hole just above the stall. Damien peered over the gate, munching contentedly on some hay as if everything was just fine indeed.

"And Peter . . . Is he dead?" Mary Lou's gaze went back to Peter, who was lying prostrate on the ground. Thorndike released her, then bent down to examine the man.

"He's still breathing," he said, straightening in relief. After picking up some rope, he bent down once more to secure Peter's hands. "I think he'll be out for a while, but I don't want to take any chances. Let's get help."

They went back to the hotel and Pierce informed the porter that the police were required, and he went himself to fetch his son from the Whitesell's. The porter raced to do his bidding, and within the hour, the Saratoga police had taken custody of an indignant and cursing Peter.

"So was it strictly because of Clarissa that Peter wanted revenge?" Mary Lou asked later, when they were comfortably ensconced in their cottage sipping brandy while Edward slept safely in his room.

Pierce shrugged. "I've known Peter since we were children. I always sensed a competition between us, and envy on his part, but never thought it would go to this extent. And actually, if Clarissa hadn't been involved, it may never have. But she was the final straw where Peter was concerned. Unfortunately, I don't even believe his feelings were reciprocated."

"You mean Clarissa didn't love him?" Mary Lou gasped, snuggling closer to him.

"I don't think she was capable of loving anyone," Thorndike said softly. "Peter was simply a means to an end. In a way, she used him as much as she did me. She was bored with marriage and never wanted to be a mother. When she understood Peter's feelings about me, it was an easy matter to ensnare him."

"So after she died, he set out to destroy you. But what did he plan to do with Damien? Surely he would have had the same problems as anyone else if he tried to race him or sell him."

Pierce's face grew cold. "My guess is he planned to have Willy kill the horse. Unfortunately for him, that plan fell through. Peter must have found out that Willy was in dire straits financially, and paid him handsomely to do his dirty work, including spying and poisoning Toby."

Mary Lou nodded. "He must have been furious when Damien disappeared."

"That's my theory. We may never know, for it certainly isn't in Peter's best interest to confess such a thing. As you know, I have insomnia and was walking the grounds late that night. Imagine my surprise when Damien came running across the fields to greet me."

"And you found—"

"Jimmy Dwyer." Thorndike grew somber. "He was dead before I reached him, the poor man, and only because he'd defended the horse. By the time I arrived at the barn, it was empty. I knew whoever had done this would try again, and that I had to protect my horse. I saddled and bridled Damien, then rode to Mrs. Norcross for help. She agreed to keep Damien at her stables, which is why I went there so frequently. I had him dyed to hide his identity, which was fortunate since someone broke into the widow's stables. I was certain they were looking for Damien."

"So that is why Damien's bridle was missing!"

Thorndike nodded. "Unfortunately, Damien's leg swelled, probably from kicking at Willy. That horse must have known the blacksmith meant him harm, and fought to protect himself. I exercised him every night, and applied ice and warm cloths to reduce the puffiness. We'll know tomorrow if he can run."

Mary Lou nodded, then took a deep breath. "So when did you deduce the reason I had come to Graystone?"

The words spilled out, and she waited uncertainly for his response. Would he dismiss her now that it was all over, especially when he understood her duplicity?

Thorndike gave her a grave look, then sighed heavily, as if unhappy with what he was about to impart. "I inquired into your affairs immediately. It would have been the height of foolishness to hire a governess without doing so. In the process, my attorney discovered that your family had invested in Damien. I really wish you had confided in me, however. It makes this that much more difficult."

"Why is that?" Mary Lou felt a shiver of fear creep up her spine.

"I'm afraid your services as governess are no longer required."

She looked at him in horror. "But you can't mean that! I know I should have told you, but I couldn't! I didn't know what happened to the horse, where you stood . . . And Edward . . . "

It took her a moment to realize his shoulders were shaking. He was laughing. Relief shot through her, along with indignation, but before she could hit him, he picked up her hand and continued between chuckles.

"But your services as a lover instead of a tutor are still very much needed, if you are interested. You see, Miss Finch, I know everything about you, which is handy, especially now."

"Why now?" Mary Lou sniffed, not entirely forgiving him.

"Because I love you. I have loved you from the first moment I laid eyes on you," Pierce confessed ruefully, smiling at his own folly. "Even when I caught you crawling around my stables. How could I not? I had never known real love, except for my son's. I never knew what it was to have someone truly care for me. You reached out to my son, touched me in so many ways . . . "

The warmth that had begun inside her blossomed and she looked at him tenderly. "But you never said—"

Thorndike laughed, then kissed her softly. "It is not my nature to blurt out my feelings with no regard for their effect. It would have been grossly unfair to you if I had confessed, particularly since I was not in a position to do so. You were a woman in my employ, and in my care. You were also in considerable danger, just by associating with me. To force my feelings and attentions on you would have been inappropriate, to say the least. But now that we know who was behind all this and can at last feel safe . . . "

"Yes?"

"Now I know I can't live without you. I want you to be my wife."

Mary Lou gasped. "But I'm your governess! Mrs. Doisneau, society . . . won't people talk?"

Thorndike looked at her in bemusement. "Mary Lou, what did you think my intentions were? We couldn't go on like this. I never wished to dishonor you. Why did you think I insisted on having you present at all those social functions? I wanted everyone to see that you were much more than a governess to me. People will talk initially, but it will die down, especially once I make an honest woman out of you."

Mary Lou giggled, but her eyes sparkled with tears. "Is that a proposal?"

Thorndike nodded. "A clumsy one, but yes."

"I believe," Mary Lou said happily, "that I'm supposed to say that."

Her words sunk in a moment later. This time when Thorndike pulled her into his arms, she joyfully returned his kiss. Mary Lou sighed, feeling an overwhelming love for this man. When the kiss finally ended, she spoke to him breathlessly.

"Pierce, can we go tell Edward?"

The look in his eyes made her heart melt. "This is why I adore you," he said softly. "Yes, of course, let's do just that."

*   *   *

The policeman arrived a short time later to take Pierce's and Mary Lou's statements. The inspector nodded, satisfied as Pierce revealed the story of Peter's misdeeds.

"It's a damned shame for everyone involved," he said, getting up a short while later, his papers tucked neatly under one arm. "I suppose this means a reduced sentence for the blacksmith."

Thorndike nodded. "It is clear Old Willy was merely Whitesell's lackey, not the brains behind all this."

"And him a gentleman," the inspector shook his head in bewilderment. "Well, I suppose I'm finished here. I will get in touch with you if any other questions arise."

"Just let me know how I can help," Pierce said, opening the door for the policeman. No sooner had he done so when another man charged in, his face florid, his white hair a stark contrast like snow on a brick chimney.

"Are you Mr. Thorndike?" he demanded.

"Papa!" Mary Lou cried out in astonishment. The policeman who'd been about to leave paused as the elderly man confronted Pierce, barely giving a glance to his daughter.

"I understand you've been involved with my girl. Intimately involved." The older man shook his hand threateningly, his spectacles slipping down his nose in the process. "I demand that you do the right thing by her!"

"Mr. Finch, I believe?" Pierce asked politely.

The rotund professor nodded furiously. "That's *Professor* Finch, from the University. I have just heard the most shocking news at the party—"

"Please, sit down, Mr. Finch," Thorndike said smoothly. "I've been wanting to speak to you for some time. I am glad to finally make your acquaintance."

The professor looked from Mary Lou, who seemed absurdly happy, to the police, then back to the suave gentleman before him. "I won't be taken in by your charm!" he said irascibly. "I'm here to see that you do the right thing by my girl!"

"Is marrying her good enough?" Thorndike asked drolly.

"Don't think because we're poor you can get away with—" Professor Finch suddenly realized what Pierce had said. He opened his mouth, closed it, then opened it once more. "Marry her? Why . . . she has no dowry . . . no position!"

"I don't give a damn about that. Please give us your blessing, for I have already asked your daughter to be my bride. She has agreed."

The policeman clapped, applauding them, while Mary Lou turned a brilliant red. The professor turned to his daughter, who nodded in verification, then his gaze swept back to Pierce. "Well then, that makes it another matter entirely." All of the thunder went out of his face, which was really only as threatening as a kettle of steam. He appeared not to know what to do with himself when Pierce extended his hand.

"Why don't you stay and have a nightcap with us?

We can tell you everything then. By the way, if you're hungry, I have a few ham sandwiches and some cake left over from tea."

Professor Finch sighed, his eyes closing just like Mary Lou's. "That sounds heavenly."

28

"Do you really think he's ready?" Mary Lou questioned anxiously as the grooms removed Damien's dye. Toby stood by, prepared to mount the thoroughbred. Both the horse and the jockey looked perfectly fit, but Mary Lou couldn't help wondering if racing him was the wisest decision.

Pierce nodded, squeezing her arm in reassurance. "He's as good as he'll ever be. He's a racehorse, it's in his blood. And Toby knows how to ride him. If the horse seems like he's having trouble, he'll pull up."

Mary Lou smiled, but couldn't stop worrying, especially as she could tell Pierce was also anxious. In spite of his reassuring words, he ran his hand down Damien's leg to check for soundness once more. Of everyone, Damien seemed the least concerned, and simply stared ahead expectantly as if he'd been waiting all his life for this moment.

"Are we going into the box now?" Edward asked in excitement as the other horses began to walk toward the starting gate.

"Absolutely." Pierce picked up his son and, with his other arm looped through Mary Lou's, walked toward the grandstand.

"I heard from my cousin Emily," Mary Lou said in an effort to distract him. "She was delighted with the result of our case, and wants to attend our wedding. She even offered me a position, as her scientific consultant."

Thorndike frowned. "You did tell her 'no,' didn't you? I don't want you involved in any more mysteries."

"Well, I don't know. It depends on what she wants to pay me. A governess's salary isn't all that much. . . ."

Thorndike gave her an incredulous look. Mary Lou giggled, and he realized she'd been teasing him. "Vixen," he whispered in her ear. "I'll make you pay for that, but not until after the wedding. And you will refuse me until then."

"I'll try," Mary Lou said, earning another amused look. Yet her heart was glad. Now that Thorndike knew Peter had been the villain, the black cloud over them was finally gone.

They found Mrs. Doisneau waiting in the stands. Mary Lou noticed she had difficulty making eye contact with either of them. Instead, she gazed out toward the field. "I hear you have an entry for the race after all. Did your missing horse suddenly decide to reappear?"

"Something like that," Pierce said smoothly. "It would be truly wonderful if he wins. I hope you thought to put a few dollars on him?"

"Certainly not!" The woman bristled. "Why, gambling is not something that I approve of at all, and you shouldn't either! That is a terrible example for you to set for Edward. Real gentlemen do not participate in such things—"

"I beg your pardon, Madam," Mary Lou stifled a giggle as her father stepped forward, assuming his best professorial manner. "But horseracing has always been a gentleman's sport. The cost and care of raising prime horses, buying and selling them, training and racing them has always put it beyond the means of the average man. It stands to reason that the biggest gamblers are the investors, wouldn't you agree?"

The woman turned to face him, indignation written all over her, but when her eyes fell on the handsome professor with his tweed jacket, pipe, silver-threaded hair and thoughtful countenance, she seemed suddenly far less sure of herself.

"I don't think we've met," she said coldly, but she had difficulty maintaining her demeanor.

"Rutherford Finch," Mary Lou's father said, taking his pipe from his teeth and giving her a broad smile. He kissed her hand like the knights of old. "Charmed. Do you agree with my thoughts?" He seemed genuinely interested in what she had to say.

"Well, I suppose there is some merit to your theory. However, you must agree that gamblers are not always gentlemen by any stretch of the imagination."

"Dearest woman," Rutherford Finch continued

smoothly. "I hope you won't criticize every man who invested or gambled on Damien. I certainly have done both, and hope you consider me something of a gentleman."

"Oh, I didn't mean you," Edward's grandmother said quickly.

"Good." He smiled again, and Mary Lou turned away, suppressing her own grin. It seemed her father still had the ability to charm a woman, and Mrs. Doisneau was definitely in need of a good charming.

The bugle trumpeted the start of the race, and everyone braced against the rail as the megaphone blasted, "And they're off!"

A dozen horses shot away from the starting gate, all of them incredibly fast. Pierce handed Mary Lou his field glasses and she peered through them. She saw Peter's horse, Rajah, pulling into the lead. The Mitchell's Western Light was right behind, and a far third ran Damien.

"Come on, Damien!" Edward shouted, as if he could urge the horse forward with his own voice. "Run!"

Mary Lou and Pierce clung breathlessly to the rail, watching as the magnificent horse passed the first post. He moved easily, although it appeared to Mary Lou that Toby was holding him back. Was Damien lame?

Her heart in her throat, Mary Lou couldn't watch as the horses rounded the bend. Instead, she turned into Pierce, holding him tightly, reveling in the safety and assurance of his embrace as the horses thundered past. Spectators screamed for their favorites, and the roar of the crowd was deafening. A moment later, Thorndike was shouting. Mary Lou glanced up from his coat and saw Damien stride effortlessly toward the front of the line, break free, and dash through the finish line a good length ahead of the other horses.

"And it's Damien, by a length! Western Light came in second, and Rajah, a distant third. Damien is the big winner today, folks, with tremendous odds against him."

The crowd cheered, and Mary Lou felt tears come to her eyes as Toby sat atop the beautiful white horse, waving and grinning. A boy ran out and placed a blanket of roses over the thoroughbred's withers. Photographers rushed forward to take pictures, and reporters surrounded Pierce as he stepped up with Mary Lou to greet Toby.

"I understand you've had the horse secreted away all this time—where's he been?"

"Was he hidden to increase the odds?"

"Rumor has it Damien was threatened."

"I hear they caught Jimmy Dwyer's killer—will he hang?"

Thorndike turned to the reporters and gave them a cool smile. "Mr. Dwyer's killer was indeed caught and is in prison today, thank God. Damien has just completed a special training, which as you can see, paid off handsomely."

"They say you trained that horse yourself, Mr. Thorndike. Care to comment?"

Pierce grinned, and shrugged carelessly. "I might have had something to do with it. But the real credit goes to Toby and Damien. I have the best rider, and the horse himself has heart and talent. It is a powerful combination."

Mary Lou looked up at him and smiled. He squeezed her hand, then turned to catch Edward who couldn't resist petting the horse. As he turned, one of the more aggressive reporters edged his way in front of him.

"Mr. Thorndike, one more question. Rumor has it that you are to wed your governess. Is there any truth to that?"

The other reporters paused expectantly, all of them waiting with poised pencils to hear his remarks. Mrs. Doisneau stood with Mary Lou's father, her brows lifted sharply, Rutherford Finch merely smiled, and Edward looked proud. Thorndike gave Mary Lou a huge grin, then turned back to the reporter. "That rumor, good sir, is undeniably true. And you can quote me. Miss Finch and I will wed here at Saratoga within the week."

The reporters pressed forward, congratulating Mary Lou. Mrs. Doisneau turned to the professor, shock and indignation all over her.

"Within the week! That won't possibly do. Why, we have invitations to write, plans to make, then there's the gown . . . "

"I hope you will allow me to help," Rutherford said. "After all, I am quite flush now with Damien's win, and can certainly provide a decent wedding and a proper dowry." He winked at Mary Lou. "It seems my investment turned out well after all."

"It certainly did, Papa." Mary Lou smiled. She gave Pierce a loving look. "It certainly did."

ABOUT THE AUTHOR

KATIE ROSE is thrilled to be a part of Bantam's FanFare program. Her first book, *A Hint of Mischief*, won Colorado Romance Writer's Award of Excellence, and *RomCom*'s Reviewer's Choice Award. *A Case for Romance* was called "A delightful love story that successfully blends mystery, humor, and a steamy romance into a western style adventure!" by *Publishers Weekly*, and was a Romantic Times Top Pick for March, 1999. A lifetime resident of New Jersey, Katie lives with her daughter in Marlton and spends her time horseback riding and researching American history. Katie has a degree in journalism from Temple University, and has been published in newspaper, book, and magazine form. Katie's website is located at www.tlt.com/authors/krose.htm. She loves to hear from readers.